DIRUS

A Novel

L.J. VITANZA

First paperback edition November 2022

Book Design and Formatting by MiblArt
Editing Services by Vicki Greer

Hardcover: ISBN 979-8-9870204-1-8
Paperback: ISBN 979-8-9870204-0-1
Library of Congress Control Number: 2022918000

Visit the author's website at www.ljvitanza.com

WORKS BY L.J. VITANZA

Novels

Dirus
Arctodus *(coming 2023)*
Red Herring Anthology *(coming 2023)*

Amazon's Kindle Vella

Arctodus *(complete)*
Dirus *(complete)*
Hayvonlar *(ongoing)*
Red Herring Anthology *(complete)*
Suchus *(ongoing)*

For Rob

Thank you for supporting me throughout this venture!

AENOCYON DIRUS

Terrible Wolf

Survived during the Late Pleistocene Epoch
and Early Holocene Epoch Periods
Lived in the Americas and Eastern Asia
Extinct 9,500 years ago... perhaps

PROLOGUE

The lone male trailed the pack from a safe distance. He stayed downwind and used trees or snow-covered brush for cover. Despite his cautious behavior, the alpha male was aware of his presence. The pack's leader would stop to make a display of his dominance towards the strange intruder. The alpha stood tall with his ears erect, hackles bristled, and lips curled back to expose his sharp canines. It only lasted a moment, but instilled fear and respect into the young adult male. The alpha repeated this intimidating exchange often, as he pushed his pack forward in search of prey.

One she-wolf, a lower pack member, distanced herself from the others when the opportunity allowed. The intruder's persistent attention altered her sense of curiosity into a feeling of attraction. She greeted him with a bump to gauge his sincerity or communicated with a low whine. She explored his face with her nose and nuzzled it against his thick, red coat for closeness and warmth. He reciprocated, showing his interest by rubbing his body against hers. They would take a brief rest, their bodies curled up against one another. This interaction became more frequent, their affection more intense.

Whenever the alpha male noticed their pairing, he charged at the two. Sometimes he nipped at the stranger, but more often than not, the intruder ran away without injury. The alpha steered the she-wolf towards the pack, glancing behind his shoulder. Defeated again and again, the intruder retreated alone to the safety of the shadows. Despite this dominant and aggressive behavior, the alpha male was fighting a losing battle.

In time, the lone male expected the alpha's constant bluffs. The she-wolf still complied with her father. She watched and waited for an opportunistic time to break from the pack. The moment presented itself one morning when they hunted and pursued an injured elk. With their attention diverted to the fresh kill, the young female retreated from her family. Unnoticed, she joined the intruder to start her own pack.

Over the next several months, the snows melted. As the weather warmed, the new pair proceeded south for vacant lands. They fled the she-wolf's former territory until the scent of her family no longer lingered in the air. When spring arrived, they stopped to mate and den. Over the next several years, they produced two litters. Their numbers grew, and the cubs became strong and independent. It was time to continue their push south. The new pack wanted to further distance themselves from any other wolves.

They chanced upon a massive and protected range, comprised of mountains and hills, flats and forests, and rivers and lakes. There were countless places to shelter during inclement weather and the deep snows of winter. The land was rich with game and wildlife. There would be no more searching. The pack would make this land their forever home.

The pack hunted and fed on the bountiful supply of bison, elk, and deer. When their bellies were full, the wolves eliminated or chased away other predators. They grew stronger and bolder, positioning their pack at the top of the food chain. But it wasn't the familiar predators that remained a threat to this young pack. They had yet to face the one that threatened their ability to thrive — the humans that frequented their home in Yellowstone National Park.

DAY ONE

The camper door swung open to a young girl standing in the frame. She glanced at the sky, pleased the sun was still shining. The girl wore the same style of clothing as yesterday, in different colors and patterns: a midriff tank top, frayed short shorts, and flip-flops. Her clothing barely covered her flawless porcelain skin. The girl was a young teenager, thirteen or fourteen.

The odd man watched her. He noticed the baseball cap and sunglasses that hid her face. But her looks didn't interest him. He focused on her youthful and exposed flesh and enjoyed the flirty way she flipped her blonde ponytail when she turned her head. Every evening, he watched as she emerged into the remaining daylight. She examined her bicycle and filled the worn tires with air. He shifted in his chair as her small breasts jiggled when she pushed down on the handle of the air pump. Sometimes he glimpsed her panties when her shorts crept up as she bent down. He blamed her and her seductive actions for his vulgar thoughts. She was sinful and vile.

Every day, she rode towards the pebbled path that led away from her campsite and into the woods. Her father noticed and yelled words of caution as he arranged charcoal briquettes in the barbecue. The laughter of women a few sites across the way interrupted his poor attempt at fatherhood. He abandoned the grill after his daughter's departure, leaving the food to rot in the heat of the intense sun. The man drank and flirted with the attractive women. Passing campers shook their heads in dissent. The girl on the bike reappeared from the forest an hour later. Her path was illuminated by lanterns and the flames of open fire pits. Angry with his drunken behavior, the girl cursed under her breath and stormed into the camper, slamming the door for attention.

No one took notice of the young teenager except the odd man camping next to them. He sheltered under an umbrella to conceal his perverted behavior. Dark wrap-around sunglasses hid his eyes, and a wide-brimmed hat shielded his short hair and the features of his face. He wore a long-sleeved, baggy shirt that hid any tattoos or scars and covered his muscular build. The man was average and forgettable.

He drove a white camper van with no identifying characteristics. It blended with the other like models that flooded the park. He changed license plates with stolen ones when he crossed state lines. During this visit to Yellowstone National Park in Wyoming, he assumed a California identity.

Nothing would draw attention to his vehicle, as there was a sea of visitors from the Golden State.

He kept a tidy campsite and packed out any potential evidence. After exiting the parks, he dumped and destroyed all the trash, receipts, and tourist brochures. He purchased new clothing and camping gear with money stolen from unattended vehicles. The odd man left nothing to tie him to the crime site. He hunted for his victims in national and state parks. These giant playgrounds offered secluded areas, little phone service, and ample opportunity. Parents kept supervision of children to a minimum, making for easy pickings. They were vacation destinations where everyone let their guard down. Happy places for the masses of smiling faces. He grinned with delight.

The odd man held a book up to his face. It warded off attention from meaningless conversations with strangers. He spoke to no one and acknowledged nothing. He watched and waited and planned in the shadows of his campsite without disruption. Every night, he observed the girl make dinner through an open window. As she cooked, her mother sat on the couch with her body leaning to one side. Her mother's mind was vacant, poisoned with opioids. The mom stared at a blackened television screen, oblivious to her daughter's presence. No one would notice this girl missing. Not yesterday, not this evening, not tomorrow.

The odd man guzzled the last of his lager. When the girl appeared in the door frame, he shoved the beer can into the mesh cupholder of his canvas chair. He stashed it in the van, his campsite now cleared of personal items. This evening, he missed the seductive bike check and tire maintenance. Instead, he jumped onto his bicycle and peddled down the pebble path that started at the edge of the forest. The odd man had scouted an area that was easily accessible and isolated. He had prepared for this moment in earlier days and was ready to fulfill his calling. The odd man planned to eliminate the evil young seductress. He took pleasure in cleansing the world of the wicked.

When he arrived at his chosen location, he concealed his bicycle amongst the thick vegetation and crouched in the bushes. He opened a cached supply bag, hidden during his previous visit to the site. He rehearsed the plan in his mind as he pulled strips of duct tape from a roll and hung them on an exposed and bare twig. The odd man remained still and slowed his breathing, waiting for her arrival. He listened for the sounds of tires traveling on loose gravel as he watched through a break in the bushes. He expected her to appear at any moment.

As he lay in wait, there was a rustling around him. The sound became louder and closer. He feared a group of people were approaching. The odd man supported his weight on the hand that held a rock. He looked for anyone that might witness his assault on the young girl. His eyes narrowed and followed the shadows dancing among the brush in the fading light. The odd man struggled to focus as something scampered about, taking their positions around him. One creature emerged from a break in the bushes. He faced a large animal that looked down upon him with hackles raised and its tail tucked under its lowered body. Its head was lowered and ears pulled back. It looked at him with large, pitch-black eyes and yellowed teeth, exposed through a snarling mouth. The man knew he was in trouble as other wolves made their presence known.

The alpha male grabbed the odd man by the neck, giving him no time to react. He struggled as the wolf's teeth tore into his soft tissue and pressed against his throat as blood seeped from the wounds. The immense pressure prevented him from breathing or screaming as he flailed his body to free himself. The rest of the pack paced around the attack in the tight quarters as the alpha female lurched forward to assist with the kill. She bit into his wrist, forcing him to drop the rock, the only weapon he possessed. Knowing the life was seeping from his body, the man stopped struggling. He was too weak to fight off the predators. When his body went limp, the pack went into a frenzy, awaiting their turn to feast. The man smirked at the irony. The predator was now prey.

During the flurry of activity, the pack failed to notice the scents and sounds of the approaching bicycle. The girl stopped and listened when she heard the wolf pack feed and decimate the odd man's body. She saw nothing in the brush, but turned her bike and pedaled back to the campsite. Her father was with the usual assemblage of women, failing to notice her return. She glanced at the rotting dinner next to the grill before shooting a disconcerting gaze towards her dad. The girl parked her bike before slamming the camper door shut behind her. With her mother asleep on the couch, the girl shook her head in disappointment and prepared her dinner. This night, she dined on reheated pizza in full view of the open window, and the absence of an odd man.

DAY TWO

A walkie-talkie crackled in one of the cup holders next to Sam's seat. She pressed the power button to her stereo, shutting off the system. Without taking her eyes off the road, she used a free hand to grab the walkie-talkie from the center console and push the button. Her passenger ignored her effort and instead stared off into the distance as the truck continued its course.

"Come again? We don't have a great connection," Sam said.

"Are you busy?"

Sam glanced at her partner as she released the talk button and moved the device away from her ear to listen for a response. The signal was weak, making it difficult to understand the woman's conversation.

"Sure am! On my way to check out calls regarding one of my bears raiding the tourons' pic-a-nic baskets."

Sam grimaced after delivering her cartoonish voice. Her passenger rolled his eyes and appeared unamused. The joke was old. It was one her friends expected Sam to say every summer. Her new protégé had already heard it countless times.

Despite the many posted warnings and pamphlets that every group received upon arrival, they continued to ignore the advice and fed the bears or left the food unattended. As a wildlife biologist and bear expert, Sam attempted to minimize contact between her bears and the park visitors. Every year, she wasted her time giving lectures and threatening fines on those with deaf ears. And through their irresponsible behavior, they forced the park to move offending bears or euthanize them. She despised those that broke the rules and kept her from her research.

"Johnson is asking a big favor of you. Where are you?"

"I'm heading to the West Bay Campground," Sam said. She groaned as her voice trailed off. Sam owed Johnson a favor, and his timing was off, as always. She needed to protect her bears from a campsite full of charcoal grills and sizzling hot dogs.

"Perfect! Johnson has a mort signal in your area and asked if you could retrieve the collar? He also needs photos of the deceased and the surrounding area?"

Sam looked at her partner with a sneer and cocked eyebrows. She felt backed into a corner, but continued her attempt to pass the job onto someone else. Sam pulled into a paved pull-out with partial views of Yellowstone Lake. She expected to lose this battle and knew her day was no longer hers.

"Why can't he retrieve the collar himself? I mean, I'm not much of a wolf person and I am shorthanded myself."

"Are you alone?"

"Just me and my boy, Dale. Your word's good with him. What's up?" Sam asked. She winked at Dale.

"There was an incident in the northwest corner of the park, in-park lines. Johnson has all his people helping him. He won't say more over the walkies, just in case someone's listening to our channel. He'll talk to you tonight when everyone returns to the cabins."

"Ooh, Dale! We have a little excitement brewing in the park," Sam quipped. The two exchanged smiles, and Sam pressed the talk button again. "What time can I expect them tonight?"

"Don't know yet. I'll text you the location. Do you have a decent signal? It's been a little spotty, with all the tourists tapping into our Wi-Fi. Okay. Sent. Over and out!"

The caller held the talk button to prevent Sam from asking additional questions. The walkie went silent. Sam slammed it back into the cupholder of the console that separated her from Dale. Her phone chimed and lit up with a notification. Sam nodded as she read the text.

"How do you like that? I shouldn't have charged the damn thing last night. Let's turn this baby around!"

The truck continued for another mile and turned onto a hidden gravel service road that led away from the lake. Close to the entrance was a large, orange sign marked Danger: All Area Beyond This Sign Is Closed Because Of Bear Danger. Dale did a double take to re-read the wording.

"My idea. I like to keep people away. I wanna give the bears a quiet place when they need a break from the tourons. It's a great place for us to hide from the visitors, too."

The washboard road was narrow and pitted with deep holes. High-clearance vehicles were necessary as large rocks jutted from the surface. Sam enjoyed this back road travel. She owned a large truck equipped with heavy tires and deep treads. The pickup flew down the winding road and only slowed for blind spots while kicking up a plume of dirt, marking the path she had just traveled. Dale sat in his chair with one hand turned white from gripping the grab handle above his side window. He locked his other arm straight, holding the seat cushion. All eyes were forward, looking for road hazards and wildlife. They left the radio off. Neither could hear the music over the sound of the roadway, anyway. Sam was deep in thought, her face red with anger. She despised having to do this work.

"What's a touron?"

Dale gazed at Sam with a dumbfounded look. He admired her smile, crinkled nose, and the little freckles on her face. Sam was older and beautiful, in a natural sort of way. Every day, she wore a short-sleeve, button-down shirt. Only a few buttons held it in place, exposing the cleavage that spilled over her tank top. Tight jeans emphasized the curves of her muscular build. Dale fought the temptation to gawk at her face and body, instead focusing on the scenery outside.

"A touron is a local term for a tourist-moron. It's someone that treats the national parks like a theme park or circus. Tourons take selfies with the bears or pet the bison. Last summer, we had one ask where we kept the animals at night. Can you believe that?"

"Okay. I lived here all my life and never heard that expression. Wonder what happened with the wolf team?" Dale asked. He stared into her green eyes as she laughed again.

"Wolf Team? Guess we're Team Grizzly? I like it, Dale. Maybe I'll order t-shirts for next year? Whoa! We have arrived!"

Sam stopped the truck abruptly, causing it to skid on the loose gravel. She put the gear into park and left it running. A deep, seasonal stream carrying the last remnants of snowmelt flowed and cut off their access, preventing them from driving further. Sam looked at her phone to verify the location before grabbing binoculars from a hidden storage compartment in the console.

"You wait here. If you see something, yell."

Sam jumped from her seat onto the gravel road, stretched a moment while tying back her thick, wavy red hair into a ponytail. She climbed into the bed of the truck. Leaning against the cab, she looked through the binoculars. The forward ground was flat, but covered with sage bushes. There were trees on either side of the small rolling hills surrounding them. She assumed the mort collar was about a hundred yards in front of the truck. Sam scanned the area again after a quick glance. She was looking for wildlife and any signs of movement. A small clearing in the sage exposed the remains of a carcass. The immediate area was dark, stained with the blood of an animal. She spotted the rib cage and scattered bones, stripped of flesh. *Who did this? Where are you?* She scanned the landscape again and spotted no activity. She hopped out of the truck and handed the binoculars to Dale.

"Keep scanning. I saw nothing, but I don't wanna walk up on anything, either."

"Yes, ma'am."

Sam walked around to the driver's side of the vehicle. After opening the back door of her extended cab, she pulled a can of bear spray from a tattered lockbox and fastened it to her belt.

"You can see better from above."

Heeding her advice, Dale moved to higher ground. With his elbows resting on the roof, he leaned forward with his eyes pressed against the eyepieces. As Dale continued his search for movement, Sam loaded her vest pockets with a small camera, large folding knife, and ammunition. She removed a small handgun from the box, loaded it, and secured it to a holster on her waist. Sam hesitated, then grabbed a rifle. Since she was approaching an active kill site, she opted for the additional protection. Sam loaded the weapon and pointed it towards the field, scanning the area again with the help of the scope. She pushed the back door shut with her hip and locked eyes with Dale. He had stopped searching and looked for Sam when he heard no movement.

"Ready for a battle?" Dale asked when he spied her armory.

"Keep your eyes on that field. I'll try to hurry." Sam reached into a pocket, pulled out a whistle, and tossed it to Dale. He caught it by the trailing string. "If you see anything, use that. I'll know it's serious. If something happens, get help. Don't come for me. It'll do neither of us any good if we're both injured. Or dead! Don't forget to look at the tree line for movement. Could be something resting close by."

Sam proceeded to the front of the truck with her rifle pointed towards the ground in front of her. She pressed the stock against her shoulder, ready to swing the weapon into action. Sam was a native Wyomingite, an experienced hunter, and understood the wildlife. The kill site would attract additional predators and scavengers. Sam hesitated before entering the field to retrieve the collar. Something didn't sit right. She stopped at the edge of the stream, scanning the area again. Sam took a step back, then jumped over the creek, landing on dry soil.

After clearing the bank, she removed the safety from the rifle and held the scope to her eye. It was difficult to locate anything from the ground level. Some of the sage was as tall as her waist. Sam looked back at Dale. He continued to stare through the binoculars as he gave her the thumbs up. Sam repositioned the butt of the rifle against her shoulder. *Rifle or bear spray? Why do I have to collect this dang collar? Johnson owes me for this. Focus, Sam, focus.* Sam positioned her finger closer to the trigger as she moved forward. With each step, she became more nervous. She would take a few steps, stop, scan, listen, and proceed.

The late afternoon rays of the sun beat down on the earth. Beads of sweat formed on Sam's brow and forearms. The winds were still, and the air smelled like rotted flesh as she closed the gap between the truck and kill site. She was familiar with this scent and wanted to avoid it. Sam walked closer and now stood at a disadvantage. She was no longer at the top of the food chain. She was in their territory and walked alone. Predators almost always attack lone prey, and Sam was alone. She stopped again to listen and observe.

Before she took another step, a sage grouse emerged from the field beyond the kill site, startling her. She heard the heavy sound of its flapping wings as it took flight. Sam looked to see what flushed it from its hiding spot. She glanced at Dale, who scanned the area more closely. Sam lifted the rifle into firing position, checking again to make sure the safety was off. She moved her finger to the trigger. All was quiet, too quiet. Sam grew more nervous and her instincts summoned her to return to the safety of the truck. Listening to her inner voice, she took a step backward.

Movement from the sky caught her attention. She watched as an unkindness of ravens emerged from the trees and circled the carcass. The birds hesitated for a moment and failed to land. They vocalized their displeasure and returned to the treetops. Ravens were scavengers and rarely passed on an abandoned kill site. They did not fear Sam; they feared something beyond her field of vision. All the voices in her head yelled at her to leave.

Sam turned to run before Dale put the whistle to his lips. When she heard the loud-pitched sound coming from the truck, she pushed herself harder. Weighed down by the vest and equipment, Sam dropped piece after piece as she avoided the obstacles in her path. Her heart pounded in her chest as her lungs struggled to process the sudden rush of oxygen. Sam listened to the predators coming towards her. She focused on one creature that approached from behind. It seemed larger than the others that moved in from both sides. The creature navigated the terrain at a quicker pace than herself.

Panicked, Sam shimmied out of the rifle shoulder strap and threw the weapon to her side. She needed to increase her speed. The mass of metal offered no protection, with an animal advancing towards her at this fast pace. When the rifle hit the ground, a malfunction caused it to fire upon impact. The blasting sound startled her pursuers, slowing them and giving her time to jump over the creek that separated her from the truck. Knowing their hunt would resume after they dismissed the threat of gunfire, she pushed herself harder until she reached the safety of the pickup.

Dale was in the passenger seat with his body stretched over the console. One hand pressed against the horn, his failed attempt to frighten the predators. He extended his free arm to help Sam into the truck, the door already ajar. Without hesitation, Sam grabbed the door handle. She swung her body up and around and into her seat. Sam slammed the door shut as Dale slid back to his side and engaged the locks with the push of a button. As Sam gasped for air with tears streaming down her face, she watched the field. She counted movement from several creatures as they slunk back into their hiding places, preparing for another attack.

"What the hell were those?" Sam asked after catching her breath.

The adrenaline was wearing off. Her body trembled and her voice crackled. Despite the hot weather, Sam was cold. Dale wrapped his jacket around her shoulders. He placed a hand on her bare and clammy arm in a gesture of support.

"I'm sorry. I blew the whistle as soon as I saw movement. They stayed hidden until you approached. I didn't see them until…"

"It's my bad. I knew they were here! I should've listened to myself. Those damn things were waiting. The hunters hunting the hunters. I'll be damned. My equipment is still in the field. Double damn!"

"I am not retrieving your equipment! You should've left the rifle with me. Maybe I could have shot them? What the hell were they?"

Dale handed her a drink after fishing it out of the cooler. He gave her another after watching her guzzle the first without pause. The truck was still running, and Sam was eager to leave. She pushed the buttons to lock the already secured doors. Sam started laughing and crying.

"I think we're both mad. Lock the doors. That'll stop 'em! As if they can work the handles. You did great. We'll retrieve my stuff tomorrow when we can round up more bodies," Sam said. She was thankful to be sitting in her truck, and thankful to have Dale by her side.

Sam turned the truck around. As she drove away, she glanced at the rearview mirror. She wanted to glimpse the predators, to identify her pursuers. Sam knew they would abandon the area at nightfall. They had stripped the wolf carcass, and there was no more reason to stay. These predators would search for a new victim at a different location. She needed to tell Johnson, now.

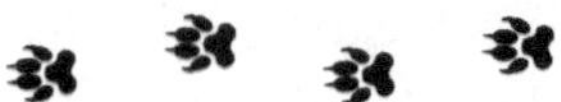

Sam sat at the kitchen table, tapping her fingers on the hard surface while shaking her right leg. She remained quiet, staring at the open window next to the front door. Darkness had consumed the land and a swarm of bugs danced in the light emitted from the porch lantern of their cabin. She watched them bounce against the screen.

Dale sat on the edge of the sofa, with his chin cradled in his hands, elbows supported by his knees. He stared down the hallway, but his eyes often drifted to the side for a peek at Sam. Dale was unsure if a conversation would be welcome, so he remained quiet. When the headlights from two vehicles approached the area, they illuminated the interior of their cabin. After the vehicles stopped, voices chattered as doors slammed shut. Sam and Dale's cabin door swung open to a towering figure.

"Shut the door. The bugs will get in!" Sam said.

The figure moved into the light after he closed the door. Dale sat up in awe of the large man; his response failed to go unnoticed. The stranger let out a deep, bellowing laugh.

"Is it my size, or have you not seen a British man of color in Wyoming?" Johnson asked. His accent was thick, and Dale had difficulty understanding him. Johnson scanned the room, looking for his device. "My collar?"

"Maybe you should have your harem join us; they are wildlife biologists, right? There's a little backstory to your missing collar."

Johnson groaned and hesitated for a moment. He knew from her behavior that something significant had happened. Johnson also knew that Sam was stubborn. She would hold out until he assembled his interns. Johnson left the cabin, frustrated by her request.

"What do you mean by harem?" Dale asked. He didn't understand how a harem applied to the studies of wildlife.

"That man has more money than we'll see during our research careers. Johnson knows how to play the system and snatch the grant dollars. People throw their money at Johnson so he can protect their favorite canine and spirit animal. Every summer, he surrounds himself with cute little college girls that love animals. Those nitwits can't tell the difference between a wolf and a fox. Anyway, we always joke about his rotating harem. The girls are his eye candy and Johnson is their sugar daddy. Both sides benefit from this odd relationship."

"If they're worthless, why do you want them here?"

"This is his problem, not ours."

The door flung open and a group of girls followed Johnson into the cabin. They screeched and swatted at the swarm of bugs they stepped through. Sam raised her eyebrows and threw a quick smile at Dale. The girls' behavior confirmed her observations. He returned her smile with an eyeroll.

"What happened to my wolf, dear Sam?" Johnson asked.

He took a seat at the small kitchen table while the girls crowded onto the sofa or leaned against the kitchen counter. Everyone watched Sam for her response.

"I found your mort collar and the carcass."

"And…"

"The creatures that killed your wolf chased me back to the truck."

"What killed my wolf?"

"I was too busy running and didn't see a goddamned thing. Your little friends were pursuing me from all sides."

"Madison, see which wolf packs might be in this area." Johnson said. He turned his attention to one of his interns. The tall and leggy blond started typing on her phone's screen.

"Mm, no," Sam said. She expected this response.

"Pardon?" Johnson replied.

"I doubt this is one of your wolf packs."

"Come again? Let us not speak in riddles."

"Before we continue, I want to know what you were doing today," Sam asked.

She turned the conversation back to Johnson. His confident demeanor turned somber. Johnson sat quietly for a moment before speaking. He realized he couldn't keep a secret from Sam any longer.

"Something slaughtered two of my wolf packs this week. And something mostly consumed them."

"Keep going," Sam said. She slumped into her chair with her arms crossed.

"This isn't the first time. Something has been striking my wolves since early spring. We started tracking the other packs more closely. My wolves are hauling arse from Yellowstone and moving into the surrounding areas. I've been retrieving collars for data and installing trail cameras throughout the park where we've experienced fatalities. I've got nothing, so far."

"Why did you keep this from me? It almost cost me my life today. I know we study different species, but we're kind of like a team. Johnson, I am disappointed."

"Sincerely, I am sorry. Tell me what happened. What did you see?"

Sam sat forward again. Her voice fluctuated as if she were telling a horror story next to a campfire. "I'm assuming they heard my truck and hunkered down for an attack. Dale and I saw nothing when we arrived or as I approached the carcass. I got spooked by birds and started backtracking. When I heard movement, I ran. In fact, I ran faster than I ever have. How many? Perhaps half a dozen of them? They were all around me. Those creatures came too close. Too close."

"How did you outrun them? Why do you refer to them as creatures?"

"I shed my gear, so it didn't weigh me down. When I threw my rifle, it went off. It startled the pack. I made it to the truck when the creature-things stopped. And no, they weren't wolves or bears."

"They are almost twice as big as a gray wolf. The ones I saw had shorter hair that appeared reddish, lighter than Sam's, but reddish," Dale said. It was the first time he had spoken. "They moved fast and hunted as a pack. I'm guessing six to ten of them? Like Sam said, they aren't wolves. Maybe some kind of hybrid wolf, but not a purebred. I only saw them for a brief second. They disappeared as quickly as they appeared. I was more distressed about Sam getting back to the truck."

"Did you get pictures?" Johnson asked. Sam and Dale erupted into laughter.

"You're kidding, right? My rifle and equipment are lying in that field right now," Sam said. "When you retrieve your collar tomorrow, you can grab my gear. Maybe you can take a picture? My camera's out there, too. That's the least you can do. Grab my stuff. It should be safe."

"Should be safe?" Johnson asked. He studied his girls for a moment. He wondered what weapons skills they possessed. Their appearance did not reassure him.

"They're on the move, looking for prey and eliminating the competition. Isn't that what you implied? Now they're doing some housecleaning on this side of the park."

"Housecleaning, that's funny," one girl said. She started laughing with another. Sam looked at Dale and they both exchanged looks of disbelief and amusement.

"Tomorrow will be a busy day. You girls should return to the cabins, get some rest," Johnson said. He watched them leave. After their departure and when they were no longer within earshot, he asked. "What's our next step?"

"Our problem? Next step? I think this is your problem. You're the wolf biologist with staff and money. Dale and I manage the bears on this side of the park. I don't have time this summer. Can you reach out to game and fish or other wildlife biologists in the park?" Sam replied. She wanted no involvement.

"My dear, I'm at a loss. It may be my problem now, but what will these creatures do after they drive my wolves from Yellowstone? Will these creatures turn on your bears? They want the other predators outed from their territory. Correct? And tourists? We had over a million in the park last July. And the children. Oh, the children!" Johnson replied. He played on Sam's emotions and knew how to manipulate her. "And you can see the girls I'm saddled with. Yes, it's my bad for hiring them for their beauty instead of brains. Lesson learned; it won't happen again. Please, Sam, I'm desperate now."

Sam became livid as he spoke. The big man had turned into a whining, helpless baby. He droned on and on with his pitiful pleas. Johnson enjoyed his elevated status amongst his peers, but Sam knew the real man that hid behind this ego. Johnson failed to handle the dirty work in the face of a crisis. Sam wanted him to reap what he had sowed, but Johnson had a point. Families packed the park, and her bears were in danger.

"What do you suggest I do?" Sam asked.

"I don't know if we're dealing with a new pack," he said, and shrugged his shoulders. "Or a new species? I'm at a loss."

"It doesn't matter how you spin it, they're here. We need to close some trails and notify the rangers. They need to engage the visitors with animal safety. With your money, invest in more trail cams and maybe a drone. See who's licensed to operate drones in the park and have them survey the area? Also, notify the park officials and get their advice. We need some direction regarding protocol. And please, have your girls sign some NDAs before they plaster this on social media."

"NDA?" Dale asked. He didn't recognize the term.

"Non-disclosure agreement," Sam replied. She looked Johnson in the eyes. "They can't talk about what they see or what they hear. You'll need to rein 'em in. Let's try to keep this under wraps before we cause panic or attract the nut cases and their cameras."

"My dear Sam, I'm lost without you," Johnson replied. He sat back in his chair, relieved to have Sam on his team.

"And don't forget, I need you to grab my stuff when you retrieve your collar tomorrow. Dale and I are going to check the bears in the area. I'm concerned about them after what happened today. I hope this is nothing, but I'm pretty certain we aren't mistaken."

"Done and done, I'll get right on it. Be safe, you two. I'll see you tomorrow night. Same time, same place. Nice to make your acquaintance, Dale. Keep your eye on that one," Johnson said. He nodded towards Sam before leaving the cabin.

Sam was hoping to move forward with her research during the brief summer season. She knew it had to wait. Something was destroying the animals in her park. Sam wanted them stopped before they could cause more damage. Johnson had a point. The park was full of visitors. Before turning off her bedside lamp, Sam recorded the day's events in a journal and checked her phone for messages. She dreaded what tomorrow would bring.

Day Three

The red canoe cut through the choppy water of the lake with some difficulty. As one person paddled the raft forward, the other fought to steer it against the pull of the winds. They fought against the weather that sought to move them into deeper waters. A cloud of mosquitos swarmed the couple as the blistering sun burned their skin. The two remained silent after bickering throughout the first half of their journey. The newlywed couple had planned this escapade to be private and romantic, although the latter eluded them. Their launch site was far behind them as they neared a canopy of trees on the western shoreline. The man turned to his new wife, pointing to a muddy and rocky beach. She acknowledged him with a nod and a somber expression.

"Careful! Please avoid those low branches. My body can't handle anymore scrapes and scratches," the man said. He turned forward and grumbled in a lower voice. "I think you're doing this on purpose."

Twice that day, she had mistakenly steered him into the thick foliage along the shoreline. Somehow, over the wind, she heard his snide quip. She lifted her oar and pretended to hit him on the head. Droplets of water hit his bare arms, leading him to turn and catch her spiteful act. This excursion was a test of the strength of their new marriage.

Once the canoe scraped bottom, the man placed his oar inside the boat and jumped into the water. "Christ, that's cold! Stay seated. You won't like this. We're not in Daytona Beach anymore."

The lake temperature was much colder than the warm Florida waters in his home state. The man pulled the canoe and the dead weight of his wife onto the gravel shoreline. Once the canoe was secure, both grabbed the picnic supplies. They headed towards the shade of the trees and doused their bodies with bug spray. The man grabbed a cold beer and returned to the shoreline. He remained distracted by views of the lake while his wife prepared the site.

"Come eat!" the lady yelled while patting the blanket sprawled on the forest floor. She served her husband a peanut butter and jelly sandwich with a side of crushed chips. "I think you owe me a do-over honeymoon!"

"Seriously? We agreed you would handle the wedding. My job was to stay out of your way and plan the honeymoon," he replied.

He grimaced as he bit off a piece of soggy jelly bread. The man hoped the conversation was over. She hadn't stopped complaining since they took their seats on the flight from Orlando to Jackson. He had no more fight in him.

"I hinted I wanted an outdoor vacation."

"This is an outdoor vacation!"

"No, like an island bungalow over the Pacific Ocean, outdoor vacation. Like walk down the staircase of your private bungalow and dip your toes into the blue, crystal-clear, salty water outdoor vacation. Like, drink from a coconut with a tiny umbrella, outdoor vacation," she replied.

"Okay, my little pumpkin. Can't we enjoy what's left of this trip? You can plan our next vacation when we get home," he said.

The man despised her whiny, high-pitched voice and second-guessed his life choice. He cracked a half-smile as she tackled him to the ground. The bride grabbed his neck and started kissing his face, working downward from his forehead to his chin. He swiped his arm to clear the food from the blanket as she straddled him. His new wife removed her shirt and exposed a white, lacy bra. He grinned and watched as she unknotted a tie from her hair and flipped her long brown curls while swaying her hips, side to side. She was quite the tease.

The woman continued her act, smacking her husband's hands when he reached out to unfasten her bra. Instead, she removed his shirt and pulled his arms above his head. Using her hair tie, she knotted his wrists together. She ran the tips of her polished fingernails over his chest before reaching behind her back. Much to his delight, she unhooked her brassiere. The woman removed it, spinning it in the air and throwing it to the forest floor. Her husband squirmed with anticipation and delight. As she bent over to kiss him, the bushes rustled behind them. They froze and listened as more movement stirred beyond their vision. The woman sat up and folded her arms across her chest as she turned to look. There was complete silence.

"Go away, you pervert!" the woman yelled. She glanced at her husband as he attempted to free his hands. "You said no one was here. This trip is not romantic. You have failed on so many levels, mister. And I thought this vacation couldn't get any worse."

"Untie me, please," her husband said.

The man shimmied himself to a sitting position, knocking his half-naked wife over. Before either could rise, the surrounding bushes erupted with movement. Ignoring her husband, the woman stood up and held her arms out, exposing her chest.

"Is this what you came to see? Show yourself, weirdos!"

A short-haired canine crept from the shadows to reveal its massive size. It watched the couple, studying its prey and waiting for them to take flight. Rather than pounce on its victim, the alpha watched a younger member of the pack step forward. Today would be his offspring's first kill. The woman's eyes bulged, and she wrapped her arms around her chest.

"Help me up. Untie me now. Don't move and don't run!" the man whispered.

Against his advice, his wife screamed and ran towards the lake. Although at a disadvantage, the man found the strength to rise and follow her lead. The man wavered as he ran, but was careful to remain on his feet. He knew that a fall could spell disaster, as he had no way to defend himself. More creatures emerged from the surrounding area to take part in the chase.

The woman reached the canoe before her husband. She pushed it into the lake, running beside it. Panicked, she lost control of the canoe as waves spilled over the side. It became waterlogged and tipped on its side, sinking to the bottom.

She tried to correct it, but only pushed it into deeper water. Her husband caught up to her and swung his tied wrists over her head, restraining her at the waist.

"Stop! You're making this worse. We need to flip this canoe. But first, untie me."

The man removed his arms from her torso and forced his bound wrists to her face. She dug her nails into the wet, thin cotton folds of the knot without success. As they struggled to untie the bindings, the fabric tightened more.

"I can't get it!"

The woman cried as the waves pushed them into deeper water. The groom noticed her shaking and shivering as her voice cracked.

"Help me flip this canoe!"

They tried to break the suction of the water, causing the raft to sink deeper and drift further. While the couple weighed their options and scanned the area, the wolves waited for them to emerge from the water. They lined the shore, communicating and exchanging glances with one another.

"I'm cold." The woman slurred through chattering teeth as hypothermia set in. Her thin frame failed to protect her from the frigid water.

Both of them shook, their bodies submerged below the shoulders. Each time they tried to near the shore, the pack stirred, forcing the couple to return to deeper waters. The man hooked his arms over his wife's head and pulled her partially nude body close to his. He relieved himself, providing a moment of warmth before the cold water returned. As they embraced, the mosquitos swarmed and fed on their exposed flesh. Neither had the energy to fight off the pests. Unable to move, the woman buried her face in the nape of her husband's neck. As his wife struggled to stay awake, his eyes darted back and forth, looking for rescue. No one was on the lake, no one was on the shore. The wolves retreated to the shade of the trees. He watched them rest while the younger ones frolicked and played. But the wolves still watched the couple shielded by the water.

As the sun started its descent from the sky, the man panicked. His wife was silent except for an occasional mumble. Until now, he had remained resilient to the chilly waters as he kept a tight grip on his wife. But all would soon change. His thoughts became clouded as he drifted in and out of consciousness. Time continued to pass, with no hope of rescue. Only when his face hit the ice-cold water did the man jerk upright to fend off sleep.

His wife was stiff and unresponsive. Her face had slipped under the water long before he noticed. To occupy time, he watched her hair dance with the movement of the waves. The groom's eyelids became heavier, his mind became blank. As his body shut down, the waves swallowed both bodies, pulling them to the lake floor and releasing the air from their lungs. The predators noticed their disappearance and watched as bubbles traveled to the surface. The alphas approached the shoreline and sniffed at the sky. Their meal had vanished. It was time to move. The pack would find sustenance elsewhere.

DAY FOUR

"What are the plans for today?" Dale secured his seat belt as Sam loaded the remaining supplies behind his seat. He listened as she fumbled with plastic cases and cardboard boxes of bullets and shotgun shells. She loaded cartridges with ammo and checked to ensure everything was loaded and ready to fire. Although she was still missing the weapons from the previous day, she seemed to have an endless supply of firepower. Dale pulled down his visor and flipped the cover to expose the mirror. He spied Sam in one corner and watched and waited for her to acknowledge his question. She busied herself and appeared deep in thought. Sam was on a mission. Dale repeated himself, "Sam, what are the plans for today?" She looked up, spotting his gazing eyes in the mirror. "Where are we going?"

Sam slammed the metal gun case shut and slid a combination lock through the round fittings before pushing the shackle into the locking latch. After it clicked, she spun the dial and disappeared from view and away from Dale's watchful eyes. The rear door closed. He listened through his open window as Sam's feet shuffled across the loose gravel and around the back of the truck. She opened her door and shimmied into her seat, sliding behind the steering wheel. Sam started the ignition as she pulled her seatbelt across her lap, locking the buckle into the latch. "We're going to let Johnson sort out his mess while we follow up with a bear disturbance. I got a message while you were inside. Someone at the West Bay Campground reported damage to a cooler. We need to check it. When we finish, I'd like to track our tagged bears. I'm hoping that Johnson's mutant pack of wolf things hasn't affected them."

For the fourth consecutive day, the pair drove north. They traveled along the same road that hugged Yellowstone Lake. Sam and Dale exchanged glances as they passed the entrance to the hidden road they traveled the day before yesterday. Both looked for movement, expecting the creatures to watch them as they drove by. But the surroundings were devoid of any animal activity. A short while later, Sam focused on the slowing traffic ahead. Dale leaned to the right, slightly tilting his head out of the window and resting it on the crook of his elbow. The wind messed his lengthy, golden-brown locks as he closed his eyes. He listened to a country song that blared from the crackling speakers, speakers that Sam had abused with her thundering music. When the truck slowed to a stop, Dale pulled himself into the cab. He sat up and stretched his limbs and the muscles in his face. Dale grabbed his thermos of black coffee for a caffeine fix and looked at the back-up in front of them. Although new to the park, he knew traffic only stopped for two reasons: the wildlife or parking spaces in the small, designated lots by the major attractions. "See anything?"

"No, I think I see lights ahead. Maybe an accident?" Dale raised his eyebrows and added a third reason to his mental list of reasons for traffic back-ups.

"How the hell does someone get into an accident at twenty to thirty miles an hour? It's a turtle race in this park." He watched as Sam leaned forward and squinted. She jerked her head forth. A pair of sunglasses fell from the top of her head to the bridge of her nose. Again, Dale was awe-struck with the actions of his mentor; his affection for her was hard to hide.

"Can't tell yet, but those are definitely emergency vehicles."

The line of cars continued to snake slowly through a dense canopy of trees that blocked most of the sun and cast dancing shadows that reflected off the newly paved and striped road. Occasionally, an intense beam of light pushed through the branches, blinding those that looked directly at it. Instead, as Sam advanced their truck, Dale fixated on the vehicles lined alongside the road as they came into sight. The first responders blocked half of their lane. There was no space for them to pull entirely off the road. They parked both on the roadway and with a set of tires resting on the sloped gravel and grassy shoulder. The tourists in front of Sam continued to zipper, having to wait until there was a break in oncoming traffic to bypass the area. Occasionally, a car might slow down, the occupants taking pictures or looking for a reason for the flurry of activity. *Nosey people*, Sam scolded them without voicing her frustrations for the unnecessary slowdowns. When it was her turn, as she slowly crept forward, Sam noticed an ambulance at the front of the procession of parked vehicles. A park service officer was unrolling crime scene tape and snaking in and out of the trees.

"I know him!" Sam jerked the wheel and partially drove off the shoulder to park with the others. "Let's go!" She was already talking to the officer before Dale could scurry through the dense brush to catch up.

"Yeah, dive teams and all," Dale caught the tail end of the brief conversation. "Not entirely sure what happened. If you go down, you know the drill. Touch nothing and watch where you tread. I'm not sure if this is a crime scene or an accident. No one tells me anything. Maybe it involves one of your bears?" He nodded his head in the right direction as he continued to unwind the yellow tape.

"Come on, stay glued to my side," Sam instructed. She and Dale followed the sound of voices that carried through the trees. They came into an open area with scattered picnic supplies and obstructed views of Lake Yellowstone. Sam and Dale stopped at the edge of a clearing to examine the site and look for safe passage; the pair wanted to avoid confrontation. In the distance, two divers communicated with one another next to a water-logged canoe before disappearing beneath the waterline. A motorboat anchored close by bobbed gently with the movement of the water. Two men leaned over the side of that boat, assisting the divers each time they breached the surface. Another man in uniform sat behind the boat's steering wheel, oblivious to the activity behind him. Officers and investigators lined the shore. Some took notes or videotaped; others took photos or talked into devices. Two investigators recorded evidence and bagged items that littered the ground in the clearing. Sam and Dale watched as one lifted a bra with a rod and placed it into a marked plastic bag.

"What happened here?" Dale whispered to Sam for answers.

"You know as much as me."

"Hey, hey. This area's closed." An officer yelled at Sam and Dale while quickly racing towards them. "You need to leave now."

Before he continued his advance, he stopped and looked towards the divers that had resurfaced and yelled to those onshore. A diver pointed downward with a gloved hand. Another was busily tethering a line to something submerged and hidden in the lake. The officer turned and joined those lined up along the shore. The men at the scene gave their full attention to the divers as they barked instructions at the watching investigators. Sam and Dale observed two bodies lifted from the water and carefully hoisted over the boat railing. Despite their isolated location and the lack of intrusive eyes, another man stood on the boat, holding a white sheet to cover the bodies. The divers remained at that location and resumed their underwater search for additional bodies and evidence.

When the men were clear of the boat, someone lifted the anchor. The watercraft slowly approached the shore until the bottom scraped against the rocks. An officer caught a mooring line thrown towards the group and secured it to a tree. When given the sign, the investigators waded into the water to make their independent observations about the couple pulled from the lake. They remained silent for a moment, taking in the sight after a man lifted the sheet from the bodies. Soon, everyone started scribbling on their spiral notebooks and taking photos. While they worked diligently, a park officer noticed Sam and approached her and Dale. She recognized him, but his name escaped her memory.

"Sam," she held out her hand to shake his. "I've seen you around, but we've never officially met. And this is Dale." Dale nodded his head.

"Peterson. I've seen you around, too. What department are you with?" He was wary of their presence.

"I'm a bear biologist for Yellowstone." He looked at her with a critical and discerning gaze. She detected his guarded behavior and continued her persuasive speech. "I received some messages regarding grizzly activity in this area. We need a quick look for scat, shredded bark, or a bear bed. Perhaps it had something to do with the demise of these people, perhaps not. We'll be a few minutes. Where is it safe to walk?" Dale knew she was stretching the truth, but played along by nodding his head in agreement.

The officer squinted an eye and gazed at the pair while trying to hold the upper hand. "Do you have an ID?"

Sam pulled a lanyard from her tank top and flashed it at the officer. He signaled to remain still as he called dispatch to verify her employment. She purposely held it below her exposed cleavage. As he spoke to someone, she watched the officer's eyes dart back and forth between the ID and her breasts. Dale smirked at the exchange. The officer sighed when a familiar voice in dispatch reassured him that Sam was indeed a biologist. If their scene involved a bear, she was the most qualified to assist. Sam was fortunate to have friends throughout the park. After the call, the officer instructed them to remain in their spots. He walked over to an evidence specialist who was wrapping up his work. After speaking to the person, the officer waved them over and gave instructions within earshot of everyone. Sam and Dale were to have a quick look, leave, and not speak to anyone regarding the activity at the lake or their investigation. Dale watched the divers stand on the shore and begin stripping out of their gear as he spoke. A separate team had righted the red canoe and secured it to an additional motorboat for transport. After his brief lecture, the officer turned his back to the pair and rejoined his colleagues.

"Come on, Dale." Sam nudged him when they were no longer under scrutiny. "Let's hurry. Look for evidence. I hope we find nothing. Especially proof that a bear's responsible for this mess."

Sam walked around with her eyes scanning the forest floor and failed to notice Dale wandering off to another area. They swiftly searched the ground and a bothersome notion crossed Sam's mind. *This location is close to the gray wolf carcass. Predators move to find prey when they require food. People are the easiest prey and tourists are an easier kill. They have no weapons, no defense, no common sense, and lots of distractions. Someone abandoned clothing pieces and picnic supplies in the clearing. Officers recovered two corpses from the lake alongside a submerged canoe. Did they go skinny dipping in a freezing lake? Stupid theory. No, the water's too cold for swimming. Why didn't they come out? Even us natives refuse to swim in that lake. Were they drinking or incapacitated? Toxicology reports can take weeks. Were they chased into the water? Did the hybrid wolf pack chase them into the water? Is that why they stayed submerged in freezing water? They must have been more afraid of what was onshore than risking hypothermia? What prevented them from using the canoe to escape? Did they sink their canoe in a panic? Did the wolf hybrids try to wait them out?* Her mind continued to race; she looked up at Dale. He stood still in the distance with his arms crossed and a smile that spanned his face. He found it!

Dale and Sam stood shoulder to shoulder and looked at the impressions in the soft dirt. A set of unmistakable paw imprints popped from amongst investigator boot prints. There were others scattered about, but none was as apparent. It was a large specimen, a wolf pad with four toe prints and deep nail indentations. Dale had already placed his phone next to it for size comparison. Sam carefully scanned the area to look for wandering eyes. Fortunately, officers were busy and heard talking and bickering over the circumstances of the death. Who tied the man's wrists? It was a crime. No, it was something kinky. It was an accident. We need bloodwork. Who are they? Is their canoe from the marina at the campground? Was this intentional? Did he drag his wife into the water to drown her? Why were they naked from the waist up? The investigators were rapid with their succession of questions, but no one offered solid answers or theories.

"Take a picture, Sam. No one's watching." Sam cautiously slipped the phone out of her pocket with her back to the investigators. She took several shots as Dale looked out onto the lake. Sam quickly scanned the snapshots to make sure they were clear and focused. She nudged Dale and nodded her head when finished. Dale retrieved his phone and used a blade of grass to measure the depth of the nail impression before slipping it into the back of his phone case. Excited with their find, the two skirted the flurry of activity and returned to the truck unnoticed. Neither said a word until they sat down with the doors and windows secured.

"I love you, Dale!" Sam wrapped her arms around his neck, tightly hugging him before releasing him from a death grip. His eyes were wide as he watched her outburst. "You found what I was hoping to find! I knew you were the right guy for this job. Intelligent and easy on the eyes!" She winked. "Let's keep this quiet until we show Johnson. Those damn creatures chased that couple into the lake. They were so scared of those animals that they froze to death. They didn't want to be eaten alive. Ha! I knew it."

Sam started the truck and turned the radio volume up as her tires kicked up gravel and gripped the pavement. She cut off a car packed with college kids that honked and flipped her off. Knowing that Johnson would be busy until evening, the pair headed towards the campground. A sick feeling hit Sam as she thought about the cooler. Was the ice chest destroyed by a bear, or did the wolf creatures move into fresh territory? She stepped on the accelerator to move them along faster.

A hostess for the campground had a vague understanding of their visit. She failed to recall which campsite had complained about the busted cooler. Sam and Dale watched her intently. While standing in the office, the young girl snapped her gum and twirled a long lock of hair. Fresh on shift and new to her summer job, she was alone in the office at that moment. She waved her hand in the campground's direction and told them it was in that general area. Of course, the wave of her hand covered almost the entire location. Frustrated with her lack of help, they thought it better to go alone. They were short on time and shorter on patience. They left the building rather than wait for another staff member, especially since the next one might be as clueless as this girl.

Sam slowly steered her truck through a sea of campers and recreational toys. They weaved back and forth while Dale unsuccessfully searched for an abandoned and broken cooler. Sam parked her vehicle in the middle of a lane and hopped into the bed for a better look. "What are you thinking?" Dale asked as he leaned out of the window with his head turned upwards toward Sam.

"The main road is that way, behind those trees. I think we look again in that area." She pointed in the opposite direction before hopping out. The campground was immense, one of Yellowstone's largest. It was open, but surrounded by a dense forest. Each site came equipped with a picnic bench and fire pit that doubled as a grill. Despite its size, the campground offered very little privacy. Camper, RV, and tent sites had little space separating one from their neighbor. This planning allowed the park service to maximize the number of people they could accommodate overnight. Those that selected West Bay for a private camping getaway chose the wrong place.

Even with its location and the flurry of human activity, bison favored the campground. The large mammals preferred to feed on the thick and overgrown vegetation. They held no fear of people and would bluff charge when aggravated. Regardless of the number of run-ins at the campground, everyone had avoided injury. Sam scanned the area for the giants. She wanted to avert potential harm to her truck; even the slightest contact would leave considerable damage. She made a mental note of their absence. It wasn't like them to pass on the lush greens amid the warmth of summer, especially with the lack of people during this time of day.

After taking her place behind the wheel, Dale probed her further. "I think we have the same suspicions."

"How so?" She furrowed her eyebrows and glanced at him while resuming the drive.

"You pointed to the tree line at the edge of the campground, closest to recent activity. The hybrid wolves would most likely approach the campground after ditching the couple on the lake. A bear will abandon an easy meal, say, an unsecured cooler, if it catches the overwhelming and unfamiliar scent of a pack of predators. While grizzlies will take on a pack of wolves at a kill site, this one might not think it worth the effort. More so if the bear has already encountered this pack. A bear will make itself scarce until the threat has left. I, and possibly you, think this campsite had a recent visitor last night. With all the strange occurrences of late, this might not be one of our bears." Dale looked at her and waited. He wanted confirmation that his hunch aligned with hers. Sam glanced at him with her familiar smile.

"You sound like a textbook, Dale. As a scientist, I do not make assumptions regarding animal behavior. I am one with common sense and one that questions everything in nature. But I wholeheartedly agree with everything you just said, one hundred percent. You are the yin to my yang!" She laughed, and her nose scrunched up. Dale blushed and looked away. "We need to find that damn cooler!"

As they approached the back of West Bay, where a line of campers backed up to the trees, Sam slowed the truck to barely a crawl. When they saw an RV door swing open, she stopped the vehicle. A much older man emerged with binoculars and a picture book of Wyoming birds. He wore a mismatched shirt and shorts with long black socks and sandals. The elderly gentleman looked more suited to a beach than the wildlands in the mountains. Sam parked the truck, released her seatbelt, and hurriedly twisted over Dale, both hands gripping the open window frame for support.

"Excuse me!" The man looked towards the truck. He put his items on a table and sat in a sun-faded fabric chair. His wife peeked out the door after hearing Sam shout. The man approached the truck after rising from his chair with difficulty. Sam was hopeful, as this couple looked like the official campground busybodies. They were the type that traveled to people-watch rather than experience local culture and attractions. They would know the comings and goings in the campground.

"How can I help?" Sam retreated to her seat as the man leaned into the window. A little on the short side, his face barely broke even with the bottom of the frame. He looked around the truck before they responded.

"We're park biologists and looking for a cooler that was destroyed by wildlife last night," she spoke loudly, unsure if his hearing was intact.

"Took y'all long enough. That family waited all morning, but got tired and went up to Mammoth for the day. They tired of waitin' for you." He tugged on his pants, pulling them over his distended beer gut. "I'll take you there."

"That's unnecessary. Just point us in the right direction and we'll be on our way." Sam disliked this man. He would withhold information unless they involved him in the investigation. She had had run-ins with this type before. The man wanted campfire fodder for the evening gossip fest. Everyone would brag about their hikes and wildlife sightings, but he would have nothing to contribute unless he accompanied the wildlife biologists. He was an annoyance. Sam fibbed an excuse. "Park policy. For the safety of our visitors, we ask that you remain here."

He cocked his head backward and scrunched his eyebrows. "Never heard of that one, but I ain't looking for trouble. You let me know what you find there." He hesitated and opened his mouth for a moment, not wanting to share the location of the cooler. "You passed it. Four spaces back." He pointed to the camper and only addressed Dale from this point further. "It's that black and tan camper. See it? They dragged the cooler to the back after you were a no-show." He stepped away from the truck.

"Thank you!" Sam immediately put the truck in reverse and Dale lifted his hand to wave. Dale gave a half-nod in a show of gratitude. Sam slammed on the brakes in front of the described camper, sending a plume of dust into the air. She discreetly slipped a handgun into her holster, unknotted her shirt, and pulled it over the weapon to hide it from view. It was probably too little firepower, but anything was better than nothing.

Once their feet hit the grass at the back edge of the site, Sam and Dale paused. They examined the location and listened for movement in the forest. As their eyes darted around, they caught sight of the trash left behind. A few pieces of shredded cellophane flapped against the tall grass blades and reflected the sunlight. Sam spotted the cooler wedged underneath the back of the camper, just as the man had described. Before they approached, she knew it reeked of stale beer and dead fish. The obnoxious smell lingered in the air. No wonder they targeted the cooler for an easy meal. Sam shook her head in disbelief as she signaled for Dale to help her pull it out.

The cooler lid was intact, but something had sheered the rubber latches away; only short nubs remained. The offending animal had also shredded the rope handles and yanked the gasket seal from the lid. After examining and lifting the lid, Sam brushed aside crumbled lunch meat bags, Styrofoam trays, and a gutted burger patty box. She noted smashed baskets of berries, bruised apples, a torn bag of granola, and an empty carton of milk. Someone had retrieved them from the ground, as bits of grass and dirt covered the contents. Sam opened and closed the lid again, noticing marks left by canine teeth. They were much too small for a bear.

"Your turn. Look, Dale." Sam stepped back and walked around the campsite, never going further than the tree line. She noticed the nosey man and his wife watching from outside their RV as Sam looked for additional evidence. She waved at the two before they retreated from sight. Sam stopped to look beyond the trees as the afternoon winds picked up. *What are you? Are you watching me right now?* She placed her right hand on her holster for comfort.

"Sam!" She turned to look at Dale. "I called you twice. Didn't you hear me the first time?" She promptly joined him next to the cooler.

"Are we still on the same page?" Sam stared into his eyes, lacking emotion.

"I think we need to bring the cooler back to the cabins. Johnson needs to see it. Our bears didn't destroy this cooler." Sam nodded. Together, they secured the oversized cooler and loaded it into the bed of the truck. As Dale took his seat, Sam rifled through the cluttered storage compartment in the console and pulled out a worn business card with her contact information. She returned to the camper door and secured it in the screen door frame.

As they prepared to leave the campground, Sam and Dale noticed a flurry of activity on a side road. They stopped to look and watched briefly as a tow truck positioned itself in front of a campsite. Thankful it didn't involve them, they proceeded towards the exit. Sam slammed the brakes when she noticed a woman leaving the office with a clipboard in her hands and eyes glued to a sheet of paper. She recognized the middle-aged woman from the previous summers; she was a friend and fixture at this campground.

"Sue!" Sam leaned over Dale and waved at the woman while displaying a big, welcoming smile. The lady perked up after recognizing Sam. She made a beeline towards the truck. She, too, beamed as she tucked the clipboard under her arm.

"How is my favorite red-head? And who is this handsome young man?" Her accent identified her as a southerner. Dale glimpsed at her name tag before it disappeared into the folds of her shirt. "How have you been? I haven't seen you in these parts this summer. Quiet on your end? I see your shirt is still on the small side. Can't you find one that fits properly? Leaves little to the imagination." She cocked her head in disapproval. Sue could out-talk Sam and was very animated as she spoke. She was one of the few people Sam adored as much as the bears. She was motherly and kind, always looking out for Sam. Sue admired the bear biologist, but always made a jab towards her wardrobe choice. She was a proper Georgia lady who failed to hold her tongue.

"This is Dale, my new intern-in-training. Dale is the next best thing to happen to Yellowstone. Smart one, he is." She winked and smiled at him as he blushed.

"Honey, let me forewarn you." She looked at Dale. "This fiery ginger is more dangerous than the bears in this park. Sam will get her claws into you. Better be careful." She winked at Dale as Sam returned to her seat. "So, what brings you to my parts?"

"I was in the area to pick up a busted cooler." She nodded her head towards the activity in the campground while adjusting her shirt. "Any news about the tow truck in the campground?"

"A couple disappeared, leaving behind their little RV. Supposedly, authorities discovered them in the lake with their capsized canoe. But you did not hear that from me. Investigators are taking the RV for evidence. It is a damn shame, but these city folk, newlyweds at that, do not understand the way things work up here." Sue shed new insight on the incident. Her husband was an employee at a sheriff's office outside the park and often aided the park rangers in Yellowstone. If something came out of Sue's mouth, there was truth to it. Sue stopped short.

"What's bothering you, Sue? I know that look." Sam furrowed her eyebrows and puckered her lips. "You're like a mom to me. Dale here is a mini-me. You can trust him."

"Well, there was a gentleman that arrived a week ago and paid for seven nights. He was due to leave this morning; I have someone waiting on his site. We're full this summer, again," she emphasized the last word. "I can't find him and I need him to move. With all the flurry about this young couple, I'm hesitant to blow the whistle on this guy. It's probably my overactive imagination. I'm sure he's out sightseeing or hiking, but then, I'm not sure. He had a bike, but that's missing, too. I was going to call my husband shortly and ask him to run the tag. No one has seen this guest lately."

"Who is he?" Sam's body was tensing up as Sue spoke.

"I checked him in when he arrived. Average looking, but a little peculiar. Acted like he was all business and no fun. Some women mentioned him one day when they came to the office for maps, called him a creep. They said he watched the little girls in the campground, especially one that liked to play on her bike. Every time I drove the golf cart through the grounds, I'd swing by his site. He was never there." She felt a pang of guilt for passing on judgment without knowing the man. "Now, he's disappeared. Sweet Jesus, I sure hope nothing happened to him. Unless he's a pedophile; God has a special place in hell for them."

"Are those women still here? When did they last see him?" Dale spoke up before Sam.

"No. They left a few days ago. I think we've had a complete turnover in that area of the campground since he became a no-show. I've asked some campers, but they don't remember him. You don't think something happened, do you?" She slid the clipboard from under her arms and hugged it tightly against her chest.

"Which site is he parked at? I'll take a quick look. Be sure to follow up with your husband. Maybe this summer is one for the record books." Sam was eager to visit his lot.

"Oh, my! He's in Loop D, site 209. Look for a small, white camper van. What are the odds, two of my campers on the same day?" She shook her head and stepped back as Sam turned the truck around.

"Thanks, Sue. Stay safe and keep your eyes open," Sam yelled as she headed back to the campground.

When they approached the site and spied the white vehicle, Sam slowed the truck. They were in the center of the loop, surrounded by other campers and small RVs. Sam stopped and parked in front of the lot's entrance. Both Sam and Dale looked around before exiting the pickup. They stopped short at the start of the gravel site and Sam swung her arm out and against Dale's chest to stop him from advancing.

"I'm thinking we should stay here in case this, too, is a crime scene. Let's not do anything to tie ourselves to this one. I don't want law enforcement breathing down our necks." Dale nodded in agreement as they did a quick scan in silence. "I'm guessing nothing happened here, too crowded. The site looks tidy, too. Maybe the pervert keeled over from a heart attack during the night in his van. We'll chalk this one up to a non-animal-related mystery. Let's make ourselves scarce before someone shows up." The two retreated to the truck.

"His bike rack was empty. Just saying." Dale stated as they buckled their seat belts. Sam frowned and looked at him with knowing eyes.

"I'm trying to stay positive."

"What's this?" Sam wrapped and tucked a terry cloth towel around her wet tresses as she emerged from the bathroom. She wore long, flannel pajama bottoms and a snug t-shirt made of thin and nearly transparent cotton material. Dale couldn't help but notice her hardened nipples through the fabric and the bounce from her breasts, no longer constrained by a bra. Sam caught his gaze and the lack of attention in the kitchen. "You're going to burn the food."

"Sorry!" Dale's eyes shot back to the griddle as his face turned a fiery red. He flipped some pancakes as Sam stole a piece of warm bacon from a plate next to the stove.

"Either you're starving or that's a lot of food for the two of us." She opened the refrigerator and poured a glass of orange juice into a glass that she snagged from the drying rack by the sink. She proceeded to a corner cabinet and removed a hidden bottle of vodka to enhance her beverage.

"Johnson texted while you were in the shower. He's on his way with the girls and should be here soon. I told him I'd have dinner ready. We have little in the cabin, so it's breakfast for dinner." He stuffed a pancake in his mouth and watched as Sam downed her drink and prepared a second. He struggled momentarily to talk with the food in his mouth before swallowing. "Take it easy with that stuff. Maybe change, too."

"My shift's over. I'm done for the evening. Johnson and I have shared plenty of drinks before. In fact," she said, holding the bottle up to look at the label, "I think I snagged this bottle from him last summer. Besides, he's seen me like this plenty of times. I'm not changing for him." She winked as she passed Dale to walk towards her recliner.

"Are you and Johnson a thing? I mean, were you a thing?" He regretted the words as soon as they left his mouth. He reacted by chewing another pancake before he could say anything else that he would regret.

"NO!" Sam laughed and placed the drink down on an end table so she wouldn't spill it. She composed herself as her mind dredged up memories. "He would love that, but it's a serious NO for me."

"Why? Aren't women attracted to a proper English gentleman?" Dale faked a horrible British accent. Sam continued to laugh as Dale picked up a glass and held it with his pinky finger extended. He pretended to drink in a dainty fashion, taking sips and rolling his eyes in delight.

He reverted to himself. "What's your story, anyway? I mean, you are hot and have a perfect body, not that I've noticed. All the men we've bumped into, well, they appear to have the same opinion. I mean, it's none of my business, but since we're spending an entire summer together..."

"No boyfriend. No husband. Never married." She resumed drinking, sitting sideways with her legs dangling over the arms of the dated and putrid green chair that faced the kitchen. "Not much to talk about. I like to flirt and all. Heck, I enjoy showing off what I have. I'll continue to do so until it expands and sags with age." She looked down and puffed up her chest before deflating it. "But I don't connect with men. No luck with relationships. Nada!" She sounded exhausted and defeated. "And before we continue, aren't you a little young? What are you, twenty, twenty-one?"

"Twenty-two and I have a girlfriend." He stuffed another pancake in his mouth to avoid digging himself into a deeper hole. Dale wasn't lying. He had a girlfriend, one he met in college, but they were spending their first summer apart.

"A girlfriend, eh? I guess you can look, but can't touch. No harm in that." She finished her drink and proceeded to the kitchen for a third. "After the last couple of days, I need a good drink to forget, reset and forge on. I have a feeling this will be the worst summer of my career. And take note, young man, this has nothing to do with you. Thank God you're here to hold me up."

Sam already appeared tipsy. She normally didn't drink and started her binge on an empty stomach. Before she left the kitchen with another screwdriver, Dale crammed a pancake in her mouth as she passed. After completing four years of college, time with friends made him well versed in the art of drinking. He finished cooking the last of the grub before preparing a hearty plate of eggs, pancakes, and bacon for Sam. Dale hoped the food would absorb the alcohol. As he handed her the plate, Johnson entered the cabin alone.

"Knock, knock! A little early for a drink, eh?" Johnson instantly spied the bottle of vodka beyond the plated food. He moved into the kitchen and helped himself to a drink. "This bottle closely resembles one that occupied my cabin last summer. Please tell me this isn't the same one?" He looked over at Sam as she lifted her glass to celebrate the moment.

"The very one." She smiled as she ate. "Help yourself to some of Dale's great home cooking. If Dale weren't here, you'd be dining on crackers and chicken noodle soup, straight from the can! I can't cook for my life." She laughed and Johnson snickered with her.

"I see you're dressed for the occasion. Mmm... mmm... mmm. Sam, you have always been one fine and delectable woman. Only you can make a t-shirt and bath towel look sexy as hell." He directed his attention towards Dale. "You are one lucky man. Don't take one moment of this summer internship for granted. You surely hit the lottery, young man!" Johnson cocked his head back and emptied the glass in one shot. He poured another, tucked the bottle under his arm, and filled a plate before topping it with more and more food. He carefully balanced his meal, a glass, the vodka, and utensils as he joined Sam in the living area. Dale watched from the kitchen table.

"Where are the girls? I made plenty." Dale poked around his plate with a fork as Johnson settled on the couch.

"They're fending for themselves tonight. I need a break from their shrieking voices and constant jabber. I'd rather spend the evening with my woman here." He smiled at Sam before scarfing down his dinner. She rolled her eyes, set her plate down, and finished her drink before reaching across the coffee table for the vodka. Johnson teasingly pulled it away from her before sliding it towards her extended fingers. "My, my, my, that t-shirt compliments your body in every way imaginable." He looked at Dale and raised his eyebrows in rapid succession. Dale blushed and looked towards Sam.

"Aren't the girls tending to your needs, Mr. Randy?" She filled the bottom third of her glass with straight liquor before sitting back. She removed the towel from her head and tossed it towards the bathroom.

"Randy? Is that your first name?" Dale inquired as he watched the exchange between the pair. Both laughed hysterically at his question.

"Randy means horny in British slang. That's my nickname for the big, old bloat." She smiled at Johnson.

"Hey, now. Let's play nicely." Johnson reclaimed the vodka.

"Fine, and my apologies. Let's get down to business."

"Fire away." Johnson's plate was almost empty. Although full, he looked towards the kitchen and contemplated filling his dish again.

"Tell me what you did today. Did you take care of everything we discussed last night?" Sam was all business, even as she continued to pound down the liquor.

"Absolutely! We retrieved the collar first thing, without incident. They picked the wolf carcass clean. Awful. We didn't see signs of any other predators, or your predator. There was a fox. Are you sure it wasn't a fox that spooked you?" He poured more vodka and took another shot before refilling his glass. "We contacted some professional drone operators. I'm waiting to hear from a few regarding their availability. And last, I had the girls sign the non-disclosure agreements."

"Not a fox. What else?"

"After we got everything sorted out, we ran stats on our wolf packs." He emptied his glass, then started drinking from the bottle. "I don't know what the hell is happening, but they have hauled arse out of Yellowstone. My surviving packs have moved to Montana, Idaho, the Tetons, east of Cody, and even to the upper Wind River. Something is scaring them. I've seen nothing like this." He drank again before wiping the rim with his shirtsleeve and passing the bottle to Sam. "Did you follow your tagged bears? What are they doing?"

"I intended to check up on my bears." Sam drank from the bottle when Johnson handed it over, wincing as the liquid burned the back of her throat. "But... the unexpected happened today. I think our little mystery is getting a little bigger."

"Oh, Sam! Please don't talk in riddles, do tell!" He bent over the table to reclaim the nearly empty bottle of vodka.

"They pulled a couple from the lake this morning north of your kill site. Dale found a paw imprint along the shore. Show 'em, Dale." She motioned for him to grab her phone that lay on the kitchen table. After swiping, she tapped the screen and expanded the photo with her fingers. "Here. This is the print. Look at the size of that compared to Dale's phone. There were lots of prints, but this was the clearest and most impressive."

"This is how deep the nail imprint was." Dale pulled the blade of grass from his phone case and bent it to a ninety-degree angle. Johnson's eyes widened at the length.

"Yes, not a fox. And not a gray wolf. What the hell is this?" He took the blade of grass to compare it to his finger length. "Four centimeters. Are you certain?"

"No mistake. And it gets better." Sam's attention turned to the cooler next to the entryway.

"How so?" Johnson twisted his head in the same direction. "What's that? Did you get a specimen?" He excitedly made his way towards the cooler as Sam and Dale joined him.

"I got a bear nuisance call about a busted-up cooler at the campground by the lake. Look." She crossed her arms and watched Johnson open the lid. All three grabbed their noses as the putrid smell of rotting food permeated the small area.

"Rotting food? More riddles, Sam?"

"What kind of food?" She egged him on.

"Fruit, vegetables, granola... I don't follow?" He closed the lid. "Are you going to let me in on your little secret?"

"Both black and grizzly bears would consume those foods. They're not picky eaters, especially when presented with such a wide variety of foods." She opened the cooler again and Johnson grabbed the lid. "Look at the empty packages and wrappers. Something ate those meats. Now, look at the cooler." Johnson released the lid from his grip, allowing it to slam shut. "Those are canine teeth marks. This wasn't a bear. Those things tore into it. They found an easy meal with your wolf. They tried to make an easy meal out of the couple in the lake, and now, they hit a cooler full of beef on the edge of the campground. It's too early to speculate, but we also got wind of a missing camper at West Bay. I think these predators are eating their way through our park. We need to draw attention to this before anything else happens."

Johnson listened intently to everything she said as he further inspected the damaged cooler. He rifled through the food items, hoping to prove her wrong, but everything was as she said. Her assumptions were right. A bear would've devoured the entire contents of the cooler. A different predator possessed the intelligence to gnaw off the latches and use their teeth to break the suction of the lid from the cooler. He had never documented a case of a gray wolf breaking into secured food items, human food items.

"Did you install any trail cams?" Johnson looked between Dale and Sam, but both shook their lowered heads.

"I didn't have any available. This wasn't in the plans today." Sam glanced at Dale.

"Should we go now? It's not too late." Johnson was eager to get video footage.

"Hell, no! I'm drunk and now it's dark. I'm not in any condition to face those things tonight."

"What if Dale drives and I install? Surely, there's enough activity at the campground to keep them at bay?" He smiled at the two, but his enthusiasm waned when neither agreed.

"Prep them tonight and we'll install them tomorrow. Let's be smart about this. And... since we're close to these areas, let's be safe in our cabins. Keep your girls inside and stay in pairs when outdoors. They can just as easily show up here. Also, keep your exterior lights on. I don't want to walk outside to a surprise." Sam crossed her arms as she barked orders.

"Agreed. Since I'm alone, perhaps I should stay here tonight?" Johnson smiled and winked at Sam.

"You don't quit, do you! I'm not that drunk. Go home! I'll watch from my doorway until you're inside. We'll regroup tomorrow. Have a good night, Johnson." She flipped on the exterior light and stood in the doorframe, watching Johnson clear the distance between cabins in record time. He couldn't hide his nervousness from Sam as his head turned from side to side and searched the darkness.

"Your gear is in my truck. I'll bring it over at first light." He yelled to Sam before disappearing behind his door.

Sam waved and locked hers before checking the window latches and drawing the curtains. As Dale finished cleaning the kitchen, Sam placed a rifle by the entry. She handed a pistol to Dale before setting one on her nightstand. Sam was scared, and for good reason.

"Mom, Brutus needs to go outside." The boy sat at the kitchen table with his back against the window. His legs rested on the vinyl of the long bench seat, his mother failing to notice the hiking boots still on his feet. He tapped his tablet in a glow of light emitted from the screen. The dog continued to beg, pacing between the table and the door.

"I'm busy. Ask your father." She chopped vegetables and leaned back to glance towards the other side of the camper. The bathroom door remained closed and she could hear his muffled singing in the shower.

"He's still in the bathroom." The boy had yet to take his eyes off the screen. Stimulated by their voices, the rottweiler elevated his assault on the door. His need intensified with every passing minute.

"Can you take Brutus out? He's going to shred the screen. Your father just replaced it, and he'll be livid." The weight of the knife hitting the plastic cutting board increased, making a loud and rhythmic noise that carried throughout the camper. She grew frustrated. Her husband wanted the dog, and she had to care for it. He wanted children, and she had to care for them. He wanted a home-cooked meal, and she had to prepare it. She had too much to juggle with her full-time job. The list of responsibilities continued to razzle her nerves. Her relaxing holiday had turned into a working vacation. The matriarch slammed the knife on the counter and refilled her glass with Zinfandel. She faced the boy and zeroed in on his feet, but held her tongue. Instead, she drank from the stemless wineglass and took a deep breath.

"Why can't Izzy?" He tapped harder on the screen, grunting as his character lost energy and met with defeat. His mother grew more annoyed with the obnoxious sound effects.

"I'm four. I don't know how. You're ten." His sister chimed in, taking her eyes away from the television screen.

"Shut up, Izzy. Who asked you?" The boy gave her an evil eye, and she responded by sticking up her middle finger.

"Mo..." His mother abruptly cut him off.

"Your sister is four and I'm about to take that darn thing away. Take the dog out! Before you do that, turn the volume off or use earbuds. I can't take any more of that noise!" She resumed preparing the dinner as the boy slid from a seating position and slammed his booted feet on the floor. He purposely stomped to display his resentment. "Take a flashlight and make sure the dog stays on a leash. Oh, and take a poop bag. Clean up after Brutus, so we don't get fined."

"I'm not picking up his poop. It's bigger than my hand. And it's hot and smells." He made a gagging face, causing his sister to chuckle.

"Stay out of the woods. I don't want ticks in our camper. Go! And hurry, dinner will be ready soon." She slid a pan into the small convection oven.

The boy leashed Brutus and walked behind the camper. They paused momentarily so Brutus could defecate while the boy watched; he had no intention of picking up the mess. Instead, he scanned the grass and found a rock to place in the empty plastic bag. He knotted the handles and stuffed it into his back pocket. He expected his mother would listen for the sound of a weighted bag, dropped in the garbage can upon their return. After completing his business, Brutus pulled the boy towards the tree line; he was a big dog and easily weighed twice that of his master.

Brutus was eager to mark the many trees that surrounded the campground and analyze the unfamiliar scents. They wandered further from their camper. At the time of Brutus' next stop, sniff, and mark the territory routine, the boy pulled the flashlight out of his front pocket and clicked the button. He required additional light as they continued to explore during twilight. The boy looked over his shoulder to gauge the distance back to their encampment. He imagined his mother would soon yell at him and wanted to stay within a safe distance of earshot. He feared her wrath more than anything in the dark. When they reached the last camper in their row, Brutus paused and stared into the woods. He let out a deep grumble, getting the boy's attention. He directed the beam of his flashlight towards the forested area and saw nothing.

"It's nothing, you big, stupid dog." He picked up a rock and threw it into the dense brush. They listened as it fell to the forest floor, hitting other rocks before resting on a bed of dried leaves. "See. There's nothing there."

He picked up another stone and threw it with the same result. Brutus's growl intensified, exposing his white canines as he snarled. This time, the boy selected the largest rock in the area, squatted, and rocked back and forth to gain momentum. He used this technique during basketball practice to throw the ball farther down the court. He tossed it underhanded into the thicket, without the benefit of his flashlight. Instead of hitting the forest floor, there was a thump and a yelp. His eyes widened, and he stood up instantly.

Before the boy could speak, Brutus lunged forward, knocking him down, and ran into the brush. He dragged the stunned youngster, who failed to stop the charging dog. The boy's face bounced against the rocky forest floor as his hand swept to the side and sought something to grab hold of. His fingers seared with pain as Brutus ripped them from the branches of low-lying bushes during the chase. Each time he opened his mouth to scream, it filled with dirt and debris, adding to his struggle. The pursuit was only interrupted as the child's shoulder smacked against a tree, stopping them both for an instant. A jolt of pain caused the boy to howl and offered enough time to release his wrist from the leash. The boy freed himself and took notice of the movement that erupted around him.

Something gave chase to his dog, and he listened as Brutus ran deeper into the darkness. With the predators distracted, he stumbled to his feet, grabbing his face to relieve the pressure from bleeding and swelling. The boy carefully backtracked towards the light from the campground, whimpering when a stumble jarred his injured shoulder. Although the race felt like an eternity, he wasn't far from the forest opening. When his feet touched the soft grass, he ran as quickly as he could, scooping up the flashlight during his escape. His mother's voice was now calling for him, but he failed to hear it. Instead, he listened as his dog emitted a disturbing yelp in the distance. He knew they were Brutus's last sounds.

DAY FIVE

Sam and Dale watched from inside the truck as the girls filed out of their cabins and filled two vehicles parked in a gravel lot to the side. The interns were oblivious to their surroundings, laughing and bumping into one another in jest. Those bringing up the rear were playing with phones, taking selfies, and shooting video clips. The SUVs left the grounds before Johnson emerged from his cabin. He appeared a short time later, slinging a large backpack over his shoulder as he locked the door. This morning Johnson sported long khakis, a cargo shirt, and a wide-brimmed Stetson hat with the chin cord tightly secured and digging into his neck. As he approached the truck, Sam prompted Dale to lower his window.

"What's with the mass exodus? I thought we had plans for today?" Sam was growing angry at the thought of everyone abandoning her plan of action. "And what's with the outfit? Going on a safari?" Although she was annoyed, Johnson's choice of clothing always provided fodder for everyone's amusement.

"You were right, always right, my dear Sam. The girls are dead weight. I gave them the day off and I sent them to Jackson. They'll pick up groceries, do some shopping, and make dinner for the lot of us. We'll accomplish more without them, anyway." He looked at Dale and motioned for him to move to the back. "Sorry chap, experience before an internship."

Dale gawped at Sam as she shrugged her shoulders. He begrudgingly removed his seatbelt and gathered his belongings before taking a position on the cramped rear bench seating. After sitting in the passenger seat, Johnson began playing with the radio, skipping through the satellite channels until he recognized Ella Fitzgerald's smooth voice performing his favorite jazz piece. He preceded to adjust the equalizer and bass, ignoring Sam's annoying huffing. They drove in silence towards the campground until they reached the heavily wooded area next to Yellowstone Lake.

"Back there." Sam pointed to the location after slowing to a crawl. She waved her other arm out the window, signaling to those behind her to pass. Eventually, her truck stopped, and no one moved from their seats.

"Are we not going to check it out? I packed some plaster for castings today. I'd love to get a true measurement of that print you located yesterday." Johnson was eager to secure physical evidence from the strange predators.

"Based on the size of your bag, I'd say you packed more than that. Any weapons?" Sam looked at his waistline and failed to see a holster poking out from beneath his shirt.

"No. You should know me by now. I enjoy observing wildlife, not executing it. I have a can of bear spray, though." He began rummaging through a pocket in his backpack.

"No way. Bear spray's worthless against wolves, you know that. I don't know where the pack is, but I'm not putting us in harm's way. Even if we walk in there with a pistol or rifle, they'll take us down before we see them. Any weapon would provide a false sense of security. I'm not doing it. Yesterday was different. There were emergency vehicles, a running outboard on the lake, and lots of men and walkie-talkies going off. They may have been watching, but they stayed at a safe distance. There was a lot of noise and activity. We'll chalk this one up as a loss and keep looking." Sam cut into the growing line of cars and resumed their course to the campground.

West Bay was a flurry of activity as campers and vehicles left the campground. If people weren't moving to another part of Yellowstone, they were heading out to explore it. Summers brought in millions of tourists each year, creating gridlocks in traffic and leaving little choice for accommodations. The competition was fierce for those without reservations and sites filled up each morning, just like today. Sam carefully weaved in and out of the sea of recreational vehicles and wayward pedestrians. She eventually turned down the lane where they spotted the abandoned van the previous day. It was missing and a different vacationer had just pulled into the pad to claim the vacant spot. A young couple failed to notice them watching as they leveled the camper after disconnecting it from their truck. Neither Sam nor Dale mentioned it to Johnson, who watched the flurry of activity in the campground from his passenger window. The trio continued towards the forest edge at the far end of the campground, stopping at the site of the old man. He noticed Sam and approached the truck, wary of the large man occupying the seat beyond her.

"Good morning!" Sam tried to remain chipper and pleasant, but craved caffeine to nurse a growing headache from last night's alcohol overindulgence. "Anything new to report?"

The man stepped on the tips of his toes to inspect the vehicle contents and eyed the passengers. He shot Dale a forced smile when their eyes met. "All was quiet since you left yesterday."

"No busted coolers? Hear anything last night? See any wildlife creeping around the campers?" She noticed the prying eyes of his wife as she peered through the partially opened screen door. Sam doubted he would offer anything useful in their quest for enlightenment.

"We heard nothing. The wife and I sleep with the windows closed and the heater on. It may be summer, but this is a Wyoming summer. It's damn cold this time of year." He was brusque and obnoxious. "Actually... I overheard people complaining about noises last night, yelping or screaming or something. They thought it was a coyote or wolf. Coyotes yip and yap. I've heard them before in Arizona. They don't yelp. It wasn't a coyote. Then I had to remind them that wolves weren't in this part of the park. They probably heard someone's dog from another part of the campground. According to my guidebook, wolves are common in Lamar Valley, not Yellowstone Lake. Too far to hear them yelping here. This generation needs to get their noses out of their phones and pick up a book. People will say anything for attention."

Johnson rolled his eyes. He could no longer take the man's insufferable yammering and misstatements regarding the animals in Yellowstone. "You realize this is their nature preserve, their home? Wildlife can visit any part as they choose. This isn't a jolly Florida theme park or city zoo." Sam dropped her head while Johnson ridiculed the man. She didn't care for him either, but needed his eyes and ears until they gained higher ground. They were still in the dark concerning the new and threatening predator. Sam cut Johnson off before he continued his rant and offended their only helper.

"We're here to install some trail cameras for video feed and research. Make sure the kids don't touch them. I'd appreciate your help. If we catch something useful, we'll be happy to share it with you." She smiled and nodded at the man as he backed away from the truck and retreated to the door of his cabin to update his wife.

"Are you mad, woman?" Johnson stared her down in disbelief.

"No, we're not sharing crap with him. Johnson, you need to learn the art of a convincing white lie and how to read people. That guy's a pain in the ass, but we need his help. If there's anyone that will keep sticky fingers and prying eyes away from our equipment, it's him." Sam stopped the truck again and parked between campers, where she previously retrieved the busted cooler. "Grab your gear, Johnson. Dale, make sure you pack one of the loaded pistols, leave the rifles so we don't instill panic amongst our guests."

As they passed on foot, Sam noticed her business card missing. The camper still looked empty. Typical tourists, she thought, too busy to give a rat's ass about the wildlife they came to see. Feed them today and they'll be someone else's problem tomorrow. When they rounded the back of the campers, they stopped at the edge of the trees. Unlike yesterday, Sam could hear birds singing and rodents scampering within the brush. Several chipmunks appeared, showing no fear as they quickly approached the humans for handouts. They had become accustomed to a consistent diet of crackers and nuts. With no shortage of food, they remained portly and lazy. She doubted they could survive without the help of the tourists and shook her head with disappointment.

Sam pointed out locations for the cameras and noticed the old man peering from behind his portable home. She ignored him today. Sam thought it might be to their benefit if he witnessed the installation. Instead of shaming him, she turned her attention to Dale and Johnson to discuss the placement height and ideal zones for catching movement. After a little back and forth, Johnson started pulling cameras and straps from the bag. He popped the case open to each device and activated the power button before handing them to Dale. The men hurriedly worked while Sam stood watch.

Despite the flurry of activity at the campground, she was nervous and feared a surprise visit from a predator. The men were too close to the brush. Sam rested her hand on her hip, close to the handle of her pistol. The men walked approximately twenty yards apart and secured the first set of cameras to trees facing wildlife trails, breaks and rugged paths that led into the campground. Each man fixed one camera to face the wooded area and two additional cameras to face the campground. They wanted sweeping views of the narrow clearing behind the campers. It was an ideal place to catch any animal as it moved away from the covering of the forest. As Dale worked swiftly, the old man started asking questions out of earshot of Sam.

"Psst. Why are you putting it by my camper? Shouldn't it be closer to the camper with the broken cooler? Why is it so low? Shouldn't it be higher? Why are you putting three cameras on one tree? Shouldn't one work? How long do they record? When are you going to retrieve them? What if they fall? What if it rains?" He wouldn't shut up, and Dale became increasingly annoyed.

"I'm sorry, did you say something?" Dale didn't like being pestered by the man as he worked. He purposely spoke in a loud voice to grab Sam's attention; she briefly glanced their way. The old man quickly retreated to the safety of his camper. Dale assumed he was going to open a window and continue the barrage of questioning from a hiding spot. This motivated Dale to work at a frantic pace. Both he and Johnson finished moments apart and reached Sam, her eyes and ears still locked on the wooded grounds.

"Do you have cable locks for the cameras?" Dale inquired. "There's nothing stopping someone from taking them. They look new and pricey, too."

"No." He chuckled as he picked up the much lighter backpack and tugged at the zippers. "I've learned over the years if someone steals something from my organization, the benefactors contribute pity money for the newest and best equipment on the market. The fools will shell out enough cash to outshine their kind in the upper-class world. People are more willing to donate for a stolen device than replace an outdated one that still works. Working for donations is a huge psychological game. It's a game I enjoy!"

"Let's go. I don't want to drain the batteries with photos of us." Sam returned to the truck as the other two followed close behind. After they took their seats with seatbelts secured, Sam backed up the vehicle to their nosey friend's camper. He was waiting at the bottom of the stairs, eager to ask additional questions. Sam yelled from her window, "Don't let anyone walk behind the campers. I don't want the batteries wasted on photos of people. Thanks!" She put the truck in drive and sped off before he could respond.

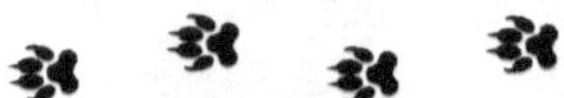

After installing trail cameras, the threesome noticed the campground was quieter and lacked human activity. Most tourists had funneled back into the park for another day of exploration. Instead of returning to their cabins, Sam, Dale, and Johnson searched the campground. They drove the truck through each roadway and looked for signs of wildlife. Sam eventually slowed and stopped at one of the marked hiking trails that led away from the lake and campsites.

"What do you think?" Johnson inquired. "Should we have a go at it? That old man said there was canine activity in the area last night."

"Hell, no!" Sam focused her eyes on the darkened abyss in the trees when she spotted movement. Her eyes dilated for a moment before a group of young adults emerged from the trail.

"Should we post warning signs?" Dale piped up from the back seat. He had remained quiet most of the day. Dale disliked Johnson and felt it safer to bite his tongue rather than start an argument. Although he had a girlfriend at home, Dale wanted to impress Sam with his maturity and intellect. He had developed a crush on his mentor and enjoyed the thought of a taboo relationship. "We can attribute it to animal activity. No one needs to know otherwise."

"Not yet. We have a fine line to balance. If we close the trail without proof, park officials will be all over us. Damned if we do and damned if we don't. Keep looking and pray the cameras catch something."

Sam steered the truck towards the opposite side of the campground and paused under a canopy of shady trees. Dozens of colorful canvas tents lay before them, gently flapping in the slight breeze. The area further housed cinder block buildings with restrooms and shower facilities, large metal lockboxes for food storage, and bear-proof garbage canisters. Sam pulled out the binoculars to better look at the campground. She searched for coolers and food debris, anything that appealed to scavengers, but she observed nothing from her angle. The sites were clean and appeared secure.

"What do you think?" Sam laid the binoculars on the dashboard.

"Looks like a smorgasbord to me." Johnson shook his head slightly back and forth. "I hope these creatures stay on the other side of the campground."

"Do you have more cameras? We may have better luck over here."

"I have more at the cabin that I can prep tonight. But..." Johnson scrunched his lips and looked at Sam.

"But what?"

"I think we should shoot one area at a time. We may panic the visitors, especially those in this location. We'll see what the cameras pick up tonight and plan from there." Johnson opened his door and remained in his seat, hesitating to move. "Since we've stopped, shall we have a look around?

Maybe we'll discover tracks? Hair? Scat? We won't find anything sitting in this truck. We should be safe here."

"Is anywhere safe in this park? You should know better than that, Johnson. Even on a good day." Sam snorted.

The three wildlife biologists hit the ground, two armed with pistols. They fanned out and stayed within eyesight of one another. Their eyes shifted constantly, scanning the forest floor, the base of trees and brush, and the distance between one another. They were unusually alert and attuned to their surroundings. No one wanted to stray off course and find themselves alone. When they reached the end of the expansive site, they returned to the truck. Sam opened her cooler in the pickup's bed and passed out bottles of water.

"Nothing. A pile of dog crap, but nothing else. How about you guys?" Sam held the cold and sweating bottle against her forehead to cool down.

"Same." Dale chugged half his bottle before taking a deep breath for air.

"No news is good news. I saw nothing. Maybe these things don't exist, and we're chasing phantoms. Perhaps a pit bull had a go at the cooler? Or an enormous wolf destroyed my small ones?" Johnson took off his hat and tossed it through the open passenger window. He poured water over his head, then removed a bandana from his pocket to dry his face off. "Let's say we head back. I have a lot of work to do and I'd like to finish before the girls return from Jackson. My place for dinner?"

"Agree. I need to track my collared bears and follow up on some emails. We'll put this on hold for now. Not much else we can do, anyhow. And yes, anything aside from my cooking sounds remarkable." Sam remained quiet during the drive as the group headed towards the exit. She glanced to her right and mumbled, "Let's make one last stop."

The men waited in the idle truck as Sam ran into the campground's office. She frantically secured the buttons around her bosom and rolled down her sleeves. When the bells attached to the door handle jingled, Sue popped up from beneath the counter and behind a computer monitor. Another woman employee looked up at Sam. Before the strange lady spoke, Sue erupted in her trademarked, cheerful expression.

"Another visit from my sweet, dear Sam?" She leaned against the counter on her elbows after removing her bifocals. They swayed around her neck as she moved, secured by a chain. "I'm about to beat this damn modem with my shoe. I shouldn't complain because this happens every summer, but our internet sucks. Excuse my brash language, that was not very lady-like. What can I do for you today?"

The other lady disappeared into a back office just as Sam spoke. "Any news since yesterday? Guest complaints about wildlife?" Sam cocked an eyebrow, waiting for a response as her body slumped against the countertop for support.

"All's quiet. No wildlife complaints and no updates on the deceased couple. I assume it'll be weeks before the autopsy and toxicology reports come back."

"So, no animal-related problems?" Sam knew Sue's mind often failed to recall important details. Sue attributed it to age, but Sam recognized she was busy and often became sidetracked during her workday. Sue stood erect and her eyes rolled up and to the side as she searched her memory. She waved her finger in the air furiously and smiled at Sam.

"Does a missing dog count? Not much to tell. A boy was walking his dog out yonder last night, and it got away from him. This happens every summer. People don't leash their dogs or they hand them over to the kids. Anyway, the family searched this morning and had to leave. The wife will email a flier for me to hang in the office. I can share it with you later. Maybe you'll come across the dog?"

"Where was their camper? Why did they leave?" Sam sought to remain calm, but grew more excited. "What kind of dog?"

"You are testing my memory, dear Sam. Their site was in the same row, the same side as your damaged cooler. The dog was a dober- no, a rottweiler. They had to leave because the boy hurt his shoulder pretty badly and got scratched up. I think he needed stitches or something. They left shortly before you pulled up. Anything else? I'm on a roll!" She tapped the countertop with a pen.

"Damn! And the white van you mentioned yesterday?"

"Ahh. Not as intriguing as the disaster on the lake. Police told me it came up stolen and was probably abandoned. Law enforcement towed it yesterday and took it to Cody, I think. Better that than losing another guest. Surely, we'll have no more shenanigans this summer. I'd rather scold guests for throwing feminine hygiene products in the porta-potties or send my staff out to douse smoldering campfires. Visitors outnumber the brain cells in the warmer months. How we've survived as a species?" Sue shook her head and turned to look at the computer monitor. Sam realized she had more pressing issues.

"Great to see you again, Sue. One last thing, we installed some trail cams in the back of the campground. I'm hoping to catch images of the bear that broke into the cooler the other night. With luck, I'll see you again tomorrow. Text me if anything comes up."

"Do we need to worry about the guests in the back? I mean, with that cooler and missing dog."

"Nope. Nothing to worry about now. Not yet, anyway." Sam smiled and winked before turning towards the door. *Nothing to worry about yet,* she struggled to convince herself.

"Sam, one last thing!" Sam excitedly looked over her shoulder as Sue yelled. "Good to see those breasts covered, leaves more to the imagination. Men may not admit it, but they prefer a wrapped present. After a ring goes on that finger, of course. Keeps a marriage strong, take my word!"

Sam waved a hand, rolled her eyes, and proceeded out the door. "See you later, Mom!" The sarcasm was heavy as she pulled at the buttons on her shirt, popping them from their holes.

Sleep eluded the alpha male. While others in his pack slept or lay listlessly on a bed of drying and decayed leaves, their leader sat and studied the stretches of the forest before him. He remained still and erect as his eyes searched for movement. His ears twitched as they detected slight disturbances in the surrounding fauna as ground squirrels darted amongst the bushes. Birds tending to their nests remained hidden in the lush treetops. They communicated across the expanse and remained unbothered by the predators that slept beneath them. The sire occasionally sniffed at the air, but it offered no leads. It smelled of pine and decaying leaves. The forest delivered nothing to the hungry predators on this sweltering afternoon.

The wolves had discovered Yellowstone Lake in their search for additional territory in the early spring. The scent of birthing deer and moose lingered in the dense forests of this part, holding up the pack's continuance for more land. They would stay and gorge instead. Working together, the wolf pack separated the newborns from their mothers and consumed their tender flesh. Unlike the bison, the wildlife at the lake lacked the protection of a herd and its bulls. The wolf pack thrived as they received the much-needed nourishment and avoided catastrophic injuries. In time, they annihilated the new population of fawns and calves.

The slaughter and scent-markings of the aggressive newcomers drove the surviving wildlife from the area. Yellowstone Lake and its surrounding forest were devoid of a sustainable food source, leaving the wolves ravenous. Before returning to the massive herds of grazing bison in the center of the park, they unwittingly stumbled across a new form of prey. It wasn't their preferred fare, but man was abundant and defenseless. Wolves observed this alternative food source gathered in a clearing during scouting missions. Their numbers and sounds were large, loud, and intimidating to the pack. Occasionally, one or two people would separate from the group. The wolves would follow and learn more about this odd creature and its habits. When the opportunity allowed, they took one life and fed. Now they sought more. This new mammal could re-energize their young pack before traveling and hunting the fattier game that carried them through winter.

The setting sun, lack of wind, and searing heat awakened swarms of mosquitos and gnats that emerged from their shelter about the vegetation. The menacing insects launched an assault on the pack, biting their exposed underbellies and swarming about their ears and eyes. In response to the jabs of pain, pack members rolled in the dry dirt or stood and shook. They rapidly blinked and twitched their ears with annoyance. This abrupt movement stimulated the sluggish pack members. Their time of slumber was over, and the wolves were now hungry and inclined to hunt. After taking a cue from their leader, the pack moved. They headed towards the lights and noises emitted from the campground in the distance. A young she-wolf, injured by a rock during the previous evening, limped and brought up the rear. Until her wound healed, she would assist in a limited capacity during the hunt and feed last.

Tonight, the pack moved to their usual spot behind a row of campers and recreational vehicles. They hid during twilight and out of sight from man. The wolf family would wait until the sun had set, the embers smoldered, and activity in the campground came to a halt. When the timing was right, they would select their prey. Patience had proven to be crucial to their success and growth.

The group continued to wait and watch for hours until the alpha moved from the cover of trees and emerged onto a grassy strip. Others followed his lead as they fanned out into the campground. The wolves stayed within a close range as they rapidly maneuvered around sites. Some stopped momentarily to examine the odors from filthy grills, but pressed forward. There were no discarded food scraps or abandoned coolers that engrossed the wolves tonight. They were desperate for sustenance to carry them into the next day.

The lead wolves paused when they reached the parcel of land occupied by tents. These were new structures in different shapes that carried unfamiliar scents. The pack watched the alphas for guidance. Not one of the family would jeopardize their safety by moving prematurely. Once deemed harmless by those leading, the group clustered closely together and pushed forward. The alien world stimulated their senses as they detected the scent of foodstuffs and observed movement within the canvas tents. They reunited amongst the trees after searching the area.

Communication was subtle, but understood by the pack members as they gazed at a particular target, partially secluded by a line of trees and thick underbrush. They yearned to feed as the aroma of beef jerky wafted through the all-mesh structure. Inside, a pile of empty wrappers and bits of snacks enticed the starved pack. They listened and watched the heavy breathing and lack of movement of a scantily dressed couple. Both were unaware of the danger that stood outside and at the edge of the tree line.

The injured she-wolf advanced towards the lone tent at the forest edge. The young female gently poked the material and pushed the fabric with the tip of her nose. It was thin and could tear easily. Careful not to stir the prey, she guardedly retreated into the darkness and took a position behind the others.

Before they advanced, an unfamiliar noise snorted above them. Startled and spooked, the pack quickly took cover in the brush. All eyes focused on the unusual sound and watched as an object swayed in the darkness. A man lay in a hammock, strung between trees, his arm hanging towards the ground. There were others like him, but only this one had exposed flesh. The same she-wolf cautiously advanced and smelled the prey's fingertips, careful not to touch or alarm the potential meal as it slept. The she-wolf slunk back toward the others, wagging her tail and expressing excitement. Other family members picked up the cues and moved into position for an ambush. The wolf pack was now ready to begin their hunt and slaughter.

DAY SIX

Sam desperately pushed forward through the burning forest despite covering little ground. Her feet were heavy and difficult to lift as she swiped the branches and thick vegetation to the side with her lacerated arms. Although Sam hustled, she failed to make progress. Her plight was like a nightmare. The more Sam pushed forward, the farther she had to move.

Dale was ahead in a clearing, sitting sideways in the driver's seat of her truck. The engine knocked, choked, and sputtered, struggling to remain running for their escape. Dale hung out the window, waving as he yelled. He watched as the wolves rushed at his beloved mentor. Sam failed to hear his voice over the crackling fire and constant howling from the pack that pursued her. His movement was slow and frantic, but she understood the fear in his expression. His lips curled over and over as he mouthed and repeated, "RUN, RUN, RUN!"

Dale was oblivious as the alpha female jumped onto the top of the truck. The tires exploded and sank into the soft ground under her weight. Only a muffled whimper escaped Sam's lips as she sought to warn Dale.

The wolf's size was foreboding, unlike anything Sam had ever seen. Its dilated pupils focused on her as it lowered its body to prepare for an attack. The alpha's lips twisted slightly, exposing pristine and razor-sharp fangs. It convinced Sam that the wolf was grinning and taunting her.

The alpha and Sam locked eyes and stared for a moment, two female gingers in a fight for control and survival. Without warning, the wolf leaped to the ground, pulling Dale from the truck. Other wolves, hidden in the surrounding brush, pounced onto the fresh kill. Blood gushed from the site, emulating an Old Faithful eruption. Sam stopped and screamed. The high-pitched shriek brought the forest to a standstill. There was silence for a moment before more heads popped up from the bushes.

Dozens of enormous wolves surrounded Sam. They slowly advanced, closing in on the defenseless human. Frozen with fear and her joints paralyzed, she watched helplessly as the predators neared. The wolves abruptly stopped and retracted as a heavy thumping began. From the flames of the fire, the alpha male emerged. He was twice the size of those in his pack. Each time his paws struck the ground, the earth trembled. His pack separated and bowed. They provided the leader a straight and unobstructed passage to Sam.

Sam faced the massive carnivore and could not move. She remained frozen in fear. The alpha stood over her, the heat from his breath intense as he sniffed her flesh. Long strings of saliva dripped from his canines into her hair and ran onto the exposed flesh covering her bare chest. The other wolves' excitement grew. They moved forward, stomping and howling in tandem. Boom... boom... boom...

Sam sprung up in bed, clutching her chest while choking on air. Sweat drenched her body in the stifling and stagnant air of her bedroom. As an oscillating fan made a pass, the air slightly and briefly cooled her damp skin. She swept the wet strands of long hair from her face and chest as she reached through the blackness for a water bottle on her nightstand.

While gulping the warm drink, a banging reverberated throughout the cabin. Sam pushed the sheet from her body and swung her feet over the side of the bed. She snatched her phone to check the time. Three o'clock, Sam grunted. The banging continued. A light came on, illuminating the space under her door. Sam heard male voices inside the cabin as she threw on a bathrobe and left the confines of her room.

"What's going on?" Sam's voice was hoarse as she walked into the living room and spotted Dale with Johnson and a man in uniform.

"There was an animal attack that resulted in fatalities at the campground tonight." The stranger rubbed the scruff on his chin as he spoke.

"What kind of fatality? Who?" Sam staggered into the kitchen, turning on additional lights as she prepared a pot of coffee.

"Not one, multiple." Sam stopped to listen with her back turned to the stranger. "They're not sure who's involved. I'm here to round up additional help. They need advice from animal biologists. You're the closest in the park. Especially at this time of the morning."

"Time of the night." She corrected him as she pulled her robe tighter around her body. "What's my involvement? Was it a bear?" The coffee maker started sputtering steam as liquid drained into the pot. Sam rubbed her eyes before pulling a mug from the cupboard.

"Johnson insists you come with us." She glared at Johnson as he shrugged his shoulders. Sam placed the mug back on a shelf and grabbed her large thermos.

"Dale, go back to bed and stay in the cabin until first light. Try to get rest. I'll need your energy later in the day. After breakfast, grab the girls and collect the trail cams. Take some firearms and ammo. Be careful." She looked at him and emphasized her request again slowly, "Be careful."

"Got it." Before he returned to his bedroom, Sam stopped him.

"One more thing, have the girls help you load the SD cards into our laptops and scan the images. Hopefully, we caught something." Sam followed him down the hall when he returned to his bedroom. She turned into hers to dress.

"Johnson," Sam's head poked out from the doorframe. "Grab your brainiest blonde. I'll meet you in the truck."

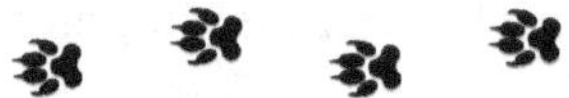

Still sleepy, Sam begrudgingly slid into her truck seat. Two more hours of darkness would prevent the sunlight from suppressing her body's production of melatonin. Resentment towards Johnson built as she cursed under her breath between yawns. She inhaled the steam from her thermos before securing it in the console. The aroma of coffee and the heat and humidity outside did little to wake Sam. She despised early mornings, especially ones that demanded her attention and expertise. When she turned the key and the interior lit up, she gasped in surprise. A girl sat in the passenger seat, measuring up Sam with a judgmental expression, a notepad resting on her lap.

"Wow! You scared the hell out of me." Sam secured her seatbelt and watched as Johnson gave her the thumbs up before taking a seat in the other car. "Please tell me you're with him?"

"You asked for Johnson's brainiest." The girl was smug and looked no older than sixteen. "And here I am. Aren't we the lucky ones?"

"I don't remember seeing you this summer. Did you arrive recently?" Sam turned around and left the string of cabins. She followed the other truck while adjusting her air conditioner for a blast of cold air.

"I've been here since day one. I'm kind of like the black sheep of the crew. No blonde hair, and I keep my legs closed." The girl snickered as she scanned the road ahead. "Seriously, I've had a sinus infection and allergy issues since I showed up. I dawdle alone, sealed in the cabin. I perform the grunt work accompanied by my air purifier and a humidifier. It wasn't Johnson or his girls, but me, that made the calls for your drone operators and other crap."

"Thank you. Much appreciated. So, where you from?"

"El Segundo, a suburb of Los Angeles. I hail from the aerospace capital of the world. Whoopee." She twirled her index finger in the air.

"That's far off from a wildlife biologist. What brought you here?" Sam turned onto the main road. It was pitch black, the road devoid of headlights and streetlamps. She was thankful that the officer led the charge. It lessened her chances of hitting wildlife.

"I like wolves. Duh. Next question in your interrogation?"

"You don't seem like the Johnson type. How did you convince him to add you to his team?" Sam glanced at the girl. She was petite, with rich bronzed skin and dark hair and eyes.

"Simple. I tricked Johnson." Both women snorted. "He was in L.A. as a keynote speaker for a fundraiser. After the function, I cornered him and asked him to join the team. He eyed me up and down and said no."

"How did you convince him otherwise? Changing his mind is not an easy thing to do. The guy is stubborn."

"I asked Johnson the same thing. But I told him not to challenge me to raise cash since I didn't have any connections. Of course, this was a lie. Before meeting Johnson, I read everything I could about him online. Coming from L.A., there's plenty like him. It's all about the money. Anyway, of course, he asked me to secure ten thousand dollars to cover my housing and other expenses for the organization. We shook on it, and here I am." The girl smirked and puffed up her chest.

"I'm still not clear?"

"At that point, he didn't know who I was. I looked like a pauper, dressed in a sweatshirt and ripped jeans. An intentional choice of clothing? Of course. So, I pulled out my checkbook and wrote a check for ten big ones. His expression was worth each zero I scribbled on that little piece of paper. I got to dangle that big carrot in front of his face until he agreed to my internship."

"So, you're wealthy?" Sam clenched the steering wheel with her knees as she unscrewed the top of her thermos to sip the scalding coffee. She returned the thermos to its place before grabbing the wheel again with her hands.

"I'm not rich. My parents are. Johnson didn't recognize I'm the only child of the largest Mexican family-owned grocery chain in southern California. My parents are busy running the business. Instead of parenting, they throw cash at me to compensate for their lack of presence. I've stockpiled a nice wad of money over the years. Saving the pity money has paid off. Here I am."

"I like you. The player got played. Perhaps you'd do better on my team?" She winked at the girl. "So, what's your name? How are you the brainiest? I thought rich kids dodged continuing education?"

"I take offense to that! Don't group me with other rich girls. I graduated high school as the valedictorian and college as a summa cum laude. I hold a bachelor of science in wildlife biology and am going for my master's in the fall." The girl tapped the top of the notebook. Despite her aggravation with Sam's barrage of questions, she respected the older woman.

"Impressive. Aren't you a little young?"

"I'm twenty. I knocked out most of my coursework during high school. My goal is to finish my education before retirement. I want to get it over with and not have it drag on. The faster, the better." She rubbed the sleep out of her eyes and readjusted her ponytail's rubber band.

"If your body's hypersensitive to the outdoors, what are your plans after school?" Sam continued to yawn despite a swig of coffee and the ice-cold air blowing on her face.

"I've created a device that will pump smog and toxins into my lungs. The machine aids my body's inability to process this fresh mountain air. Seriously, I want nothing to do with this. I'm here to list it on my resume, especially to reference Johnson's name. I want to be a curator at a science museum in southern Cal. Plus, I need to stay close to my parents' money since this job won't pay crap. If I'm a productive member of society in the Los Angeles area, Mami and Papi will continue funding my future. That, and I need reliable Wi-Fi and authentic street tacos. An unmistakable call on my part."

"Couldn't you have picked something easier? Work at the family business per se?"

"This is easy. Except for the early morning part."

There was no missing the campground entrance in the darkness. As the pair neared the turnoff, the lights of vehicles and flurry of activity illuminated the road in the park. Sam continued following Johnson as their trucks rounded a turn and made for the cluster of tents in the far-off corner. The same area they had visited the previous day. The two women remained quiet and wide-eyed as they observed the chaos from within the safety of their vehicle. When the trucks came to a stop, the girl turned to Sam and extended her hand.

"Gabriella Morales. You can call me Gabby. But only you."

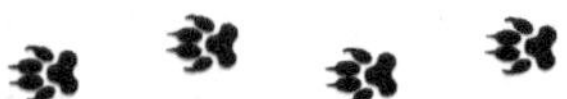

"Holy shit!" Sam whispered under her breath as she reacted to the scene that had materialized around them. West Bay was under siege by utter pandemonium. Artificial light from vehicle headlamps and free-standing spotlights illuminated most of the campground. They watched as men and women in uniform ran about the grounds with weapons drawn as they rounded up wandering and nosey campers. Sam patted her side to ensure that she hadn't left her pistol in the cabin.

She whispered to Gabby; their eyes were locked on the scene before them. "Do you know how to use a weapon?"

"I'm a single female from a wealthy family in a big city. What do you think?" Gabby pointed towards a hidden pocket in her tank top concealed by a flannel shirt. "Do you think I'd spend a summer in the wilderness unarmed?"

"Does Johnson know about it?"

"No!" Gabby rolled her eyes. "Give me a little credit."

"For the record, I don't know you possess a firearm. My advice, leave it holstered unless something's eating you alive. There will be serious legal repercussions if you discharge a weapon in the park. Your inheritance will go towards attorneys and legal fees." Sam raised her eyebrows and glanced towards her young passenger. Her words and tone were valid and significant. Gabby nodded in agreement. The truck came to a stop, and Sam scanned the surroundings before returning her gaze to Gabby. "Do you know how to fire it?"

"This firearm is the only thing my dad and I have in common. He took me out to the desert and taught me how to shoot when I was a toddler. I can handle any weapon. Seriously, I took a gun safety course. Besides, I hold a current concealed carry permit. I'm legal, and I'm good. I've got your back."

Johnson startled the women when he knocked on Sam's window. It was time to go. Sam took a swig of coffee before the two grabbed their things and locked the truck. As they passed each campsite, they observed families sheltering in the safety of their vehicles, their tents now empty. Others sobbed or cupped their faces. Some wore faces of anguish and defeat as they leaned against their cars, awaiting updates and new information.

Sam spotted a child's head poking up from a minivan's rear window. He was watching the movement of first responders until he spotted Sam. She made eye contact with the toddler as he cupped his ears, tears streaming down his cheeks. Sam turned her attention back to the path in front of her. But her heart ached for the little boy. Did he bear witness to the sights and sounds of tonight's onslaught?

"Gabby, you can wait in the truck. I won't think any less of you. I'm uneasy about what's ahead. You don't need to see this." Gabby pressed closer to Sam, only stopping when their arms brushed against one another.

"I'm terrified..." her attention turned to an officer behind them. He was yelling at campers to return to their cars until instructed to do otherwise. "But I can do this. It's just like television, but real. Right?"

"This is my third encounter with a human casualty. I don't think this or a mauling ever gets easier. Just stay close."

"Listen to her. Sam's a wise woman, Gabriella." Johnson turned to the women and inserted himself into their pep talk. He couldn't hide his anxiety, either.

They stopped short at the edge of a campsite, carefully stepping over bundles of extension cords that connected the generators to the lighting. The roaring motors muted the sounds of those chatting around the site, so Sam watched their lips. She failed to interpret what they were discussing and followed their efforts instead.

Gabby fixated on four men with high-powered rifles and scopes that occupied each corner of the clearing. They continually scanned back and forth, looking for signs of carnivores in the brush. Even with spotlights aimed at the forest, the shadows and rustling throughout the thicket deceived those on guard. Their fingers hovered around the triggers.

A gentleman wearing a national park jacket approached Johnson, Sam, and Gabby. With his head hung low, he held a walkie in his hand as he neared the three. They heard a clamoring voice through the earpiece as the man turned the dial to mute the incoming ruckus. Sam recognized the park official from photos and a previous attack in earlier years. While she was trying to recall his name, he remembered hers.

"Sam, right? I'm Tony. Tony Mancini. I think we met a few years back?" He held his hand out and shook with everyone before turning towards the operation. He stood next to Sam and addressed her, although he raised his voice for the others to hear. "I work for the NPS and serve as their eyes and ears. I'm in charge of public relations and the media. I got the call around three, but only arrived about twenty minutes ago. What do you know so far?"

"Nothing. We heard there was a fatality or fatalities." Johnson conveyed from the rear. He nudged Sam to the side, sliding between her and the park employee. Sam and Gabby flashed looks of disgust at each other.

"Guess I'll fill you in, then?" He pointed to various areas of the campsite as he spoke. "A couple was sleeping in that tent with their newborn."

Only a heap of mesh and cloth remained. Splinters of fiberglass poles poked through the material and remained scattered around the space. Gabby turned away when she recognized the dark splotches as bloodstains. Sam rubbed her back when she rejoined the briefing.

"Where are they?" Johnson squinted as Sam glared at him. She thought it ridiculous to ask the obvious.

"The woman and baby are missing. Something dragged them into the forest. Over there." He pointed toward the hammocks before swinging his arm further to the left. "The man's body is over there. You can make out his feet in the underbrush. He's deceased, but we won't retrieve his body until daylight. Too much risk in the darkness."

"Why do you assume he's deceased? Maybe he's alive?" Gabby spoke up while taking notes in the dim light. She focused on the paper to avoid looking at the body.

"His entrails end at his feet. You can see they start at the edge of the tree line." Gabby puckered her lips, puffed her cheeks, and closed her eyes for a moment. Tim continued with his findings. "We think he was too heavy for them to carry off when mayhem broke out."

"And the other two?" Sam looked for disturbances on the ground.

"We haven't located them yet. The guys sleeping in the trees heard her scream. They stayed in place during the attack, too scared to move. When the predators dragged the woman underneath their hammocks, they heard a gurgling, foamy sound, so we assume she's deceased. No one knows what happened to the baby. We checked the tent and sleeping bags, but nothing turned up. Hopefully, we can recover their remains later this morning."

"What happened there?" Gabby pointed to a hammock set off from the others. She could see the outline of an arm hanging to the side. Sam nodded her head in approval. Neither she nor Johnson had noticed it before Gabby spoke.

"He's deceased. We think the predators had a go at him. Our victim is a young man in his mid-twenties. He's entangled in his hammock. His friends said he created a netting around his bedding to ward off mosquitos because he didn't like bug spray. All the extra sheeting probably prevented him from being dragged away. Not sure how his arm got out, though?" The official shrugged his shoulders before continuing, "The predators shredded his arm and tore into his radial artery while trying to drag him away. Medics said he probably bled out within minutes. When you get closer, you can see the pool of blood. Impressive."

"Why haven't they removed him?" Gabby's eyebrows furrowed.

"Again, waiting for the first light. The bodies are too close to the brush, and the predators may be in the area. We're standing between them and their breakfast. More concerning, we have a lot of armed and jumpy men. Make the wrong move, and you'll get shot." Johnson and Sam bobbed their heads in agreement. "We need your input before we create a response team to execute the animals. There's never been a wolf attack in this park. Verify that this was a wolf attack, identify the pack and provide their history. Was this a result of injury or disease? Were they desensitized to human activity? Was someone feeding them? I want answers immediately. Yellowstone needs to approach this thoughtfully and carefully. All eyes are on us. If you need a look around, tread lightly and watch your step. The hammock survivors are in an SUV on the other side of this brush there."

"Thanks." Sam shook his hand again. "We'll get back to you soon."

A cloud of smoke escaped the van when the side door slid open. Three men frantically waved their hands to disperse the cloud as they extinguished their blunts. One took a tongue lashing for opening the door prematurely as they slid drug paraphernalia under pillows and bedding. Johnson, Sam, and Gabby watched the fiasco unfold. They patiently waited as the men tidied their small living quarters. Gabby motioned to the farthest, who forgot to remove a blunt tucked behind his ear. He responded with a smile and an affectionate wink, causing Gabby to look away and blush.

"That's enough, gentlemen. I don't care what you do in this camper." Johnson poked his head inside the door to give it a look. "How, may I ask, do four gentlemen live in something like this?"

"We're one with nature, man, living our best lives. This... this right here is our transportation. It gets us from here to there. From point A to point B. Follow? That... that great expanse behind you..." a man at the back of the van addressed them. Pillows propped him up in a make-shift bed as he rested his head against a window. He spoke with his eyes closed as he struggled to form coherent sentences, his brain fried from a lifetime of drug use. "That, man, that out there is our bedroom. And, oh shit. I forgot what I was going to — oh yeah, our bathroom." He chuckled as his head jerked forward. "All I need is my hammock and a joi... cigarette." He fell asleep. The last few words were barely audible as they escaped his lips.

"Was our bedroom. I ain't sleeping in that shit anymore!" A second boy, stoned and high like the others, shouted while pointing outside. "Fucking thing's got my brother, man."

"The fourth man was your brother?" Sam questioned.

"Not like my blood brother, but my bro brother. Follow?" He cupped his face in his hands and checked out of the conversation. "He'll help you. I'm done with this shit." He moved to the back of the van and curled up in the fetal position by the other man's feet. He cried briefly before they heard him snore.

Only one man remained cognitive. Sam pressed him for more information before he, too, fell asleep. She nudged Johnson and signaled that she'd take the lead.

"We're wildlife biologists. We conduct research on the carnivores in Yellowstone. My name's Sam. You can address me and ignore the others."

"Did you say undress you?" He cracked a smile, but quickly drew back when Johnson stepped forward. "Sorry, man. Just a joke."

"We have a few questions to ask. I see your van's registered in Colorado. Is that where the four of you come from?" Sam wanted to make him comfortable before pressing him with tough questions.

"Yeah. All four of us. We're spending the summer exploring the national parks in the lower forty-eight. Well, we were. I need to go home now." He mellowed out from exhaustion and drug use.

"College students?"

"Kinda. We're, like, taking a break." He gestured with his fingers to draw quotation marks in the air.

"How are you funding your trip?" Gabby scribbled frantically on her notepad, trying to keep up with the conversation. She struggled as she attempted to interpret their slang and slurred speech.

"Good ole Grandma. She gifted me a wad of cash for photos and the occasional postcard. Her travel days are over, so she's living through me." He pulled an ashtray close, forgetting that he had extinguished his joint earlier. He mouthed curse words as he scrunched up his face.

"Can we talk about what happened tonight?" Sam sat on the floor of the van at the edge of the door. One leg was crossed as she faced him and the other rested on the ground. Sam motioned for Johnson and Gabby to move out of sight. She thought the boy might open up better without the scrutiny of two additional people.

"Shoot away, man. Let's get this over with." He moped and rocked back and forth.

"Start from the beginning. Tell me in your words. I'm not judging and I won't interrupt. I want to know what you know so we can catch these things. Help me, help you." She gently touched his knee before withdrawing her hand. There was a moment of silence before he spoke.

"Sometimes we sleep in the van. But not tonight. This damn heatwave got the best of us. We thought a breeze might keep us cooler instead of piling up in the van. A/C's not working and all. Anyway, we don't have many large trees at our campsite, so we asked the family next to us if we could hang our hammocks at the edge of their site. We hung with them the night before and knew they were good with us. Husband even shared a joint. Wifey passed, though. She thought it would get into her breastmilk or shit. So, last night, we shared dinner with this couple and their baby. Hot dogs, yeah, fucking dogs. Typical camping fare, right?" He hesitated. "Nice family. The guy was chill. So was the gal. The baby was cute and happy. They were a hippie-like family, kind of like the older version of us. The family I strive to have." He stopped rocking and rested his elbows on his knees. "Man, I could go for another drag right now. This shit is getting intense."

Sam shook her head. "Not yet. Let's get to the incident. What happened tonight?"

"It was getting dark, so we hung our hammocks. Scott, back there," he pointed to the boy propped up with pillows, "he snagged some of his mom's sleeping pills. We smoked a joint or two, then popped some pills to help us sleep in this heat. J-boy didn't want to use the bug spray. He was afraid he'd catch on fire or some shit if he lit up another joint. Anyway, me and the boys wrapped him up so the bugs couldn't get him. He wanted an opening in the sheets and shit."

"Why?"

"To light a joint or some shit. Wait, no. He wanted a pee hole. Yeah. That's why he wanted the hole. We left his arm hanging out, so he knew where the opening was." The boy smiled as he reflected on the last moments with his friend. His mood quickly turned as he continued. "It was dark, like, you can't see your hands in front of you dark. Once the fire went out, you couldn't see a thing. We heard the baby babbling before it fell asleep. Then we heard the couple screwing. Then the drugs kicked in and everything went black. That's when the shit got real."

"You're doing great. Take your time." But Sam felt differently. She wanted him to share the details that mattered most. She didn't care about what they smoked or ate before the attack.

"She screamed first. I can still hear the terror in her voice. He yelled, too. I think he was trying to scare them away or something. Didn't hear the baby. They may have grabbed it first. Maybe that's why they screamed. I don't know." He lacked expression as he spoke. "I froze in my hammock. My bros yelled, too, but we yelled at each other to stay quiet and stay still. There was no sense in all of us getting killed. You could hear the things running around, growling, running around, growling. I stared upwards and lie still like a mummy. I didn't want to move and risk flipping out of my bed. Couldn't see a fucking thing. We didn't help them, man. Do you know what it sounds like when something rips flesh? These things were savage. You could hear everything. They ate that family." His eyes rolled upward as he attempted to stop tears from rolling down his cheeks. He looked at Sam with swollen and bloodshot eyes. "If the four of us fucking cowards had helped, they may have survived."

"No. They would've taken you, too. There's nothing you could've done. You survived to tell the story and offer us the help we need to find the family." Sam pulled his fingers towards her and pressed his hand tightly between hers. "Let's try to finish this. Afterward, you can get some rest and I won't bother you again."

He pulled his hand away and wiped his nose with his lower arm. Sam watched as a string of snot snapped as he crossed his arms and rested his fingers in his armpits. "It was a wolf. No question. A lot of wolves. I swear I could feel one of them brush against me when it dragged the woman under my hammock. The fuckers are enormous. Yeah, enormous. And to pull her like that? I didn't know they could do that? I heard her last breath, man. That woman was gurgling and shit. They dragged her under me. That was it, man. They wiped the whole family out. And poor J-boy. He yelled like a motherfucker. I thought he was joking at first, or I wanted to think he was joking. But no one yells like that unless they're dying. He faded. Yeah, he faded. Like someone turning the radio off. Loud then, not loud, but you can still hear it until it powers off."

"What happened after the attack? How did you get here?"

"Shit got real in the campground. Lights came on everywhere and people screamed and yelled. There was this mass exodus and shit from the tents. You could hear car doors slam and people laying on horns. Maybe they heard the wolves? Or the dark scared them shitless? Maybe they heard this family screaming for their lives? Fuck, man. Me and the boys were terrified. We stayed in the hammocks until someone put their car lights on us. Then we hauled ass out of there when they yelled. We saw J-boy, but he was gone. They were all gone."

"I think that's enough. You've been a great help." Sam stood up and patted her pockets for a business card. She looked at Johnson. He flipped his business card out of his palm through his fingers. She grabbed it and handed it to the kid. "If you think of anything else, call us."

"Can we get the hell out of here now?"

"Don't go anywhere until you sleep off the drugs. Park officials may pay you another visit. Hang tight until they give you the go-ahead."

Johnson, Sam, and Gabby returned to her truck as the first rays of sun peeked through the trees. The sunlight brought a false sense of security as they left the safety of armed officials. A thermos of caffeine and some exercise would wake their brains and get the blood flowing. Today was going to be a long day.

Once a bustling recovery scene, all went silent as Sam crouched over the male victim's body with Johnson. A wave of fear swept over her as she suspected a predator was approaching. Sam glanced up to find the attendees staring at her cleavage. They promptly turned and looked away.

"Don't you have more important matters to tend to?" It didn't embarrass her, but Sam didn't want distractions. She stared at Johnson. "Not a bear. I can say that with confidence."

"It was a canine. I can say that with confidence. But look at these injuries. The damage isn't consistent with our gray wolves. The bite radius looks much larger. See here." Johnson pulled back the man's mangled t-shirt to reveal a bite mark. He lifted the shoulder to show Sam the victim's back. "Whatever pulled him into the brush left a massive impression."

"I'm no expert on wolves, but was it a northern gray? Wildlife is bigger in Canada, and we're not that far from the border."

"What's that?" The park official was watching them from a distance. He noticed their furrowed eyebrows and questioning looks. They were conferring in lowered voices, but the man picked up an occasional word.

"I'm fairly certain this was a canine, but I'm baffled by this wound. It's rather remarkable for one of our grays." Johnson raised and lowered the shoulder several times. He attempted to visualize the wolf's jaw size.

"It's probably an illusion. When it dragged the body, the skin stretched and pulled. Made it look bigger than it is." The official was confident with his assessment.

"No, that's not how it works. One embedded its teeth in the skin, right here. I don't see rips or tears in this impression. What do you think?" Sam pointed to puncture marks and looked at Johnson, whose eyes remained locked on the body as he shook his head in agreement.

"Look at the way it ripped his throat out and tore open his abdominal cavity. The witness conveyed the predators silenced him quickly during the attack. These were large carnivores to inflict this sort of damage." Johnson released the body from his grip and looked at Sam and the park official.

"No chance it was a bear?" The man looked at Sam.

"Absolutely not." She glanced at Johnson.

"Which packs live in this area?" He studied Johnson, ignoring Sam.

"Several packs, but they left the area after winter. I don't think this is one of my packs." Johnson stood up and Sam followed his lead. Both brushed their hands off to clear debris from their palms.

"I want you to identify this pack so we can move forward. How quickly can you get back to me?" A whistle shrieked in the distance and the park official's walkie sounded off. "I think they found another body."

Guided by a man carrying a rifle, the three followed the sound until they spotted a group of men further in the forest. As they cleared the bushes, they noticed a partially exposed body of a woman poking out from leaves and soil. All those present remained quiet as the park official called for medical personnel.

"We'll stay with the woman. You gentlemen, continue the search for the third victim." Only an armed escort remained as the official turned to wave down the responding group of workers. The search party left in silence, fearing the remaining task. No one wished to find the remains of the infant.

Sam and Johnson scanned the small clearing. Blood, bones, and hair stained and littered the ground. The pair noticed an arm, recognizable from the elbow; a tibia spotted a short distance away. The predators had stripped all the flesh and muscle from the discarded remains. They watched as a new group of men arrived and took photos. The group carefully uncovered the body as they documented the evidence.

"There's nothing left. Why bury it?" Sam had seen many carcasses during her time spent in the park, but never one so clean in only a few hours.

"Instinct? They can still eat the marrow another time. Feast or famine? I don't know?" Johnson studied the body, but looked away when they turned the woman's torso. The corneas of her eyes were hazy, and a grimaced facial expression shocked the cowardly wildlife biologist.

Sam pulled her cell phone from a back pocket as it vibrated. She spotted a text from Dale before the notification disappeared from the screen. She walked away as she entered the password. *We got the images loaded. Need you in the cabins. NOW.* After reading the message, Sam looked over her shoulder. "Johnson, we need to go."

"What's up?" the official requested.

"We need to track the pack that did this. We won't do any good staring over everyone's shoulders." The man shot them an okay sign with his fingers when a medic interrupted. Johnson understood Sam was bending the truth. She had a way with words that, while partially true, failed to tell the whole truth.

Sam and Johnson returned to the truck to find Gabby stretched out. She slept on the rear bench and failed to notice their arrival. Without waking her, they dodged the exodus of campers and left the campground. Something was important enough for Dale to interrupt their work.

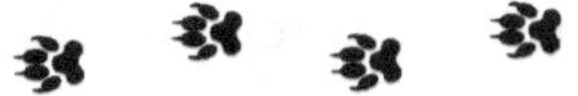

They heard the truck traveling through the gravel before it came to a stop in front of the cabin. Despite the seriousness of the situation, the girls giggled and filmed videos for their social media sites as they prepared snacks in the kitchen. Dale sat at the table with laptops open, snapping at the girls if they encroached on his space or sought to put a glass on the table. He knew their behavior and inattention would lead to spillage or damage to the equipment spread out before him.

When not throwing evil glances towards the crowd in the kitchen, Dale kept constant watch on the laptop screens. He occasionally swiped at the mouse on each keyboard to prevent the monitors from going dark. He grew impatient, as it seemed an eternity since he received a text response from Sam.

Sam was the first to enter the cabin, with Gabby and Johnson close behind. The girls barely took notice as they continued with their nonsense. When Sam slammed her belt and pistol on the countertop, the room fell silent. She spotted Dale behind a mass of charging cables and half a dozen laptops. She made a beeline toward him.

"What is it?" She was cautiously excited when Dale grinned.

"Girls, girls, gather round." Johnson pulled his team together. Everyone assembled behind Dale, awaiting the news. Sam took the empty seat beside him when Dale pulled a chair from beneath the table.

"We have images of the typical crap, the nosey man looking at our equipment and kids playing in the grassy strip behind the campers. We expected that. But look at this." He swiped the mouse over the arrow to click on the next photo. The black and white images taken after dark now replaced the colored ones shot during daylight.

"There." Sam tapped the screen when a blurred picture of a canine appeared.

"It gets better. Just wait and watch." Dale continued to the next photo and the next. Slowly, a figure appeared before the camera. It looked into the lens as if it knew the trail cam was taking photographs. The jaw was more muscular than a gray wolf, and the animal stood much taller. As the wolf smelled the equipment, the camera continued to shoot, revealing elongated and glowing canine teeth. The red flash made it look even more menacing. Dale hit the back button until it returned to the full-frontal shot of the wolf's muzzle.

"See, a giant wolf!" The girls laughed in response to their cohorts' sudden outburst. The room went silent when Johnson made a cutting gesture with his hand across his throat.

"A dire wolf. That's a dire wolf." All eyes turned to Gabby as she continued staring at the screen.

"Dire wolves are in the movies. They aren't real!" A shrill voice exclaimed from the back. The laughter continued as two slapped hands in a high five.

"GO!" Johnson snapped at the sea of blonde hair. The girls exchanged glances, as they had never heard him raise his voice. "Pack your things and go home. Your summer in Yellowstone is over. Leave, now!"

The cabin was silent as the girls funneled through the door. Sam grabbed Gabby's arm to prevent her from leaving. When the door closed, all eyes turned back to the monitors.

"There are other angles, too. These three aren't clear." Dale rapidly clicked through the shots that caught shadows and blurry images in the distance. He slowly clicked through the remaining two cameras that displayed images of other wolves at different angles. "These images support this one." He tapped the laptop screen with the wolf gazing into the camera.

"Why do you believe it's a dire wolf, Gabby? They went extinct during the ice age." Sam looked at the girl who had since pulled a chair to the table and sat by Dale.

"I took a field trip to the La Brea Tar Pits in middle school. They have hundreds of skulls displayed in the museum. They also have complete skeletons and full-size mounts. I vaguely recall seeing them as a kid, but I read up on them more recently."

"Why is that?" Sam questioned.

Gabby made a pained expression, embarrassed to continue. "I started playing tabletop games." She hoped her response would end further discussion regarding her resources. She sank into the chair.

"What kind of tabletop games?" Sam was clueless. She couldn't recall board games with dire wolves.

"Just a game," Gabby muttered. "One of my study groups played and got me hooked. Seriously."

"So, how does this relate to a dire wolf?" Johnson grew annoyed with her words and prepared to send Gabby packing, but she cut him off.

"It's a creature in my game. Anyway, while looking at the dire wolf's hit points, I became more curious. It was a pretty powerful character. Before you know it, I clicked link after link, reading about dire wolves. These pictures resemble the drawings online: large, shorter hair, reddish color. The dire wolf's coloring has researchers split. Some think they're like today's gray wolves and others think their coats were reddish. I think these photos prove the latter half correct."

The group looked back at the image as Johnson spoke. "It's a black-and-white image. How can you say that its coat is red?"

"Here. These images. Go back, Dale." She pointed to a screen at the opposite end of the table. Gabby scanned the images thoroughly when he arrived at the colored photos. "Stop! There."

"Kids playing. I'm not seeing what you're seeing." Sam shook her head.

"There." She reached across Dale and Sam to tap the screen. The faint image of a wolf in the brush was directly above her fingertip. "You can barely see the color of its coat reflected in the sunlight. I wasn't sure at first, but looking again, I'm certain it's a wolf. And not just any wolf, a dire wolf."

"The pack sent a scout to look for a victim. I'll be damned. Those kids don't even know it's there." Sam shook her head again in disbelief. "You have a brilliant eye, Gabby."

"Dire wolves went the way of other species during the ice age. How can you be sure? Gray wolves aren't always gray." Johnson drilled his intern.

"Other mammals survived the ice age. Pronghorn, for example. Why not a wolf?" Dale defended Gabby's assessment. The two quietly smacked hands under the table and out of sight.

"But how did dire wolves survive? Where have they been hiding the last ten thousand plus years?" Johnson became offensive. He felt their responses were a personal attack against his intelligence and anything schooling had ever taught.

"Think about it. Yellowstone remained quiet until this spring. The resident wolf packs started moving out of the park. Those in the park were, well, deadish. Something was scaring them off and eliminating them. This new species, possibly a dire wolf pack, took hold of the food chain. They shook things up, and now the new pack holds the top spot." Gabby hesitated with her assessment, unsure if she should continue.

"It goes back to what I said earlier, Johnson. The predators and prey are larger in Canada than those in the lower forty-eight. The gray wolf descendants in Yellowstone aren't native to the park. Biologists brought them here from Canada in the nineties. Since then, they've culled the elk herds and other wildlife, even my bears. They've remained unchallenged by other predators until now. Today there's talk to reduce gray wolf numbers in Wyoming. How can we not consider that a new species entered the park? There's always a bigger fish in the sea." Sam glanced at those around her.

"These aren't fish, and this is not the sea. Canada? It's so far. Scattered human populations would deter them from wandering past their borders. How do you explain it?" Johnson challenged her.

"Five hundred miles to the Canadian wilderness from here. Give or take." Gabby looked up from her phone.

"That's doable. Wolves have recently moved into Colorado from our parts. Despite the distance and the scattered population in Wyoming." Dale chimed in.

"Gray wolves can travel thirty miles a day. As Dale said, it's doable." Gabby held her phone up with the statistics displayed and waved it gently in her hands.

"But why? Why leave a bountiful food supply for the unknown? Especially such a great distance." Johnson crossed his arms and rubbed the stubble on his chin with a free hand.

"The same reason any wolf deviates from the pack..." Sam countered Johnson, "to start a new pack."

"How many wolves did we film?" Johnson waved a finger at the screens. Dale flipped through images at a steady pace. Everyone silently watched the pictures as they tallied the numbers with their fingers.

"Eight!" Johnson exclaimed when they reached the end.

"I got nine." Sam glanced at her fingers.

"I counted ten." Gabby objected.

"Nine with Sam." Dale insisted.

"For argument's sake, we have a new pack in the park that numbers no less than eight, but could number over ten. There's possibly more off-camera." Sam stood up to stretch and grab a drink from the fridge. She scooped up additional cans of soda before returning to the table. Dale and Gabby each grabbed one before Sam set them on the table. Johnson held up the palm of his hand when Sam offered one.

"What is our next step? How do we make certain that this isn't a gray wolf? Can you imagine presenting our theory to the scientific community? Dire wolves? I'll be the laughingstock if DNA testing determines otherwise. It'll end my career." Johnson pulled out the remaining chair, flipped it, and sat with his arms resting on the top rail.

"There's only one thing to do," Sam responded.

"Trap them!"

"Eradicate them!"

Both Sam and Johnson spoke simultaneously. They looked at one another in disgust. Dale and Gabby discreetly slid from their chairs and retreated to the kitchen. They knew this conversation was going to turn ugly. Any input from them was unsolicited and off-limits. Neither wanted the outrage redirected towards them.

"Are you fucking kidding? These things just demolished an entire family, a boy in a hammock, and a couple at the lake. They are an invasive species. We need to eliminate them before they kill anyone else. How can you even think that, Johnson?" Sam stood and turned as red as her hair while spewing at Johnson. He remained in the chair, looking off to the side. He appeared bored and unconvinced.

"Yellowstone is a national park. A national park protects the wildlife within its boundaries. Yes, these are new predators. Yes, they have hurt people. But it is our responsibility as wildlife biologists to preserve and study them."

"They didn't just hurt people! They tore into these victims before they stopped breathing. This species, whatever they are, stripped living human beings from flesh to hair and bone. I can't believe you're saying this! I've known you all these years, and this is how you react to a tragedy? You want to save them?" Sam stormed out of the cabin.

They listened as Sam screamed and ranted before returning. Dale and Gabby leaned against the counter, eating sandwiches and hiding their anxiety behind slices of bread that covered half their face. Their eyes darted between the lead biologists. Sam guzzled her soda, belched, popped the second can open, and took a seat.

"Let's be calm and reasonable. We know nothing about these wolves, and this is the perfect opportunity to study a new pack, a new species. Can you imagine, Sam? Discovered by the two of us. If we eliminate them, we may cause their extinction." Johnson stared at Sam with his doe eyes.

"They won't be extinct, Johnson. They came here from somewhere. Like other animals, they left their kind to claim fresh territory. There are more out there. I will bet my career on that fact." The sarcasm was heavy in her voice as she spoke to him slowly. "And flashing those big, innocent eyes at me is unbelievable. We need to kill them now. You can study their remains and track down their origins later."

Johnson stood up. "I think our partnership has come to a most tragic end. Let's not let this event strain our friendship, too. I wish you the best for what remains of the summer, Sam. I wholeheartedly believe that you are an intelligent, attractive, and remarkable woman." He nodded his head at Sam, ignoring Dale. "I'll appreciate the prompt return of my equipment. You can leave it in my cabin. My cabin door will remain unlocked. Come, Gabby."

"Gabriella, to you." She peered over her shoulder with a sour expression as Johnson shuffled her out the door.

"Damn! So much for dining in the air conditioning. I thought we were going to beat the dinner crowd." Sam circled the parking lot again, hoping to come across a spot at the Prancing Pronghorn Pizzeria. The joint was on Yellowstone Lake, next to the only marina and boat slip. "You should've awakened me from the nap earlier."

"I fell asleep, too. Apparently, we're not early birds." Dale scanned the next row, looking for activity within the cars or bright taillights. He was preparing to jump from the truck to save an open spot until Sam could reach him.

"Forget this. Let's go down to the marina and find a spot there." Again, vehicles or empty boat trailers filled the parking lot. Frustrated by the lack of parking, Sam drove over a curb and parked on a grassy verge. She blocked the gravel walkway, but shrugged it off. "They can walk around. We have important business. I'm starving!"

Sam slipped a bundle of expired identification cards onto the dashboard. Most of the park employees knew her, so she didn't fear having her truck towed. Sam spied a friend sitting in a national park pickup when they exited their vehicle. It was identifiable by its white paint job and green striping.

"Grab a pie and a couple of pops. I'm going to catch up with an old friend. Need cash?"

"No, I've got us covered. You can treat us next time." Dale headed for the pizzeria as Sam walked toward the West Bay Marina's reserved parking spaces.

Sam tapped on the driver's side glass with her knuckles, startling its occupant. The window rolled down, blowing cold air in her face. Sam listened to the noise of communication devices. The sound was inaudible as their transmission overlapped one another. She had hoped to pick up a bit of inside information.

"Sammy! I haven't seen you all summer. How is *e ku'u aloha*?" Kaimana exited the truck to hug her. He was a sizable man and picked her up, swinging her around before carrying her and placing her on the truck's open tailgate. Kaimana lurched upward, taking the empty spot next to her, causing the pickup to bounce until he settled.

"You look great! Any new tats?" She inspected his arm for new tattoos, running her fingers up his bicep and pushing the shirt sleeve back to expose more skin. Black tribal markings covered his muscular limbs and torso. She noticed no fresh and dark ink.

Kaimana was born and raised on the Big Island. Every summer, he would venture to the mainland to work in Yellowstone National Park. Mistakenly, he expected to escape the heat and hordes of tourists in Hilo. Aside from the landscape, there was no change between Hawaii and Wyoming. The temperatures were hot, and crowds swarmed the state.

Since his first visit, the Hawaiian had grown to appreciate the park and sightseers. His appearance and the little name tag displayed on his chest created many memorable encounters. No one expected to see a cheerful islander helping them with their vacation needs. Especially in a landlocked state. Kaimana would return to Yellowstone as long as he was welcome.

"Nah. I'm running out of space. I almost got one on my face before I left, but I wasn't drunk enough. My friend snitched on me. When she heard, māmā pulled a chain from her muumuu and started blessing me with her crucifix. You know me, I can't disappoint my māmā. No more tattoos. At least for now." There was a twinkle in his eye as he bumped shoulders with Sam. When a walkie on his belt started blaring, Kaimana turned it off. "A lot of chatter with those wolf attacks. I hope you're not affected. I heard Mr. Johnson will handle their capture."

"What do you mean, capture? Aren't they going to eliminate them?" Sam stumbled over her words as Kaimana shook his head. "I thought that was a given. They killed four people last night."

"Nah, Mr. Johnson told the park he discovered a new pack, possibly a new species. He bought some time to capture the wolves. It doesn't bode well for us to have maneaters running around. What do you think?"

"What else have you heard? I'm out of the loop since this morning." Sam pressed him for additional information.

"Not much. The campground was closed today, which is why it's especially crowded here. People have no place to go. I have to chase them out and close these parking lots in about an hour. The park service doesn't want people sleeping in cars or setting up tents here."

"Not to mention that we're only a couple of miles from the campground. Any wolf pack can easily clear that distance since last night." She looked at the crowds of people wandering the parking lot. "Do you mind if I hang out for a bit? I'm packing, and the truck is close-by." She nodded towards her vehicle and patted the holster that hung from her belt. "Do you need help this evening?"

"Nah. I'm good. A few others will swing by to help me. Just watch yourself. Be safe, Sam. *Noho me ka hau'oli*, be happy. I miss that smile." He wrapped a free arm around Sam's shoulder and squeezed her tightly before she jumped to the ground.

"Great seeing you. Take care of yourself. Be careful. I don't trust this wolf pack. And watch your back!" Sam blew him a kiss as she headed to the docks. Thinking back, Sam realized she hadn't smiled since first seeing him. There was too much weighing on her mind.

Sam stood at the edge of a floating dock in the marina. It gently swayed as waves broke against its buoyant pontoons. She stared at the lake, ignoring the peninsula to her right side for fear of spotting a dire wolf. Perhaps the wolves were watching and waiting? Sam shook when recalling her dream about the attack.

Curiosity got the best of Sam when she heard the innocent screaming of playing children. A large group took part in a game of tag in the open grassland that bordered the forest. The children were oblivious to the dangers that awaited them as they ran within feet of the dense brush. When the game ended, their interest turned to the water and they skipped stones instead. Sam's anxiety lessened when the distance between them and the forest was greater. It would be more difficult for a wolf to pluck a child from the open.

The dock bounced with more vigor causing Sam to turn quickly. Dale approached as he juggled multiple soda bottles in the crook of his arms and a pizza box in his hands. She helped him lay their dinner on the metal surface while they rested on the dock. Sam removed her shoes to dip her feet in the chilled water, but promptly replaced them. The water was too cold.

"Officials granted Johnson permission to catch the wolves. Do we call them wolves or dire wolves now? Anyway, he's already claimed it as his discovery." Sam hid her anger as she nonchalantly stated the facts. She grabbed a slice of steaming pizza.

"Are you kidding?" Dale screwed the cap open on his soda. The drink gushed, spraying them with a mist of sticky sugar. He sucked in the bubbles that continued to spill over the side. "Sorry!"

"Do you think a scout is watching the kids right now? Like the wolf in the images? There could be one at the edge of the tree line at this very moment. Maybe it's sitting and watching patiently. Is it choosing a victim for tonight's feast, hoping for the most succulent? Perhaps it's selecting the slowest or weakest? Like that kid." She pointed. "The one that just fell. Wolves are opportunistic predators. That child's life could end in an instant." Sam continued to stare, holding the pizza close to her mouth.

The two remained on the dock as visitors moored their boats or pulled them from the lake. They observed parents rounding up their children and returning to parked cars. When the sun slowly set and the swarms of mosquitos took flight, they swatted at their arms and blew the pests from their faces. They witnessed the park rangers directing visitors from the marina and listened as vehicles exited the grounds. During this time, Dale collected and disposed of the pile of napkins and an empty pizza box. He moved Sam's truck closer to the dock when she surrendered her keys. Dale returned with a rifle, flashlight, and bug spray. Sam grinned as she continued to examine the forest for movement in the fading light.

"How much longer do you want to stay? Not sure if it's a good idea to stick around in the dark. I think most people left. We might be the last men standing." He sat next to Sam and studied their surroundings.

"We'll go soon." They heard a wolf howling in the distance. Its voice failed to garner a response from other packs. "That came from the other side of the lake. Pretty far from here, too. Probably looking for a mate or the rest of his pack. Maybe the dire wolves annihilated his family?"

"How sure are you? Sounds kind of close." Dale sat erect, straining to pick up the sounds of another cry or a response from the dire wolf pack. "Do you think the dire wolves will respond?"

"Who knows? I wonder what that gray is thinking? Does it know the other pack is here?" Sam sprayed her arms with insect repellent. The mosquitos halted their assault, but flew about her face. The buzzing noise aggravated Sam as she struggled to listen for disturbances around the lake. "Maybe we should head back. Let's see what Johnson is scheming."

They left the marina and pizzeria, now devoid of activity. It was dark except for a few floodlights attached to the buildings. Sam and Dale drove south, traveling slowly in the blackness. Although they had taken hours-long naps after the fallout with Johnson, both were tired. Gluttony and exhaustion made them yearn for their beds. It would be a long drive to the cabin, despite the relatively short distance.

Just as Sam pressed the lever for her bright headlight setting, she slammed the brakes. The truck came to an immediate stop. Dale grabbed the dashboard with both hands as his body lurched forward. A dire wolf stood in the road. The massive beast with a coat of thick red hair stared at the pickup, its threatening posture a warning to Sam and Dale. Both sat wide-eyed and startled by the animal in the headlights. The alpha male remained in an attack position until the last of its pack finished crossing the pavement before it, too, disappeared into the thicket.

Now concealed by a juniper bush, the alpha male watched the glow from a vehicle that abruptly stopped on the pavement. After it had nearly missed his pack, the dominant wolf examined the pickup, unsure of its intentions. A light flicked on from a flashlight and its beam slowly scanned the edge of the forest. The dire wolf remained still as something explored the bushes in front of him. The light then continued searching the surrounding flora. Sometimes, it doubled back and stopped before proceeding with its probe.

Sensing his concern, the other members stopped. They, too, observed the strange light. Each wolf listened for noise or movement, unsure if the intruding object was predator or prey. Aside from the rumbling of the pickup's engine, the forest offered no other sound. It was silent and still.

There was no rustling as the air lacked wind. Timber critters sheltered in place, and birds and bugs ceased communication. The earth froze the moment the wolves entered this territory. Every living thing was fearful of one another.

Eventually, the spotlight shut off and the vehicle slowly lurched forward. The alpha male remained motionless until the object moved away and the headlights were no longer visible. After sniffing the air and scanning the surroundings, he rejoined the pack that looked to him for direction. The leader feared the vehicle's return and the occupants' intentions. He pushed them to travel faster to avoid detection, capture, or injury.

The dire wolves revisited the lake territory after taking flight the previous night. Their attack on a campsite had created an unexpected response from the other living things. Unsure if danger was imminent, the alpha male drove his offspring deeper into the interior of Yellowstone. He couldn't risk another injury to his pack.

Hunger forced the wolves to return to their preferred hunting grounds. However, taking down a human proved more demanding than the pack expected. Men were plentiful, but sheltered and remained protected in hardened structures. Despite the challenge, the wolves would linger near the campground until men, like deer and moose, took flight from the lake.

Before reaching the waterfront, the wolves spied a cluster of buildings in a clearing. Porch lights illuminated the figures they had grown accustomed to hunting. When the wolves neared the structures, two scouts separated from the pack. The others took cover in the darkness to study those they hunted. Again, they lay patiently, and waited, and watched. They would not take risks or go without another meal.

Bright lights, loud music, and a flurry of activity took place in front of the cabins. People darted in and out of doors. They laughed and sang or feasted and barbecued. The smells of searing flesh tormented the ravenous pack. Despite their eagerness, the wolves remained disciplined and attentive. They followed their leader for direction.

A car approached, illuminating the area as it turned and parked. When a woman emerged from the vehicle, the crowd became quiet. Her voice carried as she bellowed with rage. The people frantically packed their items and returned to the cabins. Interior lights came on as doors slammed, latches clicked, and curtains closed. Patio lights flicked off, and the forest again emerged in darkness. The prey had disappeared as their bellies rumbled. The pack glared at one another with disappointment and despair.

Before they had emerged from their hiding spots, the hinges of a cabin door squealed. Two figures egressed. The men settled on the stairs leading from the entry to the gravel. They relaxed in the dark, careful to remain unnoticed as they clicked the buttons on their vape pens and whispered to one another. The portly individuals were oblivious to any danger they faced as they inhaled vapor fumes and conversed.

When the alpha spotted the scouts, the pack moved into position on both sides of the cabin. They crept forward, slowly and silently, until given a signal. Before the men knew what had struck them, the wolf pack pounced on their victims. They dragged them from the porch, pressing their throats until the men no longer struggled or gave fight. As the wolves collected their prey, the injured she-wolf watched for a response from those in the cabins.

Rather than risk losing another meal, the pack pulled the men's bodies deep into the forest. Unlike the previous night, this attack remained unnoticed. When they reached a clearing, the wolves stopped to feed, including their wounded sibling and daughter. The alpha male stood guard and waited as his mate and offspring gorged on warm flesh and tender muscle. He would feast last and no wolf would go hungry. When they finished devouring their prey, only bones remained.

The dire wolves pushed on towards the lake. Despite tonight's success, they remained wary of man. They abandoned the area for safer ground. The pack arrived at the lake to drink, rest, and groom themselves or one another. Although it was late and the sun had yet to peak, the alphas pressed their pack to move. The shoreline provided insufficient cover and safety.

Exhaustion and full bellies brought on sleep and a need for rest. The dire wolves stopped short of a clearing and scattered amongst the thick underbrush to pause. Before lounging, the alpha male approached the tree line. A quick scan of unfamiliar territory revealed a grassy field that ended at the water. New objects floating atop the lake piqued his curiosity as they bobbed up and down. Once he determined the boats weren't a threat, he returned to his pack. Like the others, it was time to slumber and conserve energy.

Tomorrow would bring a new day of discovery and the hunt for prey.

DAY SEVEN

Sam's truck drifted over the campground's gravel roadway when she hit the brake pedal. She stopped short of Johnson and the people surrounding him. Everyone jumped or turned to look except Johnson. He was aware of her presence, but didn't flinch and appeared to be busy. Sam lay on the horn until he looked over his shoulder and lifted his sunglasses to meet her gaze. She was furious with the man in front of her bumper. When Johnson turned to ignore her again, Sam jumped from the truck and slammed her door.

"Johnson! What the hell are you doing? Sue came to my cabin this morning and was distraught. Two of her maintenance workers disappeared during the night. What are you doing about it?" Sam hollered as she moved towards him. Johnson held up a clipboard to stop her approach.

"I'm in the middle of preparing for the humane capture of my dire wolves. We already visited with Sue at the staff housing enclave this morning. There was no evidence to show my wolf pack was responsible. If you don't mind, I'm a very busy gentleman." Johnson looked over Sam's shoulder to give direction to an approaching park employee.

"No!" Sam interrupted. "Two men that never skipped a day of work are missing. They left behind supplies and equipment needed for their jobs. How do you explain that?" She stood with her hands on her hips. Dale remained in the pickup and watched from behind the tinted windshield. He silently applauded her showdown with Johnson and watched with amusement.

"Simple. According to the men's flat mates, the blokes were pissed last night and probably wandered off. That is Sue's concern, not yours. They'll turn up. Why don't you take your toy boy and do a bear thing? Let's put this to rest."

"I don't appreciate your condescending remarks, specifically from someone that hires the tramp troupe each summer. Dale is intelligent and an incredible wildlife biologist. Maybe he can teach you a thing or two?" The men helping Johnson oohed and snickered as she spoke. Sam smacked the clipboard against Johnson's chest and stormed away. After taking a seat in the truck and slamming the door again, she lowered the window. Sam slid through the opening and shouted, "Dale and I saw the wolf pack last night, closer to the marina. Your pack is on the move, you twat!"

Sam and Dale sped off towards the cabins that housed the West Bay Campground employees during the summer. Both wanted to see the area themselves, get updates, and offer Sue support. The truck turned off the main road and slowed to a crawl.

The pair scrutinized the landscape for movement and red hair. Rather than searching for the missing men, they scoured the wooded area for dire wolves. Everyone related the men's disappearance with the predators rather than their drunken carelessness. But Johnson convinced the park otherwise.

Sue stood inside the doorframe to her cabin with a hand on the lock rail. She was ready to shut and secure the door if approached by the predators. Sam shook her head when she witnessed the fear displayed by her friend. Since their last encounter, Sue had aged from the stress of her job.

The cabins and parking lot were empty except for Sue's vehicle and a few golf carts. After the men went missing, Sue reassigned her employees to other positions in the park. With the campground closed for the remaining season, there wasn't work, anyway.

Before exiting her truck, Sam did a weapons check. She and Dale were armed and carried extra ammunition. Sue waved them inside as they neared her cabin on foot. She slammed it shut and engaged the lock as soon as they entered the living area.

Sue's living quarters were just as Sam expected. A small window air conditioner cooled her half of the duplex. Houseplants and portraits of her family occupied tabletops and counters. A stack of home decor, quilting, and southern magazines lay stacked on the cushion of a sofa. Sue's cabin was immaculate and smelled of fresh-cut jasmine.

Sam removed a blanket from the couch and draped it along the back. She plopped on the worn couch as Dale took a seat at the table. Sue returned with a tray filled with mugs of coffee, sugar cubes, creamer, and cookies. Sam shot her a smile. Sue was a true southern lady.

After serving her guests, Sue sat with Dale at the small two-seater table. They exchanged awkward glances before she stared at her cup and watched the steam rise.

A notification on Sam's phone interrupted the silence. She noticed Gabby's name across the screen, but the message went dark before Sam read it. She quickly entered her password and unlocked the phone to display the text.

ctn sorry. j watching me. look under stairs. j kicked something no one saw hth gtg ttyl

"I need a decoder for this damn message. What's CTN?" Sam looked at Dale for information.

"Can't talk now."

"HTH?"

"Hope that helps." Dale furrowed his eyebrows. Whatever she was reading sounded exciting. He wanted to know more.

"GTG?"

"Got to go. What's this about?" He broke his silence, but Sam ignored his question.

"One last one. TTYL?"

"Talk to you later."

"Which cabin do the missing men sleep in?" Sam asked. She arose and unlocked the mechanism in her holster to release her pistol. Dale copied her movements and accompanied her to the door. Before they reached for the knob, Sue stepped between her and the exit.

"What happened?" She refused to move and shook with anxiety.

"Don't worry, Sue." Sam placed her free hand on Sue and squeezed her shoulder. "I just got a text that someone may have concealed something under their steps. I want to take a quick look. Dale will come with me. We'll be fine."

After moving aside, Sue opened the door and watched from the doorframe. It scared her to go any further. Sue pointed to the men's cabin, then slowly rotated her head back and forth to scan for predators.

The pair carefully and quietly approached the stairs that led into the cabin. Something had disturbed the dirt and pebbles surrounding the building. Sam wasn't sure if it was recent or old; it was hard to differentiate between all the markings. Unlike the previous attack site, no blood or impressions showed foul play.

"Watch my back." Sam lay her pistol on the bottom step and cautiously dropped to her hands and knees. She grimaced as the rocks dug into her skin. Sam lay flat to look under the stairs and activated the flashlight on her cell phone. She gradually scanned the darkness, not wanting to miss something. A flash blinded her as the light reflected off a shiny object. It was within reach, and she quickly swiped at the loose ground to pull it into the sunlight. Sam clutched the item as they hastily returned to Sue's cabin. Neither took the time to inspect it in the open.

"That belongs to Gage. That's his vape stick thingy." Sue's mind was racing faster than she could spit the words out. Her index finger frantically pointed to the device. "He goes nowhere without it. I knew something happened to that boy."

"Any chance this belonged to someone else?" Dale questioned.

"No. No. That's the only one Gage uses. He custom-wrapped it before coming back and wouldn't stop teasing me about it. He picked glittery pink so the guys wouldn't touch it. Gage had two sticks disappear last summer. I know that's his, one hundred percent. What are we going to do to find him?" Sue returned to the kitchen table and cupped her face before she started sobbing. Sam pulled a chair next to her and rubbed her back as she motioned for Dale to retrieve a tissue. He returned from the bathroom with a box instead.

"I don't want you to stay here alone. Come back with us and stay at our cabin. We'll keep you safe. We'll work on a plan to find Gage. Dale and I have our hands tied, but I'll figure something out." Sam continued rubbing her back as Sue wiped her eyes and cleared her nose.

"I'll be fine. My husband and a friend are on their way. I'm going back to Cody this afternoon. I'm going home." She grabbed Sam's hand and squeezed it tightly. "Come with me, both of you. I have enough space. Stay in Cody until they kill those things. The park isn't safe. No, the park isn't safe."

"It's getting dark. Where the hell is she?" Sam paced their cabin, waiting for Gabby. Since her earlier text, Sam hadn't heard from her.

"Maybe they're pulling an all-nighter? They had a lot of crap to set up." Dale poked through the refrigerator. He opened and closed the door as if something would wondrously appear. Dale finally settled on a cold drumstick and placed it on the counter while retrieving a milk carton. After unscrewing the lid, he smelled it, shrugged his shoulders, and poured a glass anyway. Their kitchen desperately needed food.

"Could you tell what he was up to? I mean, Johnson? Did you see what Gabby was doing? I was too busy yelling at Johnson and caught up in the moment."

"Yeah, you were definitely a fiery red. I didn't see Gabby, but I noticed a bunch of cage traps. A group was wrapping them with covers. Maybe she was with them? Honestly,

I saw little. You were putting on quite a show. I think the guys standing next to Johnson shit their pants when you pulled up. I didn't want to miss a thing." He snickered and slid along the edge of the counter to make room for Sam when she entered the tiny kitchen.

"Why would Johnson hide the vape stick? He's up to something. I just don't trust him." Sam wanted a drink, but the cabinets, like the fridge, were bare. She opened cupboards, rummaged through the shelves, and repeated her actions. After a second go at it, she gave up and grabbed a nearly empty bottle of orange juice. She drank directly from the container as she continued pacing the cabin in her pajamas and slippers.

"We both know why he hid it. Adults can legally disappear without just cause. If authorities suspect foul play, it leads to an investigation. At least, that's what I learned from a murder documentary on television. A search would lead to the discovery of two additional bodies." He talked with a mouth full of food.

"Which would lead to the park executing his dire wolf pack. They'd refuse him the grandstanding he's accustomed to. Brilliant observation, inspector!" Sam winked at Dale before finally settling in her chair. "What an ass, though. Seriously. Johnson would rather have notoriety and riches than find these men. We know they're dead. Why not return the bodies to their families? So, what can we do? How do we go about finding them? Johnson has the park wrapped around his finger so we can't approach them. And I'm not stepping foot in that forest with those damn things running around. Who's going to help us?"

"I think we should get some rest tonight and figure things out tomorrow. Today was a roller coaster of emotion for you. And me. I mean, I don't know Sue, but she seems nice and caring." Dale tossed his chicken bone into the empty trash can. It ricocheted within the interior, causing the can to rock back and forth until it reached the bottom.

"Speaking of, thanks for staying with me today. I hadn't planned to be there long, but I couldn't leave her alone. Sue is like a mom to me."

"Where is your mom? You don't talk about your personal life and never bring up your family," Dale asked while retrieving another piece of chicken. He inspected the fried thigh and plucked something off the skin before cramming the meaty part into his mouth.

"Dead," she stated without emotion. She noticed Dale's eyes widen. "No worries. Happened when I was little. My dad and his Forest Service friends raised me. He passed when I was seventeen. No siblings, little extended family. I'm mostly a loner. Therefore, there's not much to talk about."

"Why haven't you married or something? At least date?" He raised his eyebrows and lowered his face, locking his eyes with hers.

"Poor taste in men, I guess. But there's time to sort that out later." Sam sighed. "Maybe I should get a dog? Or a cat instead? Yeah, a cat. Then I won't have to walk a dog outside when it's twenty below."

"I'm good taste in men, I think?" He grinned as she threw a slipper at him.

"I think not. You have a girlfriend! Don't be that kind of guy!" she scolded him. "Remember what I said..."

"You can look, but don't touch!" Both announced at the same time before laughing.

"Ugh! You both make me cringe. The incurable lasciviousness is so damn heavy in here, I can't breathe.

Get a room. Wait, you have a room, actually two. So, pick a bed!" Gabby leaned against the wall and stuck a finger in her mouth before making a vomiting sound. Her sarcasm was harsh, causing Sam and Dale to turn red. It embarrassed both that someone had witnessed their exchange. "Maybe if you two weren't carrying away, you would've heard the door open. Anyway, I have to go in a sec. Some park employee brought me back to grab a few things for tonight. Johnson won't let me leave his side. Lucky me, I get the graveyard shift with the playa. No worries though. My brown locks and hairy legs will protect me from his sexual advances. I'm totally not his type."

Sam was relieved to see the young girl. She walked over to hug her, but Gabby moved to the side.

"Nah, I'm not that kind of girl. But Dax, Dawayne, or whatever your name? I could go for that." Gabby professed as she looked over Sam's shoulder.

"Dale," he said, still blushing from embarrassment.

"Dale isn't half bad. Looks like he came straight out of a cowboy magazine. He's the all-American boy." Gabby shot him a kiss. She enjoyed messing with people.

"He's already spoken for. We're both out of luck." Sam snorted as she stepped back to study Dale. "Seriously, Dale and I have a great relationship. Nothing's happening in this cabin."

"If this cabin's a-rockin'... anyway, I stopped by to bring you up to par. The park gave us two nights to capture these things. After that, they'll call in some hunters or something. Johnson, wait, me and a team of park employees set up cage traps around the campsites. Had to bait those damn things with rotten roadkill. That stuff stinks like ass. Johnson, wait, me again, also arranged for a wildlife sanctuary to house them once they're caught. That's his glorious master plan."

Gabby handed Sam several pieces of torn yellow paper from a legal notepad. Each scrap had Johnson's name and cell phone number written in Gabby's handwriting. Sam furrowed her eyebrows as she compared it to the number stored on her cell phone.

"I already have his number. Why do I need this? What do I do with this many copies?" Sam looked at Gabby.

"The press is snooping around. We're not allowed to speak to anyone. Johnson is keeping me on a very short leash. Be sure you don't lose those copies if you stop by the campground tomorrow. I'd hate for his number to find its way into the wrong hands." She emphasized wrong as she spoke.

"But they're in your handwriting. What if he finds out?" Sam wished to protect the younger version of herself.

"I couldn't give a damn. After tomorrow night, I'm out of here. If by some far chance Johnson catches a dire wolf, I want a picture. An image of me posing with one would garner a bit of publicity for me in L.A. Could open up some interesting job opportunities?"

"Gabby, be safe. I don't trust Johnson. He's liable to take risks in his quest for fame and fortune. And don't get caught up in his playbook. You're smarter than that." Sam extended her hand to shake with Gabby.

"What the hell is that? Just hug me. Get it over with." Gabby held her tightly and Sam responded with a similar embrace. The women feared what the following days would bring. Gabby released her grip on Sam and opened the door. A tear rolled down Gabby's cheek, and she promptly wiped it on her sleeve. "Dale, you might consider switching from bears to a different predator."

"To what?" He watched her intently, unsure what she was alluding to.

"Cougars. I hear one is creeping around your cabin. Watch your back, Dale. They'll grab you when you're not looking." Gabby pointed towards Sam, winked, and hurriedly closed the door. She listened to the boisterous laughter and Sam's denial through the open window. Gabby waited for a moment, shutting her eyes for fortitude before stepping into the darkness. It was time to rejoin Johnson at the campground and capture the wolves.

DAY EIGHT

When Sam and Dale emerged from their cabin the next morning, they noticed Johnson's SUV parked outside. They understood his attempt to catch the predators was unsuccessful. Had he captured a dire wolf, the world would already know. No declarations of victory, no phone calls or texts, and not a person in sight. All was quiet in their neck of the woods.

The two spoke briefly about the previous night's conversation over coffee and agreed it was best to maintain space between them and park officials. Sam and Dale didn't want to be the scapegoats if something went wrong. And Sam expected that was a given. It would be disastrous for their careers and neither wanted to risk being banished from Yellowstone.

During the last week, the pair had neglected their own research and instead assisted Johnson with his wolf plight. Because their help was no longer wanted, Sam thought it best to track a popular grizzly bear and her only surviving cub. The brown bears were farther north, possibly farther from danger. They looked forward to spending time away from the lake and the drama surrounding the campground.

With the wolves and their whereabouts unknown, Sam packed weapons and extra ammunition. They loaded battered trail cameras, hiking equipment, and a long-range monocular. Before she locked the cabin door, Sam hesitated for a moment. She ultimately grabbed the scraps of papers with Johnson's cell phone number. Perhaps they would come in handy?

As they headed towards Hayden Valley, Sam and Dale conversed about the rolling hills, open pastures, and the Yellowstone River. Herds of bison, scattered elk, and an assortment of waterfowl inhabited this lush and green land. If they were fortunate, they would chance upon the grizzlies they pursued. Neither mentioned the dire wolves and instead envisioned a day spent observing wildlife. Before they drove any further, their bellies rumbled. Both had eaten little that morning and they wouldn't make it until dinner. Their options were limited, but they decided a quick stop at the pizzeria for lunch fare and the marina for drinks and snacks was in order.

When they entered the pizzeria, Sam signaled to Dale. He followed her around a counter and into the kitchen. A feeble and elderly man dressed in an oversized and stiff white apron noticed the pair. His face lit up, and he dropped a bag of sliced pepperoni on the countertop before approaching Sam for a hug. The man expressed the same enthusiasm towards Sam that Dale noticed from Sue. Almost everyone in Yellowstone knew of and admired his mentor. He understood why.

"Oh, Sammy. Why have you waited this long to visit? It's been quiet this summer without you. I've missed your pretty face popping into my kitchen! Who is this handsome young gentleman? Where is Olivia?" he exclaimed with a thick Italian accent.

"This is Dale. Dale, this is Riccardo. Dale is replacing Olivia as my apprentice this summer. Olivia graduated and accepted a job on the other side of the state." Although he wore a hearing aid, Sam was articulate and loud. She realized Riccardo struggled with distinguishing words, despite the device crammed into his ear. "Sorry I haven't stopped by yet. It has been a crazy summer."

"Yes. Every summer is crazy for my Sam. Welcome to Yellowstone, Dale." He addressed Dale before coming back to Sam. "I'm happy for Olivia. If you speak to her, tell her Riccardo wishes her well. Now on to business before it gets busy. I'm presuming my favorite redhead has a bare pantry and icebox?"

"You know me well, Nonnino," Sam responded. Riccardo preferred she address him as a grandfather.

"Let me sneak some items from my inventory." He wiped his hands down the front of his chest as he yelled to the kitchen staff, "*Fammi una pizza! Veloce!*"

Although his staff didn't speak Italian, they understood his request. Riccardo looked like a pushover, but he ruled his kitchen with a heavy hand. Before Riccardo finished speaking, a woman was already preparing a pizza. Dale watched with wonder as she slid a massive pie into the restaurant's wood-fired oven within minutes.

"Pull your truck around to the back door. Your timing is perfect. I'll set you up." Riccardo waved Sam off and hobbled down a hallway with food storage on either side. At the end of the short corridor, employees left a battered metal door cracked for a chance breeze and fresh air. It wasn't long before Sam backed her truck up to that door and Riccardo prepared a pile of foodstuff.

"Wow! This is quite the stash. How are we going to eat this? This is too much!" Sam looked at piles of cans, boxes, and bags of assorted items from his kitchen.

"Take it, take it. This morning, I got word the park may force us to close. They won't commit to a reopening date and I don't want this food going to waste. I'd rather you have it. Share if you like. What am I to do?" He asked and shrugged his shoulders.

"Why are you closing?" Sam asked. Dale lowered the tailgate and started loading the items before Riccardo changed his mind. Dale was thankful for the man's generosity. He hated shopping and this would save them from making a trip to a grocer outside of Yellowstone. At least for a while.

"Something happened at the marina last night," Riccardo expressed, while still catching his breath. He had over-exerted himself from lifting boxes. "They pulled a man from the lake this morning."

"Do you know what happened? Are authorities still there?" Sam asked. Dale stopped loading the truck and exchanged concerned glances with Sam. Neither moved, but watched Riccardo instead.

"The park didn't seem overly concerned. They stated the area needed to be vacated until they ensured it was safe. They'll contact me later today. Now I'm facing closure and releasing my employees. Headquarters won't be happy with the loss, but what am I to do? I've run this pizzeria for years and never had this happen. Maybe this is God's way of saying it's time to quit and slow down?" Riccardo signed the cross with his fingers and kissed his thumb as he looked at the sky.

"Thank you, Riccardo. This food will help us and my budget. However, I hate you gave it to us for this reason. I can't thank you enough." Sam pointed to the supplies with an open hand. She gave Riccardo another hug, unsure if she would see him again this summer. Dale slammed the tailgate shut, shouted a quick thank you, and jumped into the passenger seat.

"Wait. One more thing." Riccardo grabbed Sam's arm to stop her from leaving and turned to face the door. Despite his size, his voice was thunderous as he yelled into the building, *"Dov'è la mia pizza?"*

Within a minute, someone from the kitchen ran down the short hallway with a pizza box in their hands. She handed it to Sam, who passed it off to Dale through his open window.

"Again, thank you, Riccardo. Send me the bill." Sam bent over to kiss him on the cheek.

"Payment accepted." He smiled. "Back to work, you go. Let me return to the kitchen before all hell breaks loose. When the boss is away, the children will play."

Before returning to their cabin to drop off the food, Sam drove the short distance to the marina, maneuvering around cones and yellow tape. Its placement failed to block Sam's pickup. When she spotted a parked park service truck, Sam pulled next to it. She noticed Kaimana singing and dancing in the driver's seat. His face lit up when he spotted her and he promptly lowered the window as he turned down the music. Kaimana still danced until he noticed the concerned look on her face.

"What's going on, Kaimana?" She asked.

"You missed the action this morning. A visitor found someone floating face down in the lake. They wrapped up the scene about an hour ago. I thought of calling or texting you, but don't want to tick off the wrong person. Strange things are happening and I'm just the little man on the totem pole. You know how that goes." His voice was serious, not jubilant like Sam always expected.

"Did you see the body? Did you notice anything peculiar?" She inquired.

"All I know is what I was told. The tourist was sleeping on his boat, which he shouldn't be doing. They said he was probably drunk, fell out, and hit the prop. His legs had injuries consistent with a boat propeller. Sounds odd, if you ask me? Who's running their motor after dark? But it's not my place to question anyone."

"Have you seen this guy before?" Sam asked. Kaimana was a talkative person. She only had to ask one question to stir up his memory and get him talking.

"He's a regular in Yellowstone. Widowed man, really nice guy. Lives in Arizona, but likes to fish here during the summer. We talk every year. His wife was part Samoan. I think I sort of reminded him of her. Anyway, the man normally stays in his camper shell. Over there." Kaimana pointed to a lone truck in the parking lot with an aged shell, an empty boat trailer parked nearby. "I don't think he would sleep in his boat when he has a bed. It doesn't sound like him. He was probably loading his boat with gear because he likes to fish early. You know, the early bird gets the worm. Right? Anyway, sorry, I keep getting sidetracked.

The old man just arrived yesterday. I didn't even see him yet. And drunk? Nah, never saw the guy with a beer or smelled alcohol on his breath. But everyone has skeletons in their closet. Some can keep the door closed longer than others. Right?"

"Why do you think authorities would lie about this?" Dale finally spoke.

"Not sure they're lying, but maybe they don't have answers. If you ask me, I think it's related to the campground. I'm convinced they're downplaying his death to prevent panic. Again, I'm not in charge. I'll continue being their yes man and hang out in my truck. Life is good. *Noho me ka Hau'oli*, be happy, my friends."

"Thanks, Kaimana. Do me a favor and text me next time. No one needs to know and I can keep a secret. Take care and stay safe. Don't leave that truck. Especially if you're alone." Sam blew him a kiss before she drove away.

Not wanting the food to spoil, Sam and Dale headed towards their cabin to unload the cargo. They ate pizza during their drive and speculated about the cause of death for the man pulled from the lake. Neither believed it was a boating accident. They assumed the wolves had shredded the man's leg as he jumped into the lake. His boat wouldn't provide safety, but the frigid waters might. Sam counted three victims that eluded the wolves by chancing their lives within Yellowstone Lake. Drowning and hypothermia were preferable to being eaten alive.

Dale studied the entrance of the campground as they approached it and when Sam slowed the truck. Although the area was away from the road, one could glimpse part of the property from a certain angle. He relayed what he saw so Sam could keep her eyes on the road and avoid detection.

"It's hard to see everything. It looks like the park erected barricades up and assigned security, like the marina. There are also unmarked vehicles parked at the entrance and a small group of people. I wonder if they're from the press? Is that what Gabby was hinting towards last night?"

As if she was listening, the phone chimed and a text came from Gabby, *Nada*.

Sam stopped the truck and read her message. "I think it's time we dropped a few pieces of paper. Do you think those are people from the press?"

Sam didn't await an answer, but backed the truck up and turned into the campground. She kept a safe distance, parked on the side of the road, and watched the activity ahead. Dale fished through the console and glove compartment until he found the stash of phone numbers.

Sam remained in the truck and watched as Dale approached the group. The bystanders stood separated from the campground by a collapsible blockade. Initially, they seemed responsive to Dale. Some pulled notebooks from satchels or phones from their pockets. A photographer readied his camera. They soon became disinterested with the newcomer, who hid his face in the shade of a ball cap. The spectators resumed watching over the campground, turning their backs on Dale. Sam watched as he pulled the scraps of papers from a pocket and casually dropped them on the ground. He strolled back to the truck, careful to hide his identity.

Slowly, the press noticed the papers that fluttered on the ground. One plucked a piece from the gravel. Another glanced around before stepping on a nearby note. The lady pretended to adjust her shoe as she palmed the memo and stepped away from the crowd. The oohs and ahhs from some garnered interest from those that awaited Johnson's arrival. Now the group directed their attention towards the ground. Everyone wanted a piece of discarded paper. Before Sam dove away, they witnessed a flurry of activity. Not one of Gabby's notes remained unclaimed.

Instead of spending a day in Hayden Valley, Sam and Dale returned to the cabin. They unloaded the truck, gorged themselves on Riccardo's food, fixed the laptop, and prepared for upcoming research. Without expressing so in words, both were eager to await updates from Johnson. Neither Sam nor Dale wanted to miss any action.

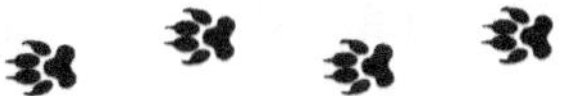

When the door burst open, a gust of air blew through the cabin. Despite Sam and Dale slamming their arms on the table to keep them in place, maps and paperwork took flight. When she looked up, Sam noticed a shadow standing in the doorway.

"Close the door, Johnson!" she yelled. He begrudgingly did so. Against the force of the wind, he slammed it even harder the second time.

Both Sam and Dale stared at Johnson when he stood over the table. They knew why he showed up, but feigned otherwise. Sam rearranged their research paperwork while Dale retrieved the pieces that drifted down the hallway.

"Why did you give them my number? My phone has been ringing since late morning. This exasperating noise is interrupting my concentration. I am a very busy man and do not have time for this!" The intensity of Johnson's voice increased as he spoke. He clenched his fists and punched them onto the table. Sam's glass of water violently shook, and she grabbed it before it toppled over.

"I don't know who you think you are? I don't appreciate you coming into my cabin and acting like a two-year-old throwing a tantrum!" Sam stood up, leaning against the table to support her body weight. Dale watched, frozen in the hallway, his hands grasping a messy pile of papers. "If you want to talk like an adult, sit down and act like one. If not, leave. Now!"

Johnson cowered under Sam's dominance. He sat in a chair across from her. Dale cautiously approached the table and quietly placed the papers down. He continued to the kitchen for a glass of water for himself and Johnson.

"I'm sorry, Sam. I'm under a lot of pressure. Gabby and I were up all night and the bloody phone woke me up. I answered the first few and they won't take no for an answer." Johnson grabbed the glass of water from Dale and acknowledged him with a nod. He glanced at this phone. "See, four missed calls since I left my place. They won't stop."

"Who's calling?" Sam asked. She faked her concern. Once Dale sat down, she tapped his leg with her toes under the table. Neither would admit their wrongdoing.

"The bloody press. Someone gave them my number. I assumed it was you. I'm sorry." A wave of shame overcame his facial features. Johnson grimaced as he prepared for a lecture and verbal assault. Sam distressed him further with her silence.

"First, I don't appreciate your behavior, your tone, or your accusations. You asked us to keep our distance, and we have done that. Dale and I have been busying ourselves with research and grant work. My normal summer duties. Second, why would I give your number to the press and how would I benefit from it? Really? Since when did I deal with news people?" She crossed her arms, sat back in her chair, and watched Johnson wiggle in his seat. He drank the glass of water in one gulp.

"Help me." Those were the only words he delivered, a whisper at that.

"Excuse me?" Sam tilted her head to the side. "And why would I do that?"

"If I don't capture them tonight, they'll kill them. I need this, Sam. I really need this." Johnson was acting himself again. After a failed attempt to capture the predators, he preferred Sam to do the dirty work. And in true Johnson form, he would relish the attention and stake a claim on her successes and discoveries.

"No. I'm busy. Don't bother me with your operation. If you want the credit, then you do the work. Simple. You're a grown man. Let's act like it," voiced Sam. Dale struggled to swallow his water without choking. He fought the urge to laugh in Johnson's face. Meanwhile, Johnson lowered his head. It bobbed as he thought up new ways to plead for help.

"I'm taking Gabby with me tonight. To the campground again. Perhaps you can pay us a visit?" Johnson asked.

"Why would I do that? And what are you planning?" Sam wondered if he had more than cage traps in his master plan to capture the wolves.

"I have cage traps. Enough to capture the entire pack." Sam rolled her eyes at his response.

"What else? How are you luring them to the campground? Where are you and Gabby hiding?" She leaned forward for a drink.

"Yesterday, we set up an observation area atop the loo facilities. The building by the tent camping area. We sat up there all night and rotated sleeping shifts. Although we didn't get much sleep. It was too bloody uncomfortable." Johnson hesitated for a response. He knew Sam would offer her opinion, and he hoped for ways to improve this night's affair.

"A cinderblock building that overlooks the campsite. Plenty of room for your equipment. Okay. How did you get up there?" She was interested and took the bait.

"A truck. We hopped in the bed. Gabby climbed up first, then I handed her the equipment. Easier than a ladder."

"Can't the wolves reach you? If a human can climb it, why shouldn't a wolf? What's stopping them? I hope someone moved the truck for your sake?" Sam was concerned about their safety. Although she had a friendly, but tumultuous relationship with Johnson, she wanted nothing to happen. Especially to Gabby.

"Yeah. Someone moved the truck. Please, Sam, I have more common sense than that." Johnson was lying. "And from what I've read, dire wolves are not as intelligent as my gray wolves. Larger bone structures, but smaller brain cavities."

Like you, Dale thought to himself.

"What else? Did you install leg-hold traps or snares?" Sam wasn't interested in a dire wolf lecture.

"I have tranquilizer guns and darts." He was proud of his non-lethal arsenal. Johnson wanted to capture them alive and uninjured.

"Seriously? You and Gabby are going to shoot an entire pack of angry wolves with a dart gun? And in the dark? Do you expect to shoot, with accuracy, all these animals at once? How about the reloading time? Or do you have a dozen guns ready to go? For argument's sake, let's say you did this within a few minutes. That gives the animals up to five minutes to scatter before the sedative kicks in, and that depends on the sedative you use. Let's say they all fall into a deep slumber at once because you hit them in the right place with the proper dosage. Now the clock is ticking. You have about forty-five minutes to get off the roof of the bathroom, locate each wolf, and secure a dozen ravenous creatures. They weigh... let's say, a hundred and fifty pounds each." Sam picked up her phone to access the calculator. "You have about forty-five minutes from first contact to secure one thousand and eight hundred pounds of dead weight. Who's doing that? You? Gabby? What if you can't find one? What if one wakes up early? They may be groggy, but they have teeth and they will defend themselves and their pack."

"That wasn't my entire plan, just part of it. The darts are backup. And we have spotlights on the rooftop. We can illuminate the area rather quickly. To catch the pack, we're going to use cage traps." Johnson spoke with confidence, although he didn't appreciate the disdain in Sam's voice.

"So, you expect a dozen wolves to enter a trap that smells foreign to them? All at the same time? Or will they take turns? Let me guess, you baited them with rancid roadkill when they've become accustomed to eating our tourists?" Thanks to Dale and Gabby, Sam was already aware of the traps and their setup. But she chose to further belittle the man that sat across from her.

"You have a negative way of looking at things, Sam." Johnson stood up to leave.

"Not negative. Just realistic. I don't want anyone to get hurt. You have a responsibility to protect Gabby, the tourists, and park employees." She sat back in her chair again.

"I thought you might help me out, but I see how it is." He opened the door, causing the papers to drift down the hall again. Sam and Dale remained still, fighting the urge to grab at the reports that rose above the table. "I can't wait to see your face tomorrow when I capture the dire wolves. Just wait and see."

"For the record, I do have one idea." Sam crossed her arms.

"Yes?" Johnson hesitated to ask.

"Kill the damn things. This will not end well. The wolves have already taken too many people. The couple in the lake, a missing dog, I'm fairly sure about those, the young family, the kid in the hammock, Sue's maintenance workers, the man at the marina. Am I missing anyone"? Should I go on?"

Johnson slammed the door during his departure. He did not appreciate Sam's condescending remarks. Yet, he knew she was slightly accurate. The dire wolves had taken too many people. But not all the deaths and disappearances were tied to his pack, so he thought. Johnson planned to stop their carnage tonight and prove her wrong. They weren't as deadly as she perceived.

DAY NINE

Johnson walked around the campsite to inspect the cage traps on the off chance a wolf had sprung the mechanism and trapped itself during his absence. An armed park employee accompanied Johnson as he continued checking each device. As expected, they were empty.

During the previous day, workers had arranged each trap next to bushes or hid them within thick vegetation. Before positioning them, Gabby wrapped the cages with green plastic to hide the steel mesh. Johnson thought it would make them less threatening. He hoped the traps would simulate a den and ease their anxiety.

Since wolves are opportunistic predators and scavengers, Johnson thought the putrid smell of rotting flesh would tantalize their senses and bring them out of hiding. Although the traps were camouflaged, flies discovered the rancid meat used to bait each trap. They feasted on the unclaimed scraps during the heat of the day. If the smell didn't attract the wolves, the sound of the swarming insects might.

As the sun prepared to set, park employees scurried about to ensure the area was secure. Only one road led into the campground, but many hiking trails fed into West Bay from outside. Johnson directed them to canvass the campground one last time. Too many people wished to witness and watch events unfold. Word spread fast, and his attempt to capture the predators was gaining popularity from within the park. Johnson didn't want interference or distractions. Tonight was his last opportunity to catch the dire wolves and unveil his discovery to the world.

Johnson ordered a park official to position a truck next to the building. It was the same one they had used the night before to stage an observation area. From atop the building, one could locate most of the traps. Gabby climbed to the rooftop before Johnson handed her supplies. They needed little tonight. The two only restocked water, food items, and their collection of non-lethal weapons. Johnson kept those in their cabin. He didn't want the tranquilizers to lose their efficacy in the heat and sun if left exposed on the rooftop.

Despite the small size of the building, it was spacious and served its purpose. The rooftop held scads of equipment and tracking devices, including collars. Johnson tasked Gabby with ensuring that everything was in working order for the night. Gabby had previously positioned dual LED spotlights on each corner. She checked each bulb and flicked the switches to ensure they still operated while rolling her eyes and shooting hateful glances at her boss. It was tedious and mindless work.

Johnson waved off the last of the park employees as they crammed into one vehicle before driving away. Only Gabby and Johnson remained behind. No one was in the vicinity to assist with their bid to capture the dire wolf pack. There was a moment of hopelessness as they stood alone atop the roof. But their self-pity only lasted a moment. There was still much work to be done.

They labored quietly in the dimming light. Gabby checked the flashlights before setting up electronics and recording equipment. She occasionally glanced at Johnson, who always chose the enjoyable tasks. But Gabby continuously reminded herself that today was her last day. She would leave Yellowstone whether they caught a wolf or not.

Johnson loaded the dart gun with a tranquilizer and peered through the scope. He set it in front of his chair alongside a container containing additional darts. Unlike what Sam had implied, he didn't have twelve dart guns. Just the one. It was old and reliable, dissimilar to the rest of the equipment he possessed.

Johnson unlatched a large metal case, opened it, and studied the contents. He looked into the case as if he had claimed a chest of gold. Instead, it contained thick padding and assorted pieces of Johnson's newest toy. Earlier that day, he received a loaner from a wildlife biologist on the opposite side of the park. Johnson was eager to assemble the device.

"What the hell is wrong with you!" Gabby shouted when Johnson aimed the net gun at her.

"Shhh. We don't want to scare the wolves." He whispered as he lowered the muzzle and inspected the mechanisms. "I think this is brilliant. If a wolf approaches, we'll use this. We only have two nets and a half dozen canisters of carbon dioxide. So don't touch."

While Johnson admired his handiwork, Gabby turned her back to him and sat in the farthest corner. Her legs dangled from the building as she cracked her back and rotated her head to stretch her neck. Gabby slipped her cell phone out and sent Sam a quick text. *Save me from this train wreck :(*

Twilight had passed, and a waning crescent moon cast little light upon the campground. Stars materialized, twinkling brightly in the absence of city lights. Gabby regretted not bringing a telescope. She was sure the Milky Way was more brilliant if viewed with the aid of a powerful eyepiece. Johnson noticed her star gazing and the glow of a cellphone resting on her lap.

"Turn that off and get over here. We need to minimize our movement now and lie low. Have a seat." Johnson pointed to her chair. Before he sat down himself, Johnson muted his phone and turned off a walkie-talkie. He wanted silence atop the rooftop.

"I have to pee." Gabby declared while standing over him. Johnson exhaled loudly, extruding any air in his lungs. She smirked, knowing how much she annoyed him.

"Hurry. Take a flashlight. Don't make any noise." He looked down at his faded cellphone screen, not offering help.

Hypocrite! She thought.

Gabby dropped from the roof to the bed of the truck. She made a loud thump noise and stopped for a moment. Again, Johnson failed to hide his discontent with her. She heard him huffing and puffing. Gabby smiled and clicked the button on her flashlight, illuminating the area. All was still and quiet as she scanned the campground. The predators were nowhere in sight.

The entrance was almost directly below where Johnson sat. Gabby heard him shuffle his feet on the gritty asphalt shingles as she reached for the doorknob of the women's restroom. But she hesitated before touching the handle. Gabby froze as a noise emanated from the thick brush around the corner of the building.

Gabby flashed her light into the darkness, yet spied nothing. She slowly turned the doorknob and slid a foot into the bathroom, propping the door open. When the hinges creaked, she grimaced. Gabby shoved the outer casing of her flashlight into her mouth to free her other hand. The light dropped towards her feet until her teeth better gripped the flashlight and corrected the direction of the beam.

Whatever was in the bushes crept closer. It rounded the corner, and the sound grew louder. Gabby removed her pistol and slipped inside, gently closing the door. She wedged a foot against the door and leaned into it with one hand. She quickly re-holstered her weapon and pulled the flashlight from her mouth.

A quick scan of the door revealed a knob lock and deadbolt, both missing the turn pieces. There was no way to secure the door without a key. She scanned the darkened interior and noticed a wooden doorstop at her side. With one foot, she slid it within reach. Gabby wedged it under the door and flipped around. She pressed her back against the door, pushing against it with all her weight. When her hands were free, she pulled the cellphone from her pocket.

Something's in the bushes — I'm in the bathroom. Help! Gabby texted Johnson.

A short while later, Gabby heard the roof creak. She listened as Johnson's weight bore down on the dry, rotted wood with each step he took. Gabby watched as a light appeared through the ventilation holes located around the exterior part of the ceiling. The beam of light moved until it stopped at the side of the door behind her. She heard a slight thud and shriek, followed by more rustling in the bushes. The creature had bolted away from the building.

It's bugger all. It's just a raccoon. Let us not waste more time. Scoot! Johnson texted.

Again, Gabby listened as his weight shifted and Johnson returned to his chair. She struggled to decipher his message, unsure of British slang. Gabby shrugged her shoulders, relieved it was just a critter. After returning to the rooftop, both continued their watch. The night was getting darker, the hours later, and soon it would be time for the pack to hunt.

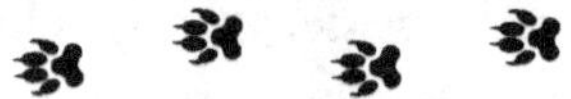

Earlier that day, but before the first rays of sunlight illuminated the area surrounding Yellowstone Lake, a scout separated from the pack. The dire wolves' attempt to seize prey during nightfall at the marina was unsuccessful. The human they pursued eluded capture by jumping into the lake. Instead of waiting for the man to emerge from the water, the wolves returned to the campground. The scout pressed ahead of the pack to hunt for new prey.

The mature male, a beta wolf, explored the far reaches of empty lots and abandoned tent sites. There was no movement except small critters that burrowed underground or took refuge in the trees. His hunger grew, yet he would not return to the others. The beta understood he must only rejoin them with information about prey and its whereabouts.

While making an additional sweep of the campground, he observed two sizable figures shift and communicate atop a small structure. These were the beings that his pack had become accustomed to feeding on. Unsure if they had seen him, he remained still and followed their interaction.

The wolf studied their behavior until a vehicle entered the campground and spooked him. Still unnoticed, the beta hastily retreated and crouched amongst the thick brush overlooking the building. More human figures and vehicles appeared as the sun rose and radiated over the landscape. Daylight had finally arrived. Rather than risk injury or death, the wolf would reunite with his pack that night. It was no longer safe to move about the campground.

For the better part of the day, sleep eluded the beta. The wolf spent the morning watching the surrounding activity, and witnessed the humans descend from the building. He continued to study the prey in sunlight and listen to their constant chatter. Sometimes, they'd walk within striking distance. He imagined the warmth of their flesh and the particular taste of their fat and muscle. But the beta remained patient and disciplined. He would not attack without the support of his pack.

On the opposite side of the building, the remaining pack members retreated further into the wooded area. They would spend the remaining daylight hours sleeping and watching one another with heavy eyelids. Like their missing packmate, the rest of the wolves reserved their energy for the hunt at nightfall.

During this time and between periods of slumber, the alpha male anxiously awaited the return of the absent pack member. His offspring, the beta and scout, was long overdue. At one point, the alpha male crept to the edge of the clearing. The campground now stood empty, except for the lure of rotting flesh scattered and hidden from sight.

Decaying meat tempted his senses, but something was off-putting. The sudden flurry of human activity forced the alpha to return to his pack. He would return later to investigate.

At twilight, the pack stirred and stretched. The alpha male cautiously led them to the edge of the campground, where they waited in hiding. The number of prey continued to decrease as the sun disappeared and the moon took to the sky. Soon, there were only two humans remaining within sight. Both figures stood atop the freestanding structure that separated them from their missing pack member.

When darkness provided adequate cover, the beta carefully maneuvered about the brush without drawing attention to his movement. A scent emitted from the wolves was strong, recognizable, and nearby. The beta hurried to meet them with news regarding his intended target. The pack enthusiastically greeted him and showed their affection by nibbling his face and licking his muzzle. Together again, the wolves watched the campground. It was still early, and their prey was still active.

Amid this watch, a human form descended from the rooftop. It quietly disappeared through a door before a light rotated around the building. The other human threw an object into the bushes, scaring a raccoon. The wolves watched as the panicked critter fled from the scene. Most likely aware of their presence, the raccoon made a hard turn. It swiftly climbed a tree opposite of their position. Shortly later, the human form reemerged from the building. It navigated a way back to the rooftop and settled next to the other person. From that point forward, all was quiet and still.

Previously, the alpha male took charge of a hunt. Tonight, the beta would lead the pack and give direction. He communicated with the others before they moved from their secluded position. The wolves' night vision and incredible sight allowed them to navigate the campground while only making the slightest noise. They weaved throughout clusters of bushes and trees until they reassembled directly behind and below the prey they stalked.

The beta imitated the human behavior he witnessed during daylight hours. He jumped onto the bed of the truck and moved forward to make room for other pack members. They understood his directive and jointly followed his lead. The pack acted swiftly to launch their attack and ambush their kill. Within moments, the pack sprung to the rooftop where the prey looked at them in astonishment. It was time for the slaughter.

Gabby pushed her hair aside to expose her ear while reaching into her backpack. Her fingers carefully poked around the interior until they brushed against the hard surface of her earbud case. She gripped it in her palm and slowly removed it from the backpack, careful not to generate noise. As she did this, she watched Johnson in the pale moonlight. He had nodded off yet again. Gabby listened to his slow and steady breathing while trying not to rouse him from sleep.

Johnson's inattentiveness gave Gabby reason to listen to music on a most boring and uneventful night. He directed her to keep watch, but there was nothing to watch on this night in the middle of nowhere. Gabby's phone afforded her the entertainment she required during the absence of human interaction. If she didn't busy herself, she too would fall asleep.

After delicately popping the lid open, Gabby removed the earbuds from her ears and placed them in the case. Like the night before, she had to re-pair them when one stopped working. Even her electronics didn't appreciate the fresh mountain air. Gabby couldn't wait to start her trek back to California the following day. Her sense of adventure was over-hyped and short-lived. She was a city girl.

While waiting for her earbuds to sync, Gabby listened to the surrounding forest. She recalled her earlier trip to the bathroom and chuckled when thinking of the raccoon. Gabby pondered whether she was more scared of the things she could or couldn't see in the dark. Johnson snorted. The distraction caused Gabby's mind to switch to tacos, street tacos. Her mouth watered as she imagined biting into tender pieces of chicken covered in spice. Her thoughts shifted to cilantro and its fragrant smell. Gabby continued to torture her senses with the foods that eluded her a thousand miles away.

Johnson snorted again as he changed position in his camping chair. The metal frame creaked and nylon fabric moaned when stretched by the movement of his weight. Gabby glanced at him and wondered how a tiny chair could support such a large man. She noticed his head had rolled backward and hung off the chair. Saliva pooled in the corner of his parted lips and glistened in the light cast off by the moon. How she wished she were in her bed right now.

A crack on the forest floor removed Gabby from her thoughts. She listened intently for other sounds, but the darkness was silent. Gabby tried to convince herself the raccoon was scampering amongst the bushes. She now admitted she was more scared of the things she couldn't see in the dark. But there was another crack, and something much larger created the sound. It wasn't her raccoon.

While concentrating on her surroundings, the mosquitos returned with a vengeance. The bug spray's effectiveness had waned over the hours spent atop the roof. But that was the least of her worries. Gabby's ears now deviated from the buzzing of mosquitos to the movement on the forest floor. She patted the pistol hidden under her jacket for reassurance before slipping her phone into her pocket and dropping the earbud case into the backpack. Gabby extended her arm and smacked Johnson on the bicep closest to her. He snorted as he roused from sleep.

"Did you hear that?" Gabby whispered.

Johnson didn't speak right away. He sat up and rubbed the sleep from his eyes before wiping his mouth with the back of his arm. Johnson looked around and listened. "Hear what?"

"Something's moving around. It's crushing leaves and cracking twigs." She explained.

"You drive me bonkers, girl. It's probably your raccoon." Sleepiness and a crackly voice hindered Johnson's effort to keep a low voice.

"It's not a raccoon. It's something larger. Listen." Gabby stood and approached a spotlight nearest her corner of the roof. Her finger hovered over the button as she waited.

Johnson grew annoyed with Gabby. He expected her movement would spook the wolves if they approached the building or traps. His hand reached into the darkness until he gripped the dart gun. Johnson pulled it closer and prepared himself to discharge the weapon. Shooting from a seated position would provide him with more stability and a better aim in his sluggish state. Johnson drew the butt against his shoulder as he lifted the muzzle and directed it towards the traps. He grew excited and anxious. Tonight, he was going to capture a dire wolf.

The noise grew closer, and no longer sounded like the forest floor. Something had emerged from the woods surrounding them. Their paws scraped and brushed against the gravel walkways behind them, rather than advancing towards the traps. There wasn't one creature moving, but many. The sound grew as the wolves neared the building. When the weight of a creature ascended onto the back of the pickup, both Johnson and Gabby turned their heads towards the enormous thump.

Additional bodies jumped onto the truck. Their toenails scraped the rigid metal flooring as they landed. When Johnson and Gabby realized what was happening, she spun the floodlight and hit the light switch. Gabby illuminated the rooftop, catching the fiery white glow of the wolves' eyes. The pack assembled before them as they adjusted to the light. Before Johnson could rise from his chair or swing the dart gun towards the predators, they raced towards him. The asphalt coating and a layer of dust kicked up from their feet as the beta lunged at Johnson. The others followed his lead.

Everything unfolded quickly, leaving Gabby little time to react. Johnson's body blocked her from the wolves, giving her time to escape. There was nothing she could do to help him. Gabby recalled the bathroom door was below them and raced to the roof's edge. She dropped over the side and grasped the ragged eave with her fingers, slicing the delicate skin of her fingertips. Gabby hung suspended a few feet above the ground, afraid to release her grip. She listened as Johnson violently fought his attackers and as a predator approached her position from the rooftop.

Unsure of the distance to the ground, Gabby said a Hail Mary and released her hold. She landed with a hard thud and rolled her ankle. Despite the shock to her body, she suppressed an urge to scream, not wanting to draw attention to herself. Gabby frantically forced herself into a standing position and pushed forward through the darkness. Her hand hit the door handle, and she quickly grasped and turned the knob. As she shoved the door open, an immense force thrust her to the bathroom floor. Gabby felt the nails of a canine dig into the flesh on her back as the creature used her to propel itself forward.

Gabby frantically closed the door and sat against it. Within the tight space, she could hear something breathing, and a slight growl reverberate from the darkness. Gabby extended her left arm, but failed to reach the light switch from her seated position. Before she drew it back, the creature lunged at her arm and held it in its jaws. Gabby howled from the intense pain as the wolf pierced the skin with its teeth. She used her free arm to unzip her jacket. As the predator pulled and shook to free the limb from her body, Gabby moved in a frenzy to retrieve her pistol.

As the creature continued its assault, additional wolves pressed against the door. Gabby faced stopping the attack and preventing additional predators from gaining entrance into the building. In a moment of desperation and with all her strength, Gabby fished the pistol from the hidden holster buried under her clothes while pushing against the attacker. The she-wolf released Gabby's arm and latched on to her throat, attempting to subdue its prey.

With her free hand, Gabby clicked the safety off and slid her finger over the trigger. She could feel the life seeping from her body as she bordered on losing consciousness. A putrid smell emanated from the predator's mouth as its hot breath pushed towards Gabby's nose. While the wolf tightened its grip, she felt the warmth of her blood trickle down her neck. Her breathing became labored from the narrowed passageway leading to her lungs. The wolf would not release its grip on her until she fell dead. Gabby had to react now.

Despair and desperation forced her to shoot blindly at the creature bearing down on her body. The popping sound of her firearm forced the animal to release its prey. Gabby flopped over to her side, only stopping when her head hit the hard and cold concrete floor. She lost her bearing in the darkness as she drifted between sleep and awareness. Gabby lingered in the same position as her ears rang from the sound of gunfire. She didn't hear the predator in her presence or the sound of Johnson pleading for his life. There was a moment of peace before something brought her back to life.

The door violently pressed against Gabby's limp body. The wolves returned to test the strength of the barrier that shielded her. Gabby forced herself into a sitting position once more. The fight wasn't over. Gabby's chest heaved as she struggled to take in oxygen, caused by a fractured hyoid. Eventually, another surge of adrenaline roused her survival skills.

Gabby set the pistol down and removed the cell phone from her pocket. After several slow and unsuccessful attempts to unlock the blood-streaked screen, she finally accessed her home page. Gabby sent a quick text to Sam, unsure if the message made sense. She then swiped her finger and activated the flashlight.

When she aimed the flashlight across from her limp body, Gabby caught the wolf's gaze. Blood matted its facial hair, but it didn't move from the floor. Gabby was unsure if she shot the beast or if the noise had scared it. As she contemplated her next move, the door continued to thump against her back. Gabby wedged the phone into the folds of her clothes and against her stomach. She needed to watch the predator in the beam of light as she reached for the pistol. The wolf's eyes followed her movement, and it slowly arose.

Gabby watched with terror as the wolf approached with slow and deliberate strides. It lowered its head and bared its teeth. A low growl reverberated from its larynx as its ears shifted downward and to the side. Gabby's arm shook as she retrieved the pistol, raised the muzzle, and slipped her finger into the trigger hold.

The predator continued its advance with its hackles raised and tail lowered between its legs. The wolf stopped for a moment and positioned itself to spring forward. Gabby recognized that stance from the beta that leaped on Johnson. Before she pulled the trigger, Gabby's phone flipped forward, casting her into darkness.

From outside the building, a series of gunshots panicked the dire wolves. They witnessed the flashes of light appear through the ventilation holes and smelled the faint odor of gunpowder. Those that pressed against the door slunk back into the darkness. They accepted a human had trapped their packmate, but were helpless to assist her. For the safety of their pack, the alpha male instructed the wolves to return to the forest. They would mourn the loss of their she-wolf. Now it was time to abandon their kill and find new prey.

DAY TEN

"He'll. That's the message I received during the night from Gabby. I assume she meant hell? This girl and her encrypted texts. Yikes!" Sam read the message to Dale as they left the cabin and locked the door behind them.

"She was probably implying hell. As in, being employed by Johnson is like working in hell." Dale stated.

"Let's play nice. Do you have everything packed?" She asked as both took their seats in the pickup. Sam started the engine and glanced over at Dale. "We'll try this again. Bears, we're only going to think of bears. Don't let me get sidetracked again. Nothing is keeping us from Hayden Valley today. Bears, got it?"

Dale shook his head in agreement. He was eager to learn more about the trade before venturing out on his own.

This summer would lead him to choose a career in either research or wildlife management. "Shouldn't we at least make a quick stop to see Gabby? She said she's leaving today. Plus, I want to see the look of defeat on Johnson's face. If they had caught something, Gabby would've let us know by now. Her he'll text doesn't sound very promising. It shouldn't take long. Afterward, it's all about the bears."

They traveled up the familiar road on this overcast day. Sam adjusted the temperature in the truck as the heatwave finally broke. The chill in the morning air was a welcome relief for the two Wyomingites. Sam and Dale were more accustomed to six months of extreme winter weather. They drove in silence as each sipped their piping-hot coffee and waited for the caffeine to kick in. As Sam reflected on a day of research in the valley, Dale thought of the disparaging remarks he would voice to Johnson.

When the truck turned into the campground, heavily armed park employees stopped them. Sam and Dale flashed their identification badges and stared at the men as they moved the barricades before waving them through. Through her rearview mirror, Sam observed the same men replace the blockade. They stopped an SUV that attempted to sneak in with her. She slowed and watched as security forced them to back up and turn around.

Probably the press? Sam thought.

A familiar and disheartening flurry of activity unfolded before them after turning the corner that led to the campsites. Sam shook her head, wondering how this involved Johnson. She recognized the usual ensemble of emergency vehicles and park employees. Dale sat up in his seat and wedged his empty mug into the cup holder. Both were eager to learn more.

Before she parked the truck, Sam spotted a pickup next to the restroom building. It was the same one she had urged Johnson to move the previous day. She watched as a few men stood atop the roof, taking pictures or collecting items. Two others hauled canvas bags and climbed ladders as those on the ground helped steady the loads. From Sam's position, the site appeared to be in disarray. Bundles of extension cords draped over the side of the building. A spotlight remained tethered by a power cord and swayed while suspended above the ground. She couldn't recall seeing anything like that before.

"This doesn't look good, Dale." Sam hadn't finished her sentence before removing the keys from the ignition and jumping out of the truck. She opened the back door and holstered a handgun. Dale met her as she was zipping up a fleece jacket. He, too, holstered a weapon and stuffed an extra cartridge in the buttoned pocket of his chore coat.

"Morning." Tony Mancini walked the short distance to greet Sam and Dale.

"Hi, Tony. What's it been? A week?" Sam slammed the door and faced the park employee. "Tell me my imagination has got the best of me? It doesn't look promising."

The three walked towards the building shoulder to shoulder. Tony glanced at his phone for updates as more vehicles arrived. There was a lull and a heavy sigh when he looked at Sam and motioned for her to stop. "How close were you to Johnson?"

"Were?" Sam felt her eyes well up with tears. She swallowed and peered at the sky to control her emotions. Portraying weakness wasn't one of her choice characteristics, especially in a career dominated by men. "Johnson and I lived in the same housing area for almost a decade. Plus, we've spent the better part of our summers together. Johnson and I have been, were, pretty good friends. What happened?"

"They attacked him like the others. His remains are up there." Tony pointed out the obvious. Sam lingered in silence as she processed the words. Dale turned and ran his fingers through his hair while mumbling. He walked a few feet before returning to Sam's side.

"What a dumbass!" Sam bawled and stomped her boot into the gravel. "I told him yesterday to have someone move the truck after they climbed onto the roof. The fucking wolves used it like a staircase. He should've known better. Look where his arrogance got him. I'm guessing Gabby's dead, too?"

"Gabby? Who's Gabby? Is that Johnson's assistant?" Tony asked. Before he got an answer, Sam rushed towards the building. Dale gave him the lowdown as they followed her.

"Hey, you up there!" Sam addressed the man closest to her on the rooftop. He looked down at Sam while pointing to his chest. "Yes, you!"

"Yes?" he warily asked.

"How many bodies are up there?" Sam held a hand over her eyes and looked at the stranger. Despite the cloud coverage, the skies were bright. She watched him approach another man, and both returned to her side of the building.

"One body. Why?" the other fellow addressed Sam.

"Are you sure? What color is the person's skin?" Sam grew restless and sounded condescending. She had more questions than answers. If Gabby were alive, they needed to find her immediately.

"I'm certain there's one corpse. I spy two legs, two arms, one torso, and one head. Those pieces are consistent with the shape of one human body. As for the second part of your question, he, yes, he, as in a male, is African-American. Can I help you with anything else, inspector?" Sam disregarded his sarcasm, knowing she brought it upon herself.

"And to be certain, you don't see any other evidence of a different person? Say, from a girl or something? Or hair, like long brownish hair?" Sam shifted and placed a hand on her hip. Dale and Tony observed and listened to her questioning from a short distance away.

The man briefly scanned the rooftop. He understood Sam's concern about additional body parts strewn amongst the other bits. "No, just the one. I'm fairly certain of that. Aside from this gentleman, there's a bunch of equipment, two chairs, and a couple of backpacks. But no, no evidence of a female corpse or her remains."

"Thanks!" Sam waved at the man as she turned to join Dale. She looked at Tony and spoke with a glimmer of hope. "Gabby might still be alive. Let's have a look!"

Tony left to assemble a group of armed men to accompany the two as Sam pulled the cellphone from her pants pocket. She and Dale stood in the building's shade because now rays of sunlight poked from the clouds. Sam pulled up Gabby's last text and reread the message as Dale looked over her shoulder.

"She texted help, not he'll." Dale pointed to the screen. "She was asking for help."

"How do you know?" Sam didn't doubt him, but wanted to understand how he came to that resolve.

"Pull up your keyboard." He watched as she followed his request. "Okay. Now swipe the word, help, quickly."

Sam followed his instruction. "I swiped, help. It comes up as help. I'm not getting it. How did she get he'll if she swiped help?"

"If she panicked or texted in the dark, it might have a different outcome. Try again." Dale urged her one last time.

"Help. Help. He'll! You were right! Gabby texted me for help at... 2:38 last night. That means they were under attack at 2:38." Sam glanced at Dale before staring at the forest. When she yelled the girl's name, all those present stopped and looked at her. "Gabby! Gabby! Where are you, Gabby! Text me if you can't speak!"

Dale put an arm in front of Sam to prevent her from approaching the wooded areas. "Wait. Text her. She must have her phone. Ask her where she is?"

Tony approached with a search party after hearing their dialogue. Sam concentrated on her phone as her fingers typed a message. All eyes watched the screen when she hit send. The text went through, and a phone chimed. Gabby's phone was somewhere near, but they needed better direction. The group remained silent as Sam texted a second time. A noise came from within the walls of the bathroom.

"There! Wait!" Sam yelled at one man that approached the door and reached for the handle. "Don't touch it. We have to make sure it's safe. Something could be inside with her."

After surveying the door and studying the building's structure, Sam sent one man to borrow a ladder. Under her direction, they positioned and steadied it below a ventilation hole. Dale helped Sam secure her cellphone with tape to a hiking pole, retrieved from a vehicle. Tony watched as she took charge of the situation, reassured by her leadership abilities.

Sam climbed the ladder and activated the video camera when the preparations were complete. She peered through the hole, but couldn't see anything. Sam slid the cellphone through a space between the cinderblocks. With a steady hand, she turned the pole to record the interior. After a slow sweep, Sam inserted the hiking stick deeper and recorded additional footage. Sam removed the cellphone and descended the ladder when she had shot sufficient footage.

The group was eager to view the video. Everyone crowded around Sam as she tapped the play button. Initially, there was darkness until the lens adjusted to the lighting. The first images revealed Gabby propped against the door and slumped over. When Sam noticed the blood pooling around her head and torso, she closed her eyes.

When Sam heard gasps from the men, she gazed at the screen. A dire wolf lay next to Gabby and looked upward at the phone. Two glowing eyes glared at Sam as her blood ran cold. She forced the camera into Dale's hand and walked away. Sam wasn't only going to kill this one; she was going to take down the entire pack.

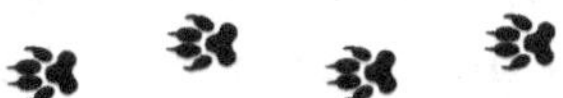

Sam watched the whitecaps form on Yellowstone Lake from the picnic bench. The waves pressed towards the shoreline in a continuous and predictable pattern. Winds had not only brought cooler weather, but stirred the waters of her favorite lake.

Footsteps shuffled through the loose gravel, headed towards Sam. The table shifted as someone sat across from her. Despite the wind and the earthy smells of her surroundings, Tony's cologne wafted through the air and stimulated her senses. Sam's self-pity party was over.

"The men are waiting for you," Tony said. His voice was monotonous and lacked emotion.

It took a moment to break her silence, but Sam finally spoke. "Gabby was young, just starting her life. She didn't deserve that. Last night was her last time working for Johnson. She was going home today, back to California."

"There's still a chance she's alive." Tony hesitated. "I'm charging you with the task. Take out the wolf and retrieve Gabby. Emergency personnel are waiting to patch her up."

"I like your positivity, Tony. If you watched the same video I did, you would realize Gabby's dead. No one survives that amount of blood loss." Sam rubbed her eyes and face. She glared at Tony as she spoke. "If you pull me into this, I want to lead the entire operation. I don't want to take down just one wolf, but the entire pack. I'm familiar with these predators and know this side of the park better than anyone. Yellowstone is my second home."

"I wholeheartedly agree. It was Johnson's idea to exclude you from the wolf capture. Now I'd like to make it up to you. There's someone that can help, a professional. She works with gray wolves on the other side of the park and is new to Yellowstone." Tony looked at his phone to verify the name. "Nicole Biller from the W.O.L.F. group. She sent over a net gun yesterday and is—"

"Are you kidding? Do you realize W.O.L.F. is an acronym for Wolf Organization for Learning and Focus? You can't make that shit up. I think she blindly pointed to words in a dictionary to create her non-profit name. If you think Johnson was a narcissist, Nicole far exceeds him. I won't work with her. I won't do it. She's new to Yellowstone because no other park wants her."

"You're backing me into a corner, Sam. I'm on your side but—"

"No buts. If you want my help, I'll give you one hundred and ten percent. You'll get your dead wolf pack and you can reopen the campground. If you want more blood on your hands, put Nicole in charge. She can have all the space she needs because I'll pack up and ship out for the rest of the summer." Sam rose from the table. "Under no circumstances will I work with that woman."

Under everyone's watchful eyes, Sam marched to her truck with Dale closely following. She loaded the chamber of her favorite rifle and passed another weapon to Dale. She stuffed extra ammo into her jacket's pocket before slinging the rifle strap over her shoulder. Dale did the same before slamming the door shut and marching back to the building. Sam was all business and ready to take down the dire wolf that guarded Gabby.

"Okay, men. Look at your weapons. Do me a favor and make sure the safety is on." The men followed her instructions and looked at one another with puzzled expressions. She pointed towards an empty campsite. "Next, you're going to put your weapons on that picnic table. Under no circumstances will you touch it until I tell you otherwise."

The men did as she said, while conveying their displeasure. They sighed and groaned within earshot of Sam or whispered amongst themselves as they walked the short distance to the table. They begrudgingly surrendered their rifles. Tony stood to the side and continued to watch, urging them to hurry. No one challenged their supervisor.

"Don't we need to shoot the wolf first?" Someone from the group asked when they returned to Sam.

"I'll be the only one shooting today. I want to ensure that no one else gets shot," Sam said before winking at him.

One man interrupted her instruction. "What if you miss?"

"I never miss." Sam informed the group. "As I was saying, I don't want anyone discharging a weapon. If my rifle malfunctions, Dale will take the shot. I don't want this turning into a Wild West shootout. Before we open the door, let's make certain there is only one wolf inside. As we did earlier, you'll record the interior. Divide into two groups and get the job done. Let's go!" Sam clapped her hands to hurry them along.

The men separated into two parties and worked quickly to record the interior from the ventilation holes. After filming, they returned to Sam. Everyone reviewed the footage on their phones and concluded the building was devoid of life. Except for the dire wolf that still lay on the floor.

Sam charged the men to stand behind her. All complied except one volunteer that took a stance next to the door. Both Sam and Dale assumed their firing positions. Sam lay on the ground with one leg straightened and one slightly bent at the knee. She nestled the butt of the rifle into her shoulder while supporting the barrel in her arm. Sam switched the safety off and peered through the scope. This position would allow her to take the most accurate shot.

Dale stood above and to the side of Sam. He raised the barrel of his rifle and watched the door. The safety was off, and his finger rested outside the trigger guard. It would only take a second to discharge his weapon if his help was required. Dale waited patiently with an eye locked on the two guidelines that would direct him to his target. He listened for Sam.

"You ready, Dale?" Sam asked.

"Yes," Dale replied. He'd spent a lifetime hunting, but felt this would be his most important shot.

"Door!" Sam yelled to the person at the door.

The man pushed the door, but it barely budged. Gabby's body prevented him from moving it further. He stopped to listen and heard nothing from inside. Again, he pushed the door until there was a slight crack and quickly stepped aside. The man wiped the sweat from his brow as he watched Sam. There wasn't enough space to take a shot. It was necessary to push the door open further. Stress rattled his nerves, but he pushed harder. Finally, everyone glimpsed the wolf.

"I think it's injured!" someone yelled when they spied the dire wolf dragging its body away from the eyes of the spectators. Everyone mumbled in agreement.

Sam instructed Dale to keep his aim while she placed her weapon down and stood up. After steadying her feet, she picked up her rifle and advanced towards the door. Like the other men, Sam felt the wolf no longer posed a threat. She slid through the narrow opening and carefully approached the predator.

The wolf bared its teeth in one last display of aggression, but failed to attack. Sam watched the predator with both awe and wonder. The creature's pitiful whimpers reminded her of the pain it inflicted on those around her. Sam lifted the muzzle of her rifle and aimed at its chest. The sound of one shot announced the ending of this dire wolf's life. Now it was time to track the others.

The afternoon skies remained threatening, and the air chilled as word spread throughout the park. Despite the low number of people working the scene and the spotty cellular reception, the press and onlookers continued to gather at West Bay's entrance. While Sam prepared to examine the wolf's body, Tony ran from group to group. He was on a quest to provide damage control. Someone was leaking information about the killings to the world outside of Yellowstone National Park.

After an agonizing wait, investigators allowed the park employees to remove the animal's carcass from the building. It now lay on a crisp tarp under the shade of trees and away from prying eyes. Dale had asked anyone present to leave and allow Sam to do her job. Oblivious to her surroundings, she shimmied her fingers into blue surgical gloves before squatting next to the remains of the dire wolf.

Before touching it, Sam and Dale admired the creature before them. Although normally chatty, Sam was silent and remained crouched in the same position. She bobbed her head while trying to process the very thing that had eluded them over the past two weeks. Its appearance and size were both impressive and puzzling.

"What do you think? Could it be a dire wolf?" Dale asked, finally breaking the silence. He wondered what thoughts were racing through Sam's mind. "Gabby made that assumption when we watched the videos. She could be right?"

"Hmm. Possible. There are creatures thought extinct and rediscovered." Sam stared at the wolf.

"Like what?" Dale asked.

"I recently read an article about a flightless bird in New Zealand. If I remember correctly, it's about two feet long and five pounds, pretty sizeable and hard to miss. Don't recall the name of the bird? Anyway, researchers thought it extinct in the late eighteen-hundreds and rediscovered them in the mid-nineteen hundreds. Think about it, they declared it extinct, but hundreds still existed. The birds somehow avoided man for all those decades, just like this wolf. At any rate, let's get to work. I want to take possession of this thing before Nicole gets here. We need to store it somewhere safe." Sam unwound a soft tape measure, and Dale grabbed his notepad and pencil.

Over the next several minutes, Sam rattled off measurements. Dale scribbled down the numbers, trying to keep up. With his help, Sam lifted the wolf to guess its weight. She continued her exam as Dale took photos. Sam inspected the muscle density before running her fingers through its coat. She pointed out bullet holes each time the tip of her finger snagged on an entrance wound.

"I'm fairly certain Gabby shot this thing about three times with her pistol. Unfortunately, none of the shots were immediately fatal." Sam lifted the rear leg to sex the animal. "Female. A she-wolf. Maybe two or three years old. Looks like a young one."

Sam pulled open the jaws and ran her fingers around the gum line. She inspected the teeth for decay, infection, and tooth loss. Its tongue was coarse, even more so than a gray wolf's. Sam couldn't help but admire the beast.

"What's your thought?" Tony had finally slipped away from everyone in the campground. Like Sam, he marveled at the wolf. He scanned the remains laid out before him.

"I'm as baffled as anyone. This specimen is not a gray wolf. The bone structure, muscle mass, and size of the skull point to a different species." Sam replied. "With your permission, I'd like to take it to a storage facility before it falls into the wrong hands. Something like this can sell on the black market to a private individual. We'd never see it again. Can you trust me with this?"

Tony watched Sam as she arose and stretched her legs before removing her gloves. He responded, "Do I have a choice? Where are you going to take it?"

"The less you know, the better. Right? I'll keep it locked up in the park. Trust me, please. My word is better than most." Sam said, trying to convince Tony.

"It doesn't leave the park, period. If you break your word, I'll have you removed from Yellowstone. At some point, I want to know where you're storing it and what you plan to do with it." Tony looked at her in all seriousness. "Now, what are we going to do about the rest of the pack?"

"We need to clean the campground. Have your men remove the traps and every piece of bait. Don't let them discard it in the wooded areas or chuck it into the lake. Every scrap leaves the campground with them. Aside from a guard at the entrance, I don't want anyone within West Bay. No one leaves their vehicles, even to pee. We no longer want the wolves to associate this spot with food and activity."

Tony interrupted Sam as she rattled off her demands. "Don't we want to use the traps one more night?"

"No. Look at this thing." Sam pointed to the wolf. "I'm guessing it's more intelligent than a gray wolf and better designed to take down large prey. I'm unsure if it's a scavenger. Not one wolf entered the traps during the last two nights for a free meal. They've been moving between here and the marina in search of prey. They'll travel for a fresh piece of meat before they settle for rancid roadkill. The traps don't work," Sam explained before she stopped and directed Dale to wrap the wolf carcass.

"So, what else do you suggest? I've received word that some surviving family members are going to arrive tomorrow. I need answers to their questions. As with previous fatalities, they'll want to know how we're responding to the attacks and want to see where their loved ones perished."

"We can accommodate them, but I don't want anyone leaving their vehicles. Bring them in, don't stop, and take them out. Impress upon them the importance of giving us space to do our job. Aside from that, I'm going to make some phone calls after we leave. I need to round up drone operators, experienced hunters, hunting dogs, and cadaver dog and recovery teams. I will only employ those licensed and listed by the park." Sam pointed to each finger as she rattled off the members she needed to aid her search.

"Cadaver dogs? Recovery teams?" Tony scrunched his face, confused about her last request.

"Two maintenance workers are missing..." Sam explained.

"Johnson convinced me the men willingly disappeared," Tony corrected her.

"And I'm convinced the wolves took them from the front porch. Witnesses saw them smoking outside the night they disappeared. We owe it to their families to find their remains. Aside from them, a large dog went missing. Not as important, but the more we know right now, the better we can understand the wolves and their hunting methods." Sam stopped to catch her breath. "Sue, who manages West Bay, explained there was an abandoned camper van towed from here. Police reported it as stolen. The occupant disappeared, but I'm unsure if it had anything to do with this. The guy could've hitched out of here to avoid law enforcement. Oh, and the baby."

"They recovered the baby. They accounted for all the bodies after that attack." Tony reassured her.

"Good. Great. Good to hear." Sam was at a loss for words. It wasn't good or great, but that bit of information provided her with some comfort. Looking at the remains of an infant would cause her great grief. "If you don't mind, I think we need to go now. Dale and I need to plan for tomorrow. Before you leave, make sure you collect and remove the traps. Transfer them from this part of the park to anywhere else, far from here. Wolves have a great sense of smell. And make sure everyone has left before twilight. That's when the pack moves and scouts for prey." Sam shook Tony's hand before gathering their items. She helped Dale lift the dire wolf, neatly wrapped in the tarp.

"One last thing." Tony stopped them. "If it brings you any comfort, the medical team said Gabby had a fatal gunshot wound to the head. She shot herself rather than let that thing take her life." He nodded towards the wrapped carcass held by Sam and Dale before turning to run for cover. The ominous skies had finally opened to release a drenching rain.

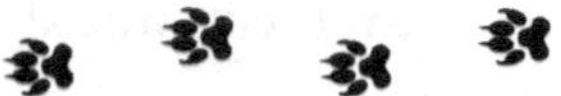

Rather than draw attention to their invaluable possession, Sam and Dale slid the wolf carcass across the rear floorboards of her truck. They covered the tarp with jackets, backpacks, and a rifle case. Sam resolved to leave the pickup's bed empty. She didn't want to arouse suspicion with any curious spectators.

Although it continued to rain, reporters and gawkers continued to clog the major artery leading into the campground. Since their arrival that morning, the crowds had grown. They stood huddled under umbrellas or donned raincoats. Most had recording devices and cameras to catch the action. The paparazzi wannabees were itching to get a shot that would propel them into the spotlight and launch their fifteen minutes of fame.

The crowd was reluctant to part ways for Sam's truck, but did so when she wouldn't stop. They tapped on her windows and glanced over the back railing. Everyone sought the latest scoop regarding the attacks. There were no markings on her vehicle, and it conveyed little importance. The horde allowed the beat-up pickup with Wyoming plates to pass.

The lower loop road that hugged Yellowstone Lake was busier than average. Although it was early, Sam suspected the rain was driving people from the park back to civilization. She could only imagine what Jackson and Cody would look like in several hours. Masses of tourists would soon stuff their restaurants, shops, and museums.

Dale sat sideways in his seat with an arm draped around the headrest. He pretended to converse with Sam, but occasionally glanced out the back window to ensure no one followed them. The continued deluge of rain made it difficult to distinguish the cars from one another.

After passing the turnoff for employee housing, Sam noticed a line of xenon headlights approaching in the opposite lane. The lights were blinding, even during daylight. Each time the windshield wiper cleared the glass, Sam got a better look until she recognized the vehicles. She spied the W.O.L.F. logo on the side of each one as they passed. A mischievous grin crossed Sam's face.

"That's W.O.L.F.!" Sam announced.

"What's W.O.L.F.?" Dale observed three black trucks pass. They traveled closely together at a high rate of speed.

"A non-profit that studies gray wolves. We want to keep our distance from them. Nothing good will come out of a partnership with Nicole and her group."

"They look more like a security detail for the president." Dale stared at the vehicles until they were out of sight, as Sam snickered.

Like Johnson, Nicole could charm money out of the chariest of philanthropists. Rather than invest those funds in research and education, she wore designer clothing, flaunted valuable equipment, and drove costly vehicles.

Unlike Johnson, Nicole didn't garner respect from those that worked for her. She handpicked her employees and kept a tight rein on their behavior and work ethics. Everything went through Nicole, and she took credit for their work. Sam had little doubt that karma would bite her hard.

Nicole was similar in age to Sam, but short and bony. Rumor suggested she had breast implants and inserted silicone butt pads under her clothing to enhance her femininity. Aside from that, Nicole wore hair extensions, received weekly spray tans, and had acrylic nails. There was little doubt that donations funded her lifestyle.

It wasn't her fake appearance that bothered Sam most, but her personality. Although they had only met a few times, Sam found Nicole seemingly omniscient and always condescending. Nicole had a knack for interjecting herself into conversations that didn't concern her. According to Nicole, no one was more accomplished or experienced than herself. Her temperament often led to her group's banishment from most state and national parks. Sam speculated about where Nicole would go after burning bridges with Yellowstone. It wasn't a matter of if, but when.

After several years of mindless and unproductive conferences and fundraisers, Sam stopped dealing with characters like Nicole. Instead, Sam delved headfirst into the behavior of grizzly bears. Sam acted independently and successfully with the limited cash she accumulated each fundraising season. Only in the past few years did she convince the state's only university to sponsor a graduate for a summer internship in the park. Sam glanced at Dale and shot him a smile.

The pizza shop was empty except for one car. Sam drove around the building and parked by the restaurant's exit. She left the truck running to check for an open door and prayed that someone was still there. The rainfall continued as Sam pulled on the locked doors and peered through the foggy glass of the poorly insulated windows. She noticed a light in the kitchen and ran back to the rear exit. Sam pounded on the door until it cracked open and a woman's face peered out.

"Yes?" the lady asked in broken English.

"Riccardo?" Sam responded. The door slammed in her face, and Sam could hear the locks click. She turned to look at Dale and threw her arms in the air. She was so close, yet so far. The rain had finally turned to a drizzle, but Sam remained in place. She didn't know where to go next. Sam had limited options on this side of the park. Again, the locks clicked, but Sam didn't hear them or the door open.

"Sammy?" Ricardo stood in the doorframe. "You look as wet as a fish. Come inside before someone throws you into the lake. Tell your boy to come, too."

"I can't stay long, but I have a huge favor to ask." Sam pleaded.

"Anything for my girl. What can I do?" Riccardo wrapped his arm around Sam and guided her into the building. She trembled when the cold air penetrated her wet clothing. Riccardo wrapped his crisp white apron around her shoulders. He still dressed the part of a chef despite his restaurant's closure.

"I need to use your freezer," Sam asked as Riccardo nodded. "Plus, I need to lock it with one of my padlocks."

"What have you gotten yourself into?" His voice reflected concern. Riccardo walked over to the freezer door and peered inside. Aside from a few items, it was mostly empty.

"I've known you all these years, and you're one of the few people I can trust. If I tell you, can you keep a secret?" Sam pulled the apron around her arms.

"You know me. The only one I share a private conversation with is the Almighty God himself." Riccardo tugged at his gold chain to pull the crucifix from his shirt. He kissed it and stuffed it back under his clothing. "At my age, there's no room for mistakes." He winked at Sam.

"I need to store a wolf carcass in your freezer." Sam blurted out. She winced, waiting for a tongue lashing. Sam would have never asked him for this favor if she weren't so desperate. Riccardo remained silent, so Sam continued to press him. "I have the creature that has been killing the tourists and park employees. If it falls into the wrong hands, it can cause problems for me. We need to keep it safe and away from prying eyes."

"I can do that, but I have one issue." He looked up at Sam.

"Yes?" Sam queried.

"I'm closing the restaurant today. We probably won't open again. I was just about to turn the freezers off."

"Can you trust me with the key to the exit door? If you show me how, I can turn the freezer off." Sam begged. Riccardo stared at her while contemplating her request.

"*Va bene.* Okay. I'm only doing this because it's you, Sam." Before he could say anything else, Sam wrapped her arms around Riccardo and kissed him on the cheek. The apron fell to the floor. She picked it up and returned it after brushing it off. "I may just let you use my refrigerator for another hug and kiss. Enough, come with me."

Sam followed Riccardo to his office. He pulled a small box from his desk and sorted through a pile of keys until he found the one labeled for the exit. After comparing it to his master key, he handed it to Sam.

"Check the key before you leave. I don't want you locked out. Before you use the freezer, let me show you how to shut it down." Riccardo shuffled through the kitchen and showed Sam how to power down the equipment. "I'll be back at the end of next month to ensure the restaurant is ready for winter. In the meantime, if you have questions, please call."

"Thank you, Riccardo. I owe you so much for your help this summer." Sam pointed to the lady working behind Riccardo.

"You can trust her. She comes from my province in Italy and barely speaks English. You have my word." Riccardo smiled and walked to the exit door with Sam. "Don't forget, check that key."

Sam gave Riccardo the thumbs-up sign after inserting the key into the lock and successfully turning it. Before pulling the wolf from the back floorboards, she and Dale scanned the area for onlookers. No one was present and the parking lot remained empty. They carried the dead weight to the freezer and laid it against the back wall.

Riccardo supervised their activity in the restaurant. He was curious about the creature concealed underneath the tarp, but remained silent. Riccardo had more pressing work to complete and convinced himself that it wasn't his business.

With Riccardo's permission, Dale locked the freezer. He used a padlock removed from Sam's gun case and tugged at it to ensure the locking device was engaged. Now that the dire wolf was secure, it was time to return to the cabin. Sam hoped no one had witnessed her visit to the restaurant, and Riccardo could keep her secret.

It wasn't the sound of Sam's feet shuffling through the gravel or the jiggling of a doorknob that garnered Dale's attention. Instead, the muffled sound of broken glass startled the young man. He dropped the items in his arms onto the backseat of the truck. As he swung around, he reached for his sidearm, but hesitated to unholster his weapon.

Sam stood in front of Johnson's cabin with her fist wrapped in an old bath towel. It glimmered from broken shards of glass caught in the loops of the terry cloth. Dale noticed a dustpan and garbage can at her feet, but overlooked the broken window behind her.

"Whoa! Nice response. I feel safer with you around." Sam shot him an adoring smile. "Don't mind me. I'm just doing a little housekeeping."

Dale was unsure of Sam's motive as he listened to her whistle and watched her punch out the remaining panes of glass in the front door. She reached through a hole to unlatch the lock before successfully pulling the door open.

"What are you doing? Why did you punch out all the panes? You could've opened the door with just one." Dale walked over for an explanation.

"If I broke one, I'd arouse suspicion. Grab me the toolbox and a screen from one of the back windows. Any window." Sam asked. She cleared the remaining pieces of glass from the window before bending down to sweep the mess into her dustpan.

"Okay?" Dale responded before heading back to their cabin. He glanced over his shoulder at Sam as he walked, unsure if he wanted to take part in her newest scheme.

When Dale returned with the items she sought, Sam nailed the screen to the inside of the door. Together, they entered the cabin. She continued to whistle as she loaded the kitchen table with computer equipment, trail cameras, and USB cards. He finally understood what she had planned.

"Do you see anything else that might hold information about the dire wolves and attacks?" Sam asked. She wanted to perform one last check of the cabin, so they left nothing else behind.

Sam and Dale collectively rustled through drawers, even pulling them out to look for hidden paperwork. Sam peered under furniture as Dale lifted pillows and sheets. They swept through the kitchen and opened cabinets and tipped mugs and bowls on upper shelves. It was a small and mostly barren cabin. When she spotted a few bottles of liquor, Sam tucked one under her arm. Before leaving, she backtracked for another bottle while hustling Dale outside, his arms loaded with the found equipment.

"Now what?" Dale asked.

"Take that stuff back to our cabin. Make sure you hide it in a closet. Don't leave it in plain sight. I'm going to double-check my workmanship and clean-up job. Can't leave any evidence of our visit. When you're finished, empty the truck." Sam placed the bottles of vodka on the stoop. She pressed against the screen and wiggled the frame with her palm to test its strength. It didn't budge. Satisfied with her handiwork, Sam scanned the floor for missed broken glass and tools.

Sam locked Johnson's door and slammed it shut. She jiggled the handle to ensure it was secure before heading back to their cabin with her newfound stash of alcohol. Although she wanted a drink now, her sobriety was more important. Sam needed a clear head for the task at hand. The celebrating would wait until she took every dire wolf down.

Together, they spent the next few hours calling those that would volunteer their services. Everyone was eager to help, as they had watched the news and read the papers. The happenings in Yellowstone were no longer a secret. It amazed Sam how quickly the world had learned the details about the wolf attacks.

The only bit of information Sam withheld from the volunteers was the species they hunted. She wanted confirmation the animal stuffed in a restaurant freezer was indeed a dire wolf. It still sounded far-fetched and unbelievable. Genetic testing was a must, as she didn't want to jump to conclusions.

"This is going to sound really stupid. They're going to think I'm batshit crazy." Sam chastised herself. Her finger hovered over the green call icon on her cell phone. "Yes? No? Yes?"

"Call before I do. We need validation from someone that knows more than us. I think it's a great idea." Dale said before reaching over and pressing her finger against the phone screen. Sam gave Dale the evil eye and listened to the call connect. She moved it to her ear before anyone picked up.

"Why do we have cell coverage today? Of all days?" Sam whispered. She stopped speaking when someone answered.

Dale listened to the one-sided conversation while preparing dinner. Sam convinced the other caller she was a wildlife biologist from Yellowstone with a new species, before pulling the phone away from her face. She worked quickly to send the images of the dire wolf by email. There was a pause in the conversation as the person reviewed the photos. Dale glanced at Sam while sliding a casserole dish into the oven. She crossed her fingers and grimaced until the other party spoke up. They both heard the excitement in his voice before the call ended.

"We have our guy!" Sam stated. She shrugged her shoulders with a surprised expression spreading across her face. "He said he'll leave in the morning and will call when he arrives."

The smell of lasagna wafted throughout the cabin as they finished their plan of attack for the following morning. Before they had a chance to enjoy their home-cooked meal, the familiar xenon lights glared through the windows. Sam walked over to the front door and watched as three trucks slowed and stopped in front of Johnson's cabin.

Nicole was the first to step outside of the vehicle. She stretched before looking at her phone to verify her location. The others followed suit and tagged along as she walked to the darkened lodge. Nicole glanced at the door and sent someone back to her truck for a knife.

"I wouldn't do that." Sam scolded Nicole, who was preparing to slice the screen. Sam leaned against her doorframe, watching the events unfold. "I'd hate to report a breaking and entering offense to park officials. This is their property. Not sure where you hail from, but we look down on that kind of behavior in these parts."

"Skank? Is that you?" Nicole's poor attempt at humoring her employees reinforced every negative thought Sam held against Nicole.

"Yeah. That was last year's nickname. Now I prefer Sam or Samantha. Heck, you can even call me Sammy," she stated matter-of-factly while crossing her arms. "I see you haven't changed a bit."

"Neither have you. Still wearing children's clothing? Don't you have anything that fits properly?" Nicole turned to her employees and laughed. They followed her lead.

"You have your flock well trained. Nice! Can you show me more tricks?" Sam asked. The group fell silent. "Make sure Nicole tells you what to do. We don't want any adults to think for themselves. Baa! Anyway, why do you want access to Johnson's cabin?"

"It doesn't concern you. Apparently, I need a word with Tony?" Nicole shooed everyone towards their trucks. "I'll return with the key."

"Quick question," Sam asked as she watched them retreat. "Nicole, how do you prop those eyelids open with lashes like that? Toothpicks? Let me get a closer look. No? What kind of adhesive do you use? I need something strong to fix the trim on my truck."

Nicole turned a fiery red and held up her middle finger. For once, Nicole was at a loss for words. Just as she closed her truck door, Dale burst out in laughter from within the cabin. He had watched the exchange from a side window, but could no longer hide his amusement. Sam grinned and offered her best princess wave as the fleet of vehicles turned around and left the area.

Sam looked towards the skies. The clouds moved swiftly as the front continued to push them overhead. A lone raindrop landed beneath her eye, causing Sam to blink. She scanned the area and listened for distant howling. All was quiet as one drop of rain led to another. Before the skies opened up yet again, Sam moved inside and secured the door. It was time for rest, as the next day would undoubtedly be busy.

DAY ELEVEN

As per Sam's instruction, only one security vehicle guarded the entrance, and the officer remained in his truck. Sam was unsure if he was following the boss's orders or feared the predators that crept around in the dark. The guard rolled down the window and used a flashlight to check Sam's identification. Both she and Dale winced when the beam of light locked on their faces.

During this time, Sam handed the man a list of volunteers. She stressed the importance of blocking access to the campground unless they provided matching identification. There were no exceptions, especially if a fleet of pickups arrived that brandished a W.O.L.F. logo. Sam suggested the press and other unscrupulous individuals might impede the park's efforts to stop the wolf pack.

After driving around the barricades, Sam parked in the center of the campground. The truck sat idle with the warm air of the defroster blowing on the front windows. Although sluggish, she gazed outward to scrutinize any movement caught in the glare of the headlights. Dale had nodded off, but sleep eluded Sam in the silence. She found it hard to believe that so much bloodshed could happen in such a beautiful park.

When the sun rose, Sam scanned the surroundings. Knowing this was their preferred hunting ground, she hoped to catch a glance of the dire wolves before they settled for the day. It would help her choose a direction to start the search. But, on this morning, there would be no luck. She would need to send volunteers in opposite directions, divide and conquer.

By this time, Dale had awakened. They each hugged a hot thermos of coffee and sat silently in their seats. The rains held off, although it remained overcast and cool. Sam pulled her flannel blanket around her body, wondering what kind of winter they'd face. Her thoughts drifted to the grizzlies in the park. She and Dale would spend the rest of summer tracking them and hoping the wolves didn't affect their numbers.

Hours felt like an eternity as they waited and watched. Sam had insisted on an early arrival. She wanted to ensure the area was safe and direct the volunteers when they arrived. She didn't want anyone waiting for her. Sam and Dale passed their time eating granola bars, telling corny jokes, and dreaming the nightmare would end before twilight. But they understood this was most likely only a beginning to the end of the pack. They would be fortunate to take out a few wolves before sunset.

"How many do you think there are?" Sam asked.

"Not sure. When we get back, I can review the footage we shot with Johnson's trail cams." Dale responded.

"What if we miss one? Do you realize how hard it'll be to find just one wolf in thousands of square miles?" Sam took a swig of coffee. She needed caffeine to fuel her thoughts.

"If we miss one, it should die off. It will lack protection from its pack and will be forced to hunt alone. But that's assuming there aren't other dire wolves within Yellowstone. Hopefully, it'll fear people and keep its distance. Like I said, without other dire wolves in the park, we should be okay." Dale projected a tone of confidence.

"If we're lucky, a grizzly will do it in." Sam smirked at Dale.

A vehicle pulled beside them, breaking off their conversation. Sam noticed a bed full of dog crates and burly men wearing hunting jackets. She turned the ignition off, and they exited her pickup. Another vehicle pulled up, followed by another. Soon there was a sea of bright orange and camouflaged clothing. Volunteers finished their coffee, cigarettes, and friendly exchanges. Most had previously worked together or knew of one another.

In just a short time, the campground was a flurry of activity. Aside from vehicles, volunteers brought campers and trailers loaded with all-terrain and utility task vehicles. The men and women unloaded the equipment, checked fluids, and revved their engines. Upon Sam's direction, those on the ATVs and UTVs circled the perimeter of West Bay before disappearing in pairs on trails that led into the wooded areas. She hoped the noisy vehicles would flush the pack out of hiding.

Hunting dogs barked continuously as their handlers removed them from cages. The canines pulled at their leashes, eager to follow the distinct odors that overwhelmed their senses. Dale divided the heavily armed huntsmen into several teams and directed them to different areas. The hunters extended the leads attached to their dogs. Soon, the men and women disappeared into the brush.

Cadaver dogs and recovery teams brought up the rear. Sam tasked them with the search for additional victims that may have gone unnoticed and unreported. Their dogs were eager to start, leading them towards the south part of the campground. Sam didn't take that as a good sign, but kept her thoughts to herself. Extra volunteers took up arms and followed the search and rescue groups. They would ensure everyone's safety if the wolves doubled back during a chase or emerged from their hiding places.

While Sam marveled at the enthusiasm of volunteers and the organized chaos, a helicopter appeared above the lake. Sam glanced around and noticed Tony leaning against his vehicle. She pointed to the chopper, and he grinned and nodded his head. The FAA and National Park regulations prohibited low-flying aircraft in Yellowstone. Pulling off this operation in such a short time frame was no small feat. Sam returned an even bigger smile with a simple wave. She hoped the helicopter could aid in their search, despite the thick canopy of trees.

As Sam waited in the center of the campground to respond to radio chatter and oversee the operation, Dale moved to the shoreline with the drone operators. He knew the odds of finding anything were slim, but wanted the operators to scan areas they couldn't reach. Dale hoped they might discover the predators hiding from the commotion.

Before noon, Sam received word from a search and rescue team regarding their discovery of a human body. She waved Tony over while listening to the details spewing from the handset. They found a set of remains just off a popular hiking trail to the south of the campground. The wolves and scavengers had picked the corpse clean, but the victim's hair and clothing led the team to believe it was a middle-aged man. They found no identification at the site.

"Who is it?" Sam asked Tony. "The only missing person I'm aware of abandoned a stolen van. Police think he hitch-hiked out of the park. Is anyone else missing? Tourists? Park employees? This area is too far from employee housing to be one of our maintenance men."

"I'll make some calls. I'm not aware of any other missing person cases." Tony yelled as the helicopter passed overhead. Sam didn't hear his response, but understood his gesture. He held his thumb and pinky fingers to his ear and mouth.

By mid-afternoon, the volunteers had yet to spot the wolf pack. They returned to the staging area for a headcount before visiting the catering tent for sandwiches and drinks. Sam listened to conversations and took notes regarding their finds and opinions. Volunteers discovered the carcass of the missing rottweiler, remains of deer and moose, and many scat piles. But with the previous day's rain, no one could say with certainty that the excrement was fresh.

After the volunteers refueled their bodies and rested, Sam delivered instructions for the remaining daylight hours. They were to install trail cameras in various positions around the campground. Those spending the night would circle their campers like the settlers' wagons of old western times. The interior would provide extra protection to their caged dogs. Added spotlights would deter the wolves from approaching the campers. From what Sam had learned about their behavior, the wolves preferred to stalk and hunt during darkness.

"You look defeated." Tony declared. He had spent most of the day by Sam's side. Her organizational skills and the respect she garnered from volunteers impressed him.

"Yeah. I didn't get the outcome I hoped for today. We found another victim and zero wolves. Even the helicopter and drones didn't catch sight of them. Tomorrow's going to be another day of searching and guesswork. Depending on what the trail cameras catch, I think we'll start at the West Bay employee housing. The wolf pack has been making runs between here and the marina. I fear they've moved north," Sam said with a long face.

"You've done great. Don't be hard on yourself. If this is a new species, they've remained undiscovered for who knows how long? Evolution aided them with some great camouflage and survival skills. You'll crack their code in due time. They can only run so long," Tony said as he put a hand on Sam's shoulder. She grinned at Tony, pleased with his support and optimism.

"Much appreciated, Tony. I'm going to wrap things up before I head out. I'm expecting one more person today. He may help us better understand these wolves and their behavior. Hopefully, he's waiting at my cabin." Sam thanked Tony before heading back to the groups of volunteers for evening instruction. She would impress upon them the importance of staying inside during dark and avoiding alcohol. Both could lead to poor decisions and risk injury to themselves and one another. Unlike Johnson, Sam didn't want to assume that liability.

The headlights of Sam's truck reflected off the shiny red paint job of a compact car parked at the start of the darkened cabins. Despite Sam's attempt to leave the campground before dark, her plans played out differently. Sam slowed the truck as they passed the rental car, and Dale looked into the vehicle. A fog had formed on the glass, but he could make out the form of a man in the light cast by the stranger's cell phone.

"Is it him?" Sam asked. She parked in front of their cabin and watched the car from her rearview mirror.

"Not sure?" Dale responded.

"Be careful when you get out. Go straight inside and turn on the lights. I'm not sure if we chased the wolves into our area. Take your sidearm," Sam instructed. She observed the headlights switch on before the vehicle started its approach towards them.

"I'll be back shortly." Dale disappeared behind the front door of their cabin. In a short while, he illuminated every light inside the cabin.

Dale reemerged to empty the truck as Sam greeted the visitor parked next to her. She aimed a flashlight into his car and scanned the interior while keeping a hand on her pistol. If it were a reporter, Sam wanted to intimidate the man. The window rolled down, and a face moved towards the light when he stretched over the passenger seat.

"Sam?"

Sam squatted and rested her arms on the window frame to scrutinize the stranger. He wore a long-sleeve button-down shirt with pressed trousers and a pocketed vest, all in earthy tones. A bucket hat lay atop a messenger bag on the passenger seat. Everything looked as if he had newly purchased it for the trip.

"That's a fishing vest you got there." Sam pointed downward with her index finger. "I'm guessing you aren't here for trout? And yes, Sam's the name."

The man let out a huge sigh. "Lee In-su from the La Brea Tar Pits and Museum. You can call me Aaron. Sorry, but I didn't catch your full name. I was excited to get your call and didn't think to ask." He wiped his sweaty palm on the side of his pants before extending it towards Sam for a handshake. She grimaced and shook it anyway.

"Let's save the formalities for later. There's a wolf pack running around, and I'd rather not be outside. Gather your stuff and lock up your car. I'll meet you inside."

Aaron nervously glanced around the area, looking for shadows and movement. He did as Sam said and grabbed his items and a suitcase from the trunk before stumbling inside with loaded arms. Dale finished clearing out the truck and watched Sam head towards Johnson's cabin. She flashed her light on his door and noticed someone had torn the screen she tacked in place the previous day.

"Nicole. Like the rat she is, she took the bait. Too damn predictable." Sam stated when she heard Dale approach from behind. A quick scan with her flashlight revealed nothing out of place. "I'll report this to Tony in the morning. I'd love to get her out of my hair. Dale, go make sure she wasn't in our cabin."

Dale left for their cabin, with Sam close behind. When she reached the entrance, Sam made one last scan for Nicole and the dire wolf pack. The surrounding forest stood silent and still. The evening air had chilled, but the clouds had cleared and a little sliver of moonlight cast light upon the earth. Sam closed the door and secured the locks.

"Welcome to my humble abode!" Sam exclaimed when she entered the cabin. Aaron was sitting at the kitchen table. Sam's arms flung in the air to showcase her living quarters. "Given the chaos going on in the park, this is the best I can offer you. The kitchen is here. Eat what you like, but don't touch my vodka. That's reserved for the celebration."

Aaron was unsure what she had meant and cut her off. "What celebration?"

"To celebrate the execution of the wolf pack. We're going to keep our brains clear and sober in the meantime. Anyway, the bathroom is down the hall, and that there is your bedroom." Sam pointed to the couch. "We'll round up some blankets and a pillow, and you'll think this is a five-star kind of joint. So, that wraps up my tour."

"Despite my appearance, I have slept on and in worse conditions," Aaron responded.

"You're clean-cut and look like you just stepped out of a catalog. I thought you looked more like an all-inclusive kind of guy, but I'll take your word for it." Sam winked. "What can I get you to drink? Are you hungry? If you like Italian food, I have plenty."

"Are you Italian?" Aaron asked.

"With this red hair? Nah, I'm full-blooded Irish. The food came from a pizzeria up the road. They had to close because of the attacks in this area. We were the lucky recipients of a massive cache of pizza supplies. Dale here, say hi, Dale." Dale held up his palm from inside the hallway, where he leaned against the wall and listened to their conversation. "Dale is a superb cook and can create dishes that don't require a crust."

"Thank you, but I'm not hungry." Aaron smiled at his host and hostess.

"Nice vest. Going fishing?" Dale asked when he spotted Aaron's pile of personal effects. Aaron winced; his attempt to look like a local had backfired. Dale made his way to the kitchen. "Also, it doesn't look like anyone was in our cabin. No one messed with the stuff in my room."

"Good," Sam responded. "So, Aaron, tell me what you've heard on the outside."

Sam listened to Aaron as she stripped from her outerwear and checked her weapons. She placed everything on her recliner before returning to the table and taking a seat across from him. Dale worked in the kitchen, reheating leftovers from the previous night. He juggled plated food and drinks as he made his way to the table to join the others.

"I need you to sign this," Sam said. She slid a confidentiality form across the table while stuffing a fork full of lasagna into her mouth. Aaron took a moment to read the document. He looked up at both Sam and Dale before grabbing a pen from the table and signing the paper.

"Why is that necessary?" Aaron asked.

"It's for our protection, as well as yours. We don't know you or your motivation for assisting us. If you have good intentions, help us, and cooperate, I will gift the museum with a carcass, not just any carcass. We preserved this one in one piece. I will also allow you to take full credit for the discovery, blah, blah, blah." Sam said. She pulled the signed document away from Aaron and slid it underneath a pile of paperwork on the table. "So, now you're officially one of our gang."

"Why don't you want credit?" Aaron asked.

"I want them dead. This isn't my field, and I'd rather have nothing to do with them." Sam replied.

"Then why are you in charge?" Aaron further probed her.

"Because I was the first one pursued by the pack and my good friend next door blundered their capture." Sam stuffed another morsel of food into her mouth.

"Can I talk to him? I'd like to learn more about his experience as well."

"There's a minor problem with that. They transported his body to the morgue yesterday. He and his partner were the last victims. The last we know of, anyway." Sam watched Aaron wiggle in his chair.

"I'm sorry for your loss. If possible, can I see the images you sent me? Do you have more photos? Any video footage?" Aaron inquired. Sam set her fork down and pulled the laptop towards her. She entered the password and pulled up the file before turning the screen towards him. Aaron's eyes lit up.

"No videos. The photos aren't that impressive. They don't show the true magnitude of these creatures. I have something better." Sam grinned.

"A real specimen?" Aaron replied.

"The very one I mentioned before. Dale, do you want to go for a ride?" Sam asked her partner.

"If it's okay with you, I'll hang back. I'm going to shower and better secure our stash. When you're finished, leave the dishes. I'll clean up." Dale responded. He looked tired and drained from the early start and full day of activities.

"Thank you!" Sam stuffed the last bite into her mouth and bolted from her seat. "Grab a jacket, Aaron, and let's head out. We have a long day tomorrow, and I don't want to be out late."

During the drive, Sam relayed every bit of information she could recall regarding her experience and observations concerning the wolves. Each time she mentioned dire, Aaron would stop her. He reminded her that dire wolves went extinct thousands of years ago, and this could be a new species. Sam couldn't help but roll her eyes. She could hardly wait to see his reaction.

When they arrived at the pizzeria, Sam drove around the barricades. Unlike at the campground, and much to her relief, the park hadn't posted a guard. Sam didn't want anyone to witness her evening visit. Her truck stopped at the back of the building, and she parked as close to the rear door as possible.

"Come out my door when I give the word. Don't forget to close it. I feel we're more exposed here and less safe. The marina over there..." Sam said as she pointed in the right direction, "is where the wolves chased one victim into the lake."

Sam took a deep breath after scanning the area with her flashlight. With the key in hand and the truck door left open, she stepped onto the loading ramp. Her hands trembled as she slid the key into the lock. The knob turned, and she quickly entered the building and waved for Aaron to follow. He maneuvered around the center console and slid across her seat. She had seen no one move as quickly as he did.

The interior was pitch black, but Sam swiped her hands across the wall. A finger eventually caught the light switch and flipped it on. Florescent lightbulbs flickered and buzzed along the hallway ceiling until they cast a golden hue. Sam peeked out the back door one last time to check that the truck was closed. She knew the wolves were intelligent and feared one might hide inside and await their return if they left a door open.

"This way." Sam led Aaron to the freezer door and unlocked the padlock. "Right there."

The interior of the freezer was just as she had left it. No one had tampered with the lock. Sam pulled the carcass away from the wall and peeled back the layers of tarp. Dale had wrapped it in such a way to prevent bodily fluids from leaking out. Aaron helped when he observed her struggle with one section. They worked together until the body lay in the center of the tarp Sam handed her flashlight to Aaron.

"Holy shit! That is most definitely not a gray wolf. And you said there are more?" Aaron asked, without taking his eyes away from the carcass. His teeth chattered as he spoke. Sam was unsure if it was from the cold or his excitement.

Aaron didn't hear Sam's response as he swept the beam of light over every inch of the wolf. He poked at certain areas and tried to brush the hair back with his fingertips, but it was hard to manipulate. The short time locked in the freezer had preserved the body as if they had just discovered it on the Siberian tundra. It would take days to thaw.

Sam bent down beside Aaron. She held the flashlight while he collected specimens and took measurements. He worked feverishly and grunted or whimpered and snickered. Sam could only imagine what was running through his head. Occasionally, Aaron would look at her with a big grin and an enormous sigh. Sam returned his gaze with a similar smile.

After taking photos, they wrapped the carcass and returned it to the back corner of the freezer. Aaron gathered his items, and Sam replaced the lock, tugging at it. They both collapsed against opposite walls and stared at one another with rosy cheeks and red and runny noses. Sam rubbed her hands along her pants to warm them and get the blood flowing.

"So, what are your thoughts? A dire wolf or new species?" Sam asked.

"Without DNA testing, I can't be a hundred percent certain. I've worked at the museum for almost two decades and handled and cataloged thousands of skulls. Dire wolves are the most common species recovered in the pits. Based on what I just observed, well..." Aaron expressed, "I think it could be a Canis dirus, a dire wolf. I need to correlate my samples against those in the museum, if that's even possible."

"You've got this. I'm putting my faith in you," Sam replied. "Let's get back to the cabin and get some rest. We'll make plans on the drive back and I want to know everything you know about dire wolves."

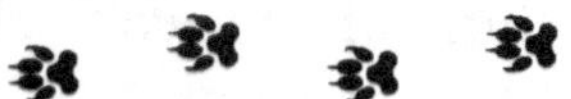

The wolf pack examined the truck parked behind the pizzeria. Warmth radiated from its engine, and the vehicle reeked of burnt motor oil. The human scent was strong, yet the wolves detected no sound or movement in the area. After a few moments of exploration, the alpha male pressed the pack onward.

Because of the day's turbulent events, the dire wolves fled the forest that surrounded the campground. They would look for new land abundant with wildlife and devoid of man. While mourning the loss of their she-wolf, the alpha pair became more guarded. Until recently, a human form provided temporary sustenance for the pack. Now they viewed humanity as a threat. They would protect their remaining offspring and expand their territory.

A companion joined the scout, and the two advanced before the others. No wolf would travel further alone without protection from another. The pair followed a narrow game trail into the densely wooded area, identifying the faded scents of prey and dried-out scat. The forest lacked new animal activity, giving them no reason to stay. They advanced further north, with the pack close behind.

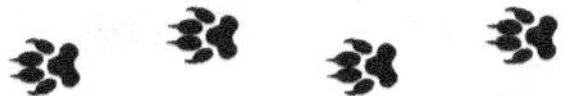

"Did you hear that? We're going to get in so much trouble if they catch us. I swear there are more people this summer than the last one," expressed one man. The tall and lanky fellow looked over his shoulder and into the darkness.

"You say that every summer, and I tell you the same damn thing. We won't get caught. We can see in both directions from here. If you see headlights, give me a warning. We'll drop the rods behind the guardrail with our goggles. If they slow down, we tell them we're looking for a set of keys we dropped earlier today," he said. The man was stocky and hobbled as he walked. Despite his bulging size, the lanky man had trouble keeping his pace. "This year, not one person has driven by this spot. We're already ahead of last year's game. Let's hurry so we can drop our lines."

The men parked their car at the base of a hill on the west side of the Piscary Bridge. It was here that the Yellowstone River ended, and Yellowstone Lake began. The bridge was popular with tourists as they could walk across the wooden structure to view the fish gathered in its shade. Although the piscary was known as a place to fish, the park forbade fishing from the old Piscary Bridge.

As with previous summers, the men would fill their ice boxes with fish collected through illegal means. They would clean the trout before selling to restaurants outside of the park gates. No one questioned where it came from when there was money to be had. It was a win-win for both parties.

The men always snuck into the park after sunset, when the rangers retired for the day. Few witnessed them enter, and no one saw them leave. Tonight, like their previous visits to the park, they donned night-vision goggles and wore camouflage. They preferred goggles over headlamps and flashlights. These devices allowed them to work in the dark and avoid detection.

From the bridge, they strived to hook as many fish as possible. The two worked quickly, setting poles along the railing and baiting the hooks with live minnows. No sooner had they finished dropping the lines than they caught their first fish. A moment later, they hooked another, followed by another.

"Shit, I'm going to need to take a load back to the car in a minute. I bet this will be our best summer yet!" the lanky man asserted. He smiled, and half his teeth were missing, the others half-rotted. "Maybe this year, I can finally afford a float boat. Or maybe that camper I told you about?"

"First, you need a damn car!" the portly man said. He wiped the sweat from his forehead on the long sleeve of his shirt.

They worked in silence, filling bags and dropping hooks. Water rushed below the bridge and fed into the lake, carrying additional fish for them to poach. Occasionally, the men would scan the shoreline for bear and animal activity. But tonight, they were too busy to keep a watchful eye.

"So, how many charges will tonight's fishing trip bring if we're caught?" the lanky man asked. He knew the answer to this question, but prided himself on eluding the law.

"Fishing without a license, fishing from the bridge, using barbed hooks, another for live bait, one for under-sized fish, exceeding the bag limit. I'm sure there's more. If we're going to break one law, why not break them all? They'll cap our fine and jail sentence, anyway. Another slap on the wrist for me," the portly man answered. "Look at these bags. Why don't you dump them in the cooler?"

"Sure thing," he acknowledged.

The lanky man lifted the bags and slid a strap over each shoulder for balance. He hurried back to the car, only stopping to light a cigarette. The goggles bounced about his face, making it difficult to see. He pushed them to the top of his forehead and proceeded in the dark, guided by the sliver of moonlight.

Working quickly, the lanky man emptied the bags of trout into a cooler in the car's trunk, covering them with a layer of ice. He looked around the side of the car, spotting the silhouette of his partner on the bridge. The lanky man ducked behind the open trunk to finish his cigarette and down a small bottle of liquor he had hidden amongst the mess. It was the best substitute for a hot cup of coffee on this chilly night.

The cigarettes in his shirt pocket beckoned for another drag. He contemplated staying longer, but didn't want to face the wrath of his boss. The lanky man closed the trunk and pulled the goggles over his eyes. After his vision had adapted to the darkness, he adjusted the straps for a tighter fit. He shook his head to test the goggles' comfort and noticed figures on the hill above him.

Through the green glow of the night vision, the lanky man counted two canines. He watched, unsure if they were coyotes or dogs. Other figures emerged beside the two until there were almost a dozen standing together. The wolves studied the man as he watched them, both parties frozen in place. When the man bent down for the fish bags, the wolves charged down the loose dirt of the hillside.

The lanky man abandoned the fish bags and struggled to pull the keys from his pocket. The wolves cleared half the distance before he finally extracted the keys. His hands trembled with fear as he tried to line the key with the lock. He dropped the keyring and bent down to retrieve the set, watching for the predators as his hands frantically swiped the soil. With little time to lose, he collapsed to the ground and started crawling underneath the car for protection.

Despite the testosterone coursing through his body, a loud, high-pitched shrill escaped from the lanky man's lungs. Two wolves clamped onto his calves, their sharp canines tearing into his flesh. As they pulled and jerked his body away from the car, the man dug his long, bony fingers into the soft earth. He struggled to grasp anything that would prevent the wolves from extracting his body from the hiding place.

The portly man cursed under his breath, knowing the lanky man was smoking or drinking or doing both. His partner took longer than usual to unload the catch and return the empty bags. Although they had worked together for many years, he felt stuck with the guy. The portly man feared animosity and loose lips would bring legal trouble if he severed ties with the lame duck. He would tolerate his careless behavior until he figured out a new game plan.

While waiting for the lanky man's return, the portly man amassed a pile of fish. He feared they would flop over the side of the bridge in their struggle to return to the water. Even with his size, the portly man moved with the grace of a dancer. He repeatedly kicked the flopping fish into the pile while pulling others from the river and baiting hooks. Aside from his patience running out, the bait was running low. He grappled with a minnow before it slipped from his fingers onto the bridge.

It wasn't the presence of the wolf that caught his attention, but the low grumble that emanated from the predator. The portly man had bent down for the dropped bait when he heard a sound unlike the babbling river below. He was face to face with the creature, its teeth glowing an intense white in the green glow of his goggles. The portly man failed to notice the other wolves that closed in around him. Before he could react, the wolf lunged at him.

There was nothing he could have done to stop the attack. Like other victims before him, the portly man lay helpless on the cold ground and stared at the sky above him, the wolf's mouth wrapped around his neck. The clouds had all moved out, allowing the portly man to focus on the twinkling stars. As the wolves ravaged his body, his life slipped away. Eventually, the stars faded and twinkled no more.

DAY TWELVE

Sam stood over the remains of a human, trying to convince herself it was the work of a different predator. They crushed the bones for marrow and picked them clean of muscle and flesh, just as they did with the other victims. A gray wolf or grizzly bear would take days or a week to do the same work, even with the help of scavengers. But this was the signature behavior of the dire wolf pack she sought.

Yellow identification markers littered the ground to identify the locations of limbs and other body parts. There were too many to count on this sunny day. The cold front and rainy weather that offered a moment of relief from the searing heat had moved on, allowing summer to unleash its wrath.

Sam wiped the sweat from her brow and waved her hands at the bugs that flew around her face. They had undoubtedly been feasting on the bits of scattered flesh before her. Now the flies searched for a place to rest and groom themselves. Someone handed Sam a can of bug spray when they noticed her annoyance with the pests. She sprayed her body with a cloud of insect repellant before offering the can to the next passerby.

"Well?" Tony began. "Does this look like their work?"

"It was them," Sam said, glancing towards the hill where they stood. She noticed the tracks where the pack descended. The grooves and paw prints stood out in the soft dirt. "We probably chased the wolves away from the campground yesterday. You said there was another body?"

"On the bridge. By that group of investigators." Tony continued, "Should we call for the volunteers to meet us here?"

"No. Dale will stick with our original plans. He'll take charge of the operation today. We need to find the bodies of the maintenance workers for their families. Who knows what else they'll uncover? Say, what are the odds that we can close this side of the park to prevent any more of this carnage?"

"We're minimizing pedestrian traffic in these parts. We've also banned camping and recreational activities in the campground and the marina. I can't allow the closure of roadways. You know that."

"It doesn't hurt to ask. Say, what's with the night vision goggles? Who are these guys, anyway?" Sam asked Tony.

"Poachers. Police told me these two have had previous run-ins with the law. They illegally harvest the waters in Yellowstone and sell the fish to local restaurants and outfitters. This wasn't their first time poaching from the park."

"Hmm. But it is their last time. It looks like karma caught up to these scofflaws." Sam responded.

Before heading to the bridge, Sam crouched and looked around the vehicle. She noticed markings in the soil where the victim crawled underneath the car. A set of car keys, half-buried in the sand, lay next to a yellow marker. Sam imagined the scene playing out after he dropped the keys. The victim knew what was coming at him.

The Piscary Bridge was a short distance from the main road. It remained closed to traffic while investigators conducted their search into the deaths of the two men. The noise of vehicle engines and squealing brakes suppressed the soft sound of gurgling water rushing over the smooth rock in the Yellowstone River. Although it was early in the day and far from overnight accommodations, onlookers already clogged the two-lane road. Sam wondered how many vehicles carried summer tourists versus those that had driven out of their way for a chance encounter with the notorious and ravenous wolf pack.

Rather than take the pedestrian sidewalk that spanned the bridge, Sam and Tony walked single file along the right lane, peering over the railing. The nearer they came to the body, the more bones, flesh, and blood staining they encountered. Bloody paw prints marked the movement of the wolves.

"Is that normal? I mean, do wolves eat fish?" Tony asked with a grimace on his face. Scattered remains of trout littered the pedestrian path. Tony had only witnessed wolves eat bison or elk in the park.

"Absolutely. Wolves are opportunistic predators. Maybe you should get out of the office more?" Sam acknowledged his question. She shot him a quick smile before resuming her search.

"I don't mind an occasional field trip, but this isn't my cup of tea."

"Tea? You seem like a single malt scotch kind of guy. I imagine you sitting in a velvet robe and leather slippers by the fireplace. Grasping a whiskey tumbler while staring at the mountains from an enormous picture window."

"Maybe in the next lifetime. I can only hope I win the lottery between now and then."

Tony stopped next to a group of investigators as Sam continued walking the bridge. She scanned the pavement before disappearing into the right shoulder of the road. Tony next noticed her on the river's embankment. Sam looked up and down the shoreline before disappearing under the bridge. A short while later, she walked onto the shoulder of the opposite lane. Sam made her way back, still scanning the pavement while glancing over the railing.

"Sorry, I was looking for tracks and other signs. I want to make certain the wolves continued on the west side of the river. The bloody prints end right there," Sam said, and pointed to the outer boundary of the kill site on the pedestrian path of the bridge. "There's nothing on the shoulder of the road or next to the river. Hopefully, they moved back towards the campground or marina after feeding, where we can better track them."

"Didn't you mention yesterday that someone was coming into Yellowstone to help?" Tony asked. They began walking back to his vehicle when a group of men started bagging the man's remains on the bridge.

"Yeah. Our new helper arrived last night. He's a paleontologist that specializes in the study of dire wolves. Aaron, something or other. I can't remember his last name. Anyway, he came to us from the La Brea Tar Pits and Museum in Los Angeles. There's no one more qualified than him."

"Where is he today? Can I meet him?" Tony asked. He swatted at a fly that hovered above his nose.

"Aaron left early this morning for Billings. He took samples of our she-wolf to compare to DNA samples from the museum. One school in Billings has the equipment he needs for testing. It was the closest to the park."

"I thought I told you not to take the wolf carcass out of the park?"

"Technically, he didn't take the wolf, just samples. I promised him the wolf carcass after we take down the pack," Sam articulated. "Aaron signed an NDA last night and understands how important this is to us, to me. I trust him."

"Sam!" Tony vocalized his dissatisfaction with her decision. "How do you know this guy? How do you know we can trust him?"

"Gabby mentioned the museum, which gave me the idea to contact him. I kinda found his information on the internet and called the museum," she replied. Sam didn't give Tony time to respond. "Aaron is a professional and knows how important this is. In exchange for his help, I've promised him the she-wolf carcass and all credit for this discovery. We can't do this without him. He knows everything about dire wolves, and I know the park. Trust me on this one."

"I'm putting my faith in you, Sam. Dire wolves are extinct."

"Thought extinct." Sam quipped.

"I don't understand how Aaron knows everything about a creature from its bones, especially those recovered from a tar pit. Please don't screw this up, Sam. Don't force me to call upon someone else. I'm impressed with your knowledge and work so far."

They arrived at Tony's car as the conversation wrapped up. Like the previous day, Sam felt battered and beaten. The dire wolves were still running loose, there were additional victims, and she received a tongue lashing from the park boss. Sam had bought additional time for her hunt, but needed to produce results quickly. The pressure was mounting.

"One last thing. I chased the W.O.L.F. group away from Johnson's cabin the other night. When we returned last night, someone had broken into his place. Not sure if this has anything to do with Nicole, but something tells me she's up to no good."

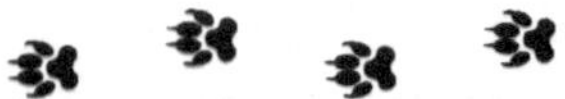

Tony parked behind a long line of vehicles, off to the side of the dirt road. Like the previous day, there was a flurry of activity. As Tony and Sam walked towards the cluster of employee cabins, they stayed close to the parked cars to avoid the small recreational vehicles that buzzed by and kicked up dirt and gravel.

"What's the latest?" Sam vocalized over the noise.

Dale twisted around when he heard her voice. He appeared relieved when he spotted Sam. There were too many search parties for one person to manage, especially one new to the game. Dale was ready to give up control of the operation. He preferred to focus on one task instead.

"It's about time. Things are going as well as they can go, given the circumstances," Dale expressed while glancing at his watch. "They found the remains of the two maintenance workers immediately. Their bodies were in the brush to the side of their cabin. We're looking for the wolf pack now.

How about you? Are the guys at the river connected to this mess?"

"Yeah. Two more notches on the alpha's belt. If we don't find the pack today, I'm guessing they've moved on to greener pastures. Do you know if the trail cams at the campground caught images of the pack?"

"No, nothing. Those that camped last night said it was quiet. One guy kept an overnight vigil on top of his camper while the others slept. He said there was no activity on the ground. Even the dogs slept through the night," Dale communicated.

Sam rubbed her eyes with her fingertips before lowering them to cover her nose and mouth. She was at a loss, not knowing where to go from here. If they didn't find the pack today, she planned to send the volunteers home. Sam feared the noise and activity were scaring the pack farther from the area.

"Sam, I'm going back to the office. My phone's buzzing and chiming with messages. The Wi-Fi must work better in these parts, but I need something a bit more reliable." Tony observed as his finger scrolled down a list on his phone. "You have a ride, right?"

"Yeah, my truck's here. Thanks, Tony."

"Let me know if you make any progress? I'll catch up with you later."

Dale watched Tony walk away as Sam checked her phone. There were no texts or emails from Aaron. She cared less about anything else that came through in her messages. After she pocketed the phone, Dale handed her the clipboard.

"What next?" Dale asked.

"Let's see how the rest of the day plays out. I'm guessing the pack is lying low and out of sight. I'm not feeling as optimistic as yesterday. We need to come up with a new plan tonight."

The late morning soon turned into late afternoon. Sam was grateful for the canopy of trees and a limitless supply of insect repellent. As the day progressed, she stripped from her outwear to combat the heat. The mosquitos became more aggressive when the sun started its decline, forcing her back into heavy clothing.

Before leaving the area, Sam thanked the volunteers for their service. She was unlike herself. Like the volunteers, Sam felt drained, defeated, and mentally exhausted. Two days of work turned up more bodies and not one wolf, not even a sighting. After the last vehicle pulled out, Dale and Sam returned to her truck.

They drove through the marina for a glance, then proceeded to the campground. Sam followed the perimeter of the forest, acknowledging those that spotted her. The volunteers worked quickly to secure their equipment and load their trailers. She suspected they shared the same vision of tackling the beasts when they arrived. Now, they would return home with fully stocked ammunition cases and empty fuel tanks. They would have no stories to tell their friends and family.

The truck stopped by the restroom building where Johnson's life ended, and her journey began. She turned her face away from Dale as she struggled to hold back tears. Sam's father taught her crying was a display of weakness during her childhood. Her thoughts switched to his death. Before he passed, tears streamed down his face as he held the hand of his teenage daughter and slipped away with a smile on his face. Weakness or strength, she wondered.

"Sam, are you okay?" Dale uttered in a whispered voice. He listened to Sam sniffle her nose or gulp or gasp for air. Dale suspected she was crying and put a hand on her shoulder. "We didn't kill the wolves today, but I'm sticking with you until we do. You'll have your revenge. Remember, very few hunters get the ten-point buck on their first hunt."

Sam turned and stared at Dale for a moment. She hadn't been crying, and Dale pulled back his hand. "You bagged a ten-pointer? Even I haven't bagged a ten-pointer. Quite the hunter you are, Mister Dale Wright. Maybe you should get the first shot at this pack? Mister Wright can't be wrong."

"Blah! As if I haven't heard that one before. You just gave me flashbacks of middle school."

"How about we cut this pity party short and head back to the cabin? We have some planning to do."

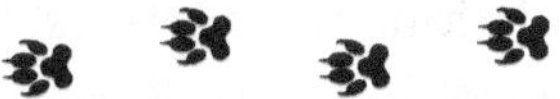

"I thought you were saving the vodka for after we kill the wolf pack?" Dale voiced.

Dale had just emerged from the shower, wearing a t-shirt and boxers. His hair was still damp and in disarray, but he was clean-shaven and smelled of the musky scent of cologne. Sam gave him a second glimpse with a drawn-out whistle, causing Dale to blush.

"The vodka was for the celebration. Now I've reassigned this bottle, this here bottle, to the planning department. My brain needs a jump start so I can figure out a way to eliminate the damn wolves." Sam slurred. The alcohol had already worked its way through her system.

"Let's eat first. You're going to get sick drinking that crap on an empty stomach. How much did you drink when

I was in the shower?" he asked, not expecting an honest answer, if one at all.

Dale swiped the bottle from the table without opposition from Sam. He stored it in a cabinet after checking the volume against the full bottles. While planning dinner, Dale occasionally glanced at Sam. She stared forward, deep in thought. Tonight, she looked especially alluring. Long, wet strands of hair hung past Sam's bare shoulders. She wore a spaghetti strap tank top that barely covered her flesh and exposed the muscle tone in her arms. Preparing dinner was the perfect distraction to hide his lust for the woman sitting a few feet away.

"I'm thinking..." Sam trailed off.

"What's your idea?"

Dale brought dinner to the table, taking a seat opposite Sam. He slid a plate with utensils wrapped in a napkin across the tabletop before taking bites from a heaping pile of pasta. Working outside in the sun and heat had drained his energy. A plate of carbs would replace what he lost and prepare him for another day of activity.

"Yesterday and today, we chased the pack from their feeding grounds. They didn't return last night. Instead, they moved further north. Dang! I forgot to check for more tracks opposite Tony's car. I looked on the other side of the river, but got sidetracked when I returned."

"Should we have a look after dinner? I can drive."

"Nah. Let's wait for daylight," Sam remarked. After Dale reached across the table and shook her plate, Sam stuffed her mouth with food. She spit out short sentences between chewing. "The wolves already annihilated the wildlife around the lake. We cut off their human food supply. There's no reason for them to stay. A pack that big needs big game to avoid starvation."

"Where do you think the wolves are enroute to next?"

"If they stay the course, the next stop on their park tour should be Hayden Valley. It's the roaming grounds for a herd of bison. Big open fields with a creek that feeds into the river. That's it!"

Sam stood and slammed her hands on the table, shaking the dishes and rattling the silverware. Although startled, Dale couldn't help but look at her breasts that shook with her movement. When she sat down, Dale concentrated on staring into her eyes. He was unsure if she caught his gaping expression and the pathetic gaze directed at her chest.

"What's it?" he asked.

"The Yellowstone River hugs the main road. I highly doubt the wolf pack will cross it. This obstacle will prevent them from moving east, into a thickly forested area. Alum Creek runs through Hayden Valley and dumps into the river."

"Forcing them to move into Hayden Valley?"

"Yes! We need to convince Tony to close the road over the waterway at that intersection. With the help of mother nature and a few man-made obstacles, we'll force the wolves into the open fields of the valley. If we can get ahead of the pack, we can wait there to pick them off."

"And what if they move west, into the forested areas south of Hayden Valley? Maybe they're already there?"

"We need to lure them towards the valley. What can we—"

Sam's phone chimed with a message. She stopped mid-conversation when she noticed Aaron's name pop up. Dale watched her jubilant expression change to one of frustration. Her eyebrows furrowed as she concentrated and typed her response.

"What gives?" Dale asked after Sam set the phone down.

"The DNA testing will take up to seventy-two hours before he can give us an answer, if he can provide an answer. We don't have that kind of time. I need his help now."

"Let's not get hung up with those kinds of details. It doesn't matter the species, anyway. We need to focus on how to eliminate them."

"You're right. Where were we?" Sam remarked.

"How do we lure the wolves to the open fields of Hayden Valley?" Dale responded.

"Easy. Me."

Day Thirteen

"We talked about this yesterday, Sam. I cannot and will not close any road within the border of Yellowstone National Park! Closing the roads is a decision for the superintendent and deputy superintendent. They refuse to budge on your request. Their reason? The people pay for the park with their tax dollars. They own it. We will not inconvenience the citizens of our great country. Therefore, the road will remain open."

Sam sank into the armchair facing Tony's desk. She and Dale had driven to Mammoth Springs in the north part of the park. They hoped someone at headquarters would permit them to close the Grand Loop portion by Hayden Valley. Sam tapped her fingernails on the arms of the faux black leather chair, struggling to muster the courage to repeat her question. She refused to take no as an answer. During this time, Dale waited outside of Tony's office. He listened to the conversation through the thin and hollowed door.

"I need the road closed, just one night. We need to force the wolves into Hayden Valley. Once we have them in our sight, Dale and I can eliminate the pack. We're both experienced hunters and carry the proper firepower. We won't inconvenience anyone, I promise."

"The only thing that closes the Grand Loop is snowfall or wildfires. We don't even close the roads for bison. And this is their natural range."

"Let me ask another question. Has an accident closed the Grand Loop?" Sam asked. She continued to scheme, thinking of other ways to shut down the road.

"Sam, I like your plan, and I'm on your side. But I'm under a lot of pressure today. Do you hear the phones ringing outside my office? I've had to pull together all available staff to field calls from the media and press. Yesterday, the savage creatures roaming Yellowstone evolved into global heroes. Once the world learned they killed two poachers, everyone decided they were worth saving. I have animal rights activists flooding our servers with emails and crackpots applying for permits to conduct research on these wolves. This morning, I must've had a dozen whack jobs stop me and offer advice while I walked from my car into the building. And don't get me started on Nicole, your friend from W.O.L.F.," Tony quipped. He stopped talking to take a swig of coffee and clear his throat.

"What is she up to?" Sam asked. She sat upright, eagerly awaiting his response.

"Nicole's vindictive and a pain in my ass! That comment stays within the walls of my office, mind you. After I questioned her about her involvement with the break-in at Johnson's cabin, she stormed away. The next thing you know, she's rallied throngs of Native American tribes from the lower forty-eight to support her cause. Wolves are spirit animals. Right? I thought it was only in theory. Wrong! It's a real thing. It turns out Nicole is pushing the tribes to pressure local politicians to stop the hunt. She links the wolf's importance to their ancestral beliefs. She's using the Native Americans as puppets. It gets better. This morning, I heard about a proposal to list them as a critically endangered species. These damn things are an invasive predator in Yellowstone. Politicians will offer these wolf creatures more protection than gray wolves and grizzlies. I'm telling you now, Sam, you are running out of time."

"Fuck!" Sam expressed as she smacked both hands on the arms of the chair.

"This suggestion doesn't come from me. Listen and listen well. Go back to your corner of the park, drain the batteries in your walkies, leave the cell phones in the cabin, and disappear. Go off the grid with your guns, knives, whatever you need. I don't know where you're going. I don't know what you have planned. When you step out of this building, you're working on your own accord. My best advice to you, get those damn wolves before they force me to stop you. End this hysteria today!"

"What does this mean for my future in the park?" Sam asked.

"We'll cross that bridge when we get there. Take care of yourself, Sam. I'm rooting for you and have your back! I'll do my best to protect you."

The cyclists spotted the herd of bison running through a field and towards the road. If the animals cut off their route, it would delay their arrival at the park's south entrance. The captain of the cycling team encouraged the others to keep his pace. To gain speed and outrun the beasts required all their focus, strength, and endurance.

The captain's strategy to avoid the bison did not go as planned. The herd switched direction, coming straight towards the men. He yelled for his team to stop and shelter in place. They could not go any further without risk of injury.

The men split up and ducked between the cars stopped in the roadway. Some drivers offered protection within their vehicles, but they left most team members outside, exposed to the danger.

It was a large herd that pushed through the cars. The bison nudged some vehicles and swiped at others with their massive skulls and hardened horns. Metal siding crinkled, a bumper fell to the ground, and windshields splintered and cracked. The bison lashed out at the vehicles that slowed their progress.

One bicyclist watched the herd's movement. He listened to the hooves clicking on the pavement. The noise and the vibration left in their wake fascinated him. He was oblivious to the activity behind him as he watched the bison pass a few feet away. A tremendous force knocked the man down, slamming his face onto the blacktop. He struggled to stand, having to support his weight with the bumper of a car. The man wiped the blood from his nose and swayed on his feet until something knocked him over a second time.

The charging bison distracted the passengers, who remained unaware of the wolf pack that moved along the shoulder, opposite their line of sight. The dire wolves pursued a bison calf until the herd surrounded the youngling to offer her protection. Rather than risk injury to its pack members, the alpha male switched its target to the scattered men between cars.

A couple witnessed the predator jump onto the cyclist this second time. They lay on their horn, trying to draw his attention to the creature behind him. One dire wolf jumped onto the hood of their car, watching its packmate latch onto the prey. The cyclist curled into a ball and pulled his bike over his body for protection. The second wolf jumped to the ground, helping to drag the man onto the soft grasses beyond the road's shoulder. It was there they consumed his body after prying it away from the twisted metal and rubber tires.

While the two young dire wolves fed, the other pack members plucked the remaining men from their hiding places. They worked quickly, giving no one time to react. The horrified tourists witnessed the gruesome events unfold, unable to offer help or save the men. Passengers and drivers lay on horns or threw objects from their windows. But it was all for naught. The wolves had found the fruitful lands of Hayden Valley and enjoyed their first feast on its lush green plains.

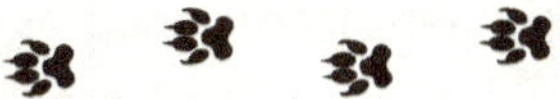

"This doesn't look promising, or does it? Maybe there's an accident that will close the road. Cross your fingers! Maybe something will finally go our way?" Sam said.

A third emergency vehicle sped by her parked truck, heading south toward Yellowstone Lake. Sam and Dale had just passed the Canyon Village intersection when traffic came to a screeching halt. Sam lowered her side window and poked her head out. A line of vehicles, a dip in the road, and a curve blocked her field of vision. She noticed no one was traveling northbound. A fourth and fifth vehicle passed just as Sam's phone rang.

"Dare I answer this call, Dale?"

A sixth emergency vehicle passed, its sirens blaring and lights flashing. Sam took the call when she recognized Tony's number. Dale struggled to listen to the conversation as Tony's boisterous voice erupted from the receiver. He feared Tony was ending their involvement with the wolf pack. When Sam completed the call, she turned to Dale.

"They just attacked a group of cyclists down the road. In front of tourists that sat in their cars during a bison stampede."

"Now? In broad daylight? In front of people? Are you sure it's our pack?" Dale asked. He was just as excited as Sam.

"Yes! Yes! Yes! And yes! Witnesses described them as a ferocious pack of red-haired wolf-like creatures. The wolves plucked the cyclists from between vehicles when everyone stopped. I think this pack just bought us some time and sealed their fate."

Sam restarted the truck and pulled into the opposite lane, traveling the eight-mile distance as quickly as possible. When she passed the line of parked cars, she honked at those that waited outside their vehicles. If they only knew about the creatures that hunted ahead, they would have remained behind locked doors. But there was no time to warn them.

"What's the plan?" Dale asked.

"Let's see where it happened first. Tony mentioned the attack occurred about a half-mile north of the Mud Volcano. He's already enroute and will meet us there shortly. If we're lucky, we can eliminate the wolves now. We can finally get our park back!"

During the drive, Sam made a mental checklist. They had crossed the Alum Creek tributary, where she had planned to block the pack. Soon they crossed both the Trout Creek and Elk Antler Creek tributaries. They, too, were great options for blockades. Both creeks fed into Yellowstone River, close to the Grand Loop.

The truck traveled past the open fields of Hayden Valley. A herd of bison had assembled close to the road, presumably the one that had stampeded. Their behavior confirmed Sam's suspicion. The bison had formed a ring to defend themselves against predators. The females and adult males encircled the young to protect the herd. They had fled during the attack and now stood their ground to protect the vulnerable.

Sam's optimism wavered when she spotted the tree line ahead. It was impossible to track the wolf pack in the forested areas. Despite their size and red coloring, they were skilled at hiding and avoiding those that hunted them. She wanted to lure them from the shadows and the safety of the trees. The pack would have retreated after the feeding. They always did.

"I'm not sure how I feel about this, Dale. The open fields would have made our job much easier. I think they may be in the trees ahead? This area gives me campground vibes. We're going to keep playing this game of cat and mouse."

"I agree. During the drive, I envisioned us standing in the back of your truck, picking the wolves off one by one. After everything we've seen, I'm not walking in those woods."

At the edge of Hayden Valley, they stopped and parked with the emergency vehicles that flooded the area. Not only had first responders converged on the site from the north, but others had traveled from the south. Sam grabbed her identification and loaded her weapons. Dale followed her lead. He holstered a handgun, stashed ammunition in a pocket, and selected a rifle. They carried more firepower than was necessary to eradicate the pack.

Sam and Dale walked through the crowd of first responders. Each time she asked someone for direction, they pointed her to someone else. Sam was looking for the head of the operation, wanting to know more about the incident. They finally happened upon a group of men and women that watched a video shot by a witness. Sam listened to them gasp when they played the attack. She waited until there was a pause in their exchange.

"Where are the wolves?" Sam asked.

They turned in unison to scrutinize the person who interrupted their investigation. One man moved forward, glancing at Sam and looking at her weapons. She didn't recognize the man that approached.

"And you are? Can I see some identification?"

Sam pulled out her lanyard and flipped through the cards attached to the clip. He bobbed his head after reviewing each one. Afterward, the man signaled to Dale to produce identification. He repeated the measure before speaking with them.

"What can I do for you?"

"The park has tasked us to eliminate this pack. I have a few questions. They killed how many people? Did anyone survive? Can I see the video? I want to confirm this is the pack that we're pursuing. Last, did witnesses see which direction the pack fled after the attack?" Sam asked.

"You get right to the point. There's no dancing around the facts with you," the man replied. "Yes, we have five fatalities, no survivors. Witnesses said the pack disappeared into the tree line after the attack. Jolene can show you the video. Anything else?"

"Nope. I think we're good. Thanks!"

Sam and Dale watched the recording of two wolves dragging a man into the tall grass beside the witnesses' car. They heard children screaming from the back seat during the grainy video feed. A woman pleaded with her husband to stop filming. She also yelled at her children to shield their eyes and take cover. Despite happening only a few feet away and being protected by only a thin pane of glass, the husband remained calm throughout filming.

"That's enough," Sam said. "Make sure you keep officers on watch. Today is the wolves' first attack during daylight. They're becoming more fearless as time passes. The two of us are going to check out the tree line. Make sure we don't get shot by anyone here."

Dale followed Sam from the bustling scene of bloodshed to the tranquil edge of the forest. They spotted the trail where the wolf pack trampled the soft grasses leading into the wooded area. Sam stopped at the pathway and stared through the trees, scanning for movement. She listened for subtle sounds that might give a clue to their position. But all was still and quiet. There was no crackling of branches or leaves, no whimpering or communication between the pack members. Although she couldn't see them, she knew the wolves were watching.

"You're not going in there, are you?"

"No. It's tempting. I'd love nothing more than to end this now. So, how do we persuade the wolves to come out of hiding? Johnson's rancid roadkill was untouched. They like to stalk and chase. The bison, for example. They pursued the herd, but abandoned them for the bicyclists. Easier kill? Less risk of injury to the pack? We need to come up with something new."

"Don't even consider using yourself as bait," Dale said.

"Yeah. I got over that idea pretty fast. It's still on the table, though. Table. That gives me an idea." Sam said. She grew more excited as she spoke.

"What's on your mind? Do I want to know? No, don't tell me."

"Let's head back to the truck. I need to make a call. I think this idea might work. You lead, and I'll watch our backs. We'll take it slow in case they spring on us. Stay quiet now."

"A culvert trap?" Tony asked.

"Yes. The large cylinder traps with the metal grate door. The ones normally used by the park for the safe capture of bears." Sam said. She misunderstood his question.

"I know what a culvert trap is. How does this apply to the wolf pack?"

"Similar to a shark cage. If it were possible, I'd use one of those instead. Anyway, this pack showed no interest in the bait Johnson used in his traps. Unlike gray wolves, we have yet to witness these predators scavenge. They prefer the thrill of the chase and a fresh kill. Their numbers and intelligence have allowed them to thrive in the park."

"I'm following," Tony replied.

"I'll use myself as bait."

"Nope!"

"I'm not finished. Keep listening, please. I'll sit in the culvert trap, safely behind bars. They can't penetrate the grating. For added safety, Dale can lock the door. There is no way in or out."

"What if something goes wrong?"

"The trap is too heavy to knock over, plus it's welded to a trailer. The metal is too thick to penetrate. If it can keep a grizzly bear contained, it can keep a pack of wolves out."

"What's the plan once you're locked up?"

"We'll hook-up lighting to a generator so the pack can see me and my movement. Once the wolves are visible, I can take the shots," Sam said.

"How will you attract them to the trap?"

"I'll play audio recordings of animals in distress. We know they select those that are weaker than themselves. Today, they pursued the bison herd. Once they spotted the cyclists, they changed course. Man can't defend himself like an adult bison. We're easy pickings. I believe if they see and hear activity in the trap, it'll stimulate their senses. We know they can't resist an easy meal."

"Where will you put the trap?"

"We've identified their game trail leading into the forest. I'll position the trap away from the tree line. The location will cause the wolves to leave the safety of the brush. The trap will be close enough to draw them into the open. But not too far. If we position it away from the forest, the trap may raise their suspicions. I'm certain they'll fall for it. I bet anything they're watching us now."

Tony looked towards the tree line, watching for movement. He sat in Sam's passenger seat with Dale in the back. Dale listened to their conversation and remained silent. Like Tony, Dale thought Sam's plan was flawed and risky. There were too many unknowns about the predators and their hunting strategy.

Outside, first responders and investigators were wrapping up their work. They had opened one lane to ease the back-up created by the wolf pack. Sam had moved her truck earlier to the opposite shoulder. She hoped the wolves might reemerge, tempted to hunt the people working at the scene. They were ready to spring into action with their loaded rifles.

"Can you shoot a weapon from inside the trap? You're sitting in a metal can. Can your rifle fit through the grating? Do you want to be near the entrance? What if they pull you through? Will the gunfire scare them? What about hearing loss?" Tony asked.

"Once inside the trap, I'll sit against the grating to fire my rifle. The barrel will fit through the grating and provide for better aim and stability. This position will allow me to take accurate shots at a rapid pace. I'll do my best to mow down the pack. As for my hearing? Yes, a blast inside will amplify the sound. To combat hearing damage, I'll wear both earplugs and earmuffs."

"How about your safety?"

"The grating will protect me. The wolves can't grab my limbs or pull me out because the gaps are too narrow. A padlock will prevent the door from accidentally opening."

"When do you plan to do this?" Tony asked.

"Right now. Friends will deliver the culvert trap this afternoon. We'll set it up after the trailer arrives."

"Sam, I'd call you impulsive, but you addressed all my questions. Your brain works in mysterious ways. Dale, you've been quiet. What do you think of this plan? Where will you be after they lock Sam in the cage?"

Dale shifted in the backseat and was hesitant to answer Tony's question. It was a double-edged sword. His response could shut down Sam's plan, resulting in his termination. He was certain that Sam would be livid. Or, he could agree with Sam, put her in harm's way, and keep his job. He took a deep breath and mustered his courage.

"Sir, this is a loaded question. If I may be honest, I don't like it one bit. I'm sorry, Sam, but your plan terrifies me. If you grant Sam clearance, and with everyone's permission, I'd like to stay nearby. I'll hang out in her truck, ready to swing into action."

There was a long pause before anyone spoke. Tony replayed the variables in his head, looking for an out. Sam made her case, and he felt backed into a corner. She would be in a secure location and Dale would remain in the area.

"Okay. Sam, do as you describe. Don't be a hero and cost someone their life. Make sure all safety precautions are in place. Dale, I want you nearby in case something goes wrong. For the record, I'm siding with you on this matter. It reeks of desperation and modest planning. I'll repeat what I said earlier, Sam. I am not privy to anything you say or do. You're acting on your own accord. I'm only sitting in this truck to reiterate the park policies and procedures."

"I appreciate your support, Tony. We need to try this."

Tony left and returned to his vehicle. Sam glanced at Dale in the rearview mirror. He sat in silence and stared out the window, ignoring Sam. When she observed his behavior, she second-guessed her plan. It sounded good in theory, but could she pull it off? Instead of sulking longer, Sam turned on the ignition, shifted gears, and pulled into traffic. They needed to return to the cabins to pick up additional equipment and prepare for a long night.

Colleagues of Sam parked the culvert trap close to the forest's edge. The group worked quickly to set up a generator and lighting. While they prepared the site, Dale straddled the culvert trap. He watched for movement and aimed his rifle towards the wooded area. Another person stood guard, scanning for the pack in the opposite direction.

Sam arranged her cramped quarters before someone closed the trapdoor and secured it with a padlock. The group completed their work and said their goodbyes. They planned to sleep in Johnson's cabin and return at first dawn. Even they were hesitant to leave Sam locked in a bear trap in the middle of the park.

Dale stood by the door of the culvert trap with his backside to Sam. He continued to aim his rifle towards the forest. At sunset, the bugs emerged for their feeding. They swarmed around Dale and the artificial lights placed around the trap. The generators drowned out the sound of their buzzing wings and Dale's voice. Sam detected the gloom in his voice as he spoke louder.

"I'll be in the truck. Let me know if you need anything."

"Be safe. Stay inside and don't leave for anything, even if you hear gunfire. If I get one or some, there may be others that escape. Use your walkie to communicate. I added fresh batteries before we left the cabin and extras are in the console. Hurry, before the wolves spot you. Let me know when you're inside. I'll watch from the rear window."

"Yeah. You stay safe, too. It's not too late to back out. No one will think any less of you."

"I know, Dale. I want to give this a shot. If it doesn't work, you pick the next course of action."

Dale glimpsed at Sam. She sat on a pile of pillows and sleeping bags, with her face against the grating. When she spoke, her voice was low and sorrowful. Even in the shadows of the culvert trap, Sam exuded beauty and intellect. Dale's heart sank at the thought of the vulnerable girl locked behind a cage door. He moved forward to kiss her through the grating.

"Dale! What the hell are you doing?"

"Nothing. I thought I heard you say something. It's hard to hear over the generators."

"You puckered your lips. You weren't trying to kiss me, were you?"

"Absolutely not. Remember, I have a girlfriend."

Dale turned a bright shade of red, even noticeable in the absence of sunlight. He looked towards the ground and kicked at an embedded rock with the tip of his boot. She didn't mean to embarrass him, but was pleasantly surprised with his advance. Sam watched with a wide grin spread across her face. If he were anyone else, Sam would send him home. But his innocence flattered her.

"Sorry, my bad. I misinterpreted your movement. How dare I even consider it? If you forgive me, let's wrap it up. I want you to leave for the truck now. Don't forget, message me when you're behind locked doors."

Dale acknowledged her with a wave and disappeared into the darkness. Sam crawled to the back of the culvert trap and struggled to follow his movement through a small window. She noticed the interior lights of her truck when he opened the door and watched as his shadow slid behind the steering wheel. In a moment, her walkie-talkie crackled to life.

"I'm safe and the door's locked. Sorry about that, Sam. You were right. I shouldn't have tried to kiss you. Guess

I got caught up in the moment. Can we start over?" Dale asked.

"I'm flattered by your words and attention. If I were a little younger and you were single, I would have let you kiss me through that grating. You're a good man, Dale. Let's cut this conversation short. I need to work, and you need to rest. We have some wolves to kill. Over and out."

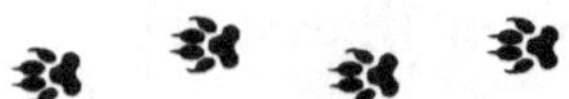

Sam's head jerked when she nodded off. The sounds of the generator and the audio transmission of distressed wildlife lulled her to sleep. She glanced at her cell phone for the time and any missed messages. There were dozens of emails from unknown addresses and unfamiliar people. Sam opened one, scrolling until she reached the signature. It was sent by someone at a small newspaper in the Midwest. Delete. She selected all the messages and deleted them, too. There was no time to respond to these people and their meddlesome inquiries.

"How the hell did they get my email? My website? It's too late for this, and my brain needs rest. Why am I talking to myself? I must be crazy," Sam said. She mumbled to herself, trying to keep herself awake.

To prevent herself from sleeping again, Sam crawled to the back of the trap. She peered through the little window to check on Dale. The interior of her truck was dark, the windows fogged. Sam was relieved that one of them was getting rest.

Sam's muscles ached, and she longed to stand and stretch. Instead, she lay flat on the cool metal, pushing her bedding against the door with her feet. She extended her limbs while tightening her muscles. Oxygen coursed through her veins, waking the sleepy woman. Sam rearranged the pillows and sleeping bags before grabbing her thermos filled with hot coffee. A jolt of caffeine would help at this time of night. She cracked the lid and inhaled the aroma of her worm dirt. It was so thick and dark; it teetered on pouring like sludge. Sam grimaced at the bitter taste. But it worked.

The audio recording went silent. While gripping the thermos, Sam scrolled through the catalog of wildlife calls. She hesitated when the highlight bar stopped over a distressed fawn. She was unsure if the noise would interest a wolf. The bleat of a baby deer sounded like a dog's squeaky toy. Sam selected it anyway. In the wild, this noise attracted other deer. Maybe the fawn would attract the wolves if they knew there were larger prey in the area? Perhaps dire wolves liked squeaky toys? Soon the speaker transmitted the fawn's distress call. If the coffee didn't wake her, the annoying cry of a baby deer would.

When the thermos was empty, Sam crawled to the grating. She wiped the sleep from her eyes and kneaded the muscles of her face. With her nose pressed against the grating, Sam took a deep breath. The fresh air was a reprieve from the rancid stench of bears and scat within her confinement. She fantasized about returning to the cabin for a long, hot shower.

An initial scan of the illuminated grassy area and forest revealed nothing. Something wasn't right. Sam's eyes snapped back and caught the gaze of a dire wolf. The fiery white glow of his eyes locked on Sam. It stood at the edge of the tree line, watching her movement. Sam pulled earplugs from her shirt pocket and crammed them into her ear canals. She slid the earmuffs from her neck onto her head. When the world went silent, she was ready to act.

"There you are," Sam whispered. "Where are your buddies?"

This dire wolf was much larger than the she-wolf carcass in her possession. Sam engaged the beast's gaze while she prepared for battle. Her hand swept the area by her side until her fingers hit the cold metal of a rifle's barrel. Not wanting to startle the wolf, she slowly raised the weapon and slid the muzzle through the grating. Sam disengaged the safety and looked through the scope. The wolf continued to study her.

With the butt of the rifle pressed against her shoulder, Sam slid her finger over the trigger. Before she took the shot, the wolf turned its head. Sam looked away, hoping to spot additional pack members. The surroundings were devoid of other wolves. Not wanting to miss this opportunity, Sam aimed the crosshairs at her target. She pulled the trigger, hitting the wolf in the center of its chest, below the neck. The dire wolf dropped to the ground. Sam reloaded the rifle and scanned the forest edge again.

"Sam! Sam! Did you fire a rifle? Are you okay?"

Sam was oblivious to Dale's frantic voice crackling over the walkie-talkie. Her ears remained covered. When her phone vibrated, Sam glanced at the message. She responded to Dale with one hand while the other still gripped the rifle.

Seconds turned to minutes and minutes into hours. Sam continued to watch the dead beast and scan her surroundings. While she didn't consider herself an expert on the species, Sam assumed she killed the scout. Hopefully, the remaining wolves would scour the area for their missing packmate. One death was satisfying, but the additional loss of wolves would make for a euphoric next day. Sam was locked, loaded, and still high on adrenaline or caffeine. She wasn't certain which of the two was fueling her energy.

Shortly before sunrise, Sam spotted a new dire wolf in the forest. It stayed within the shadows and watched her from the game trail. The wolf sniffed at the air. Sam was unsure if it was interested in her or the carcass that lay on the grass. She lifted the rifle and found the creature in her scope.

Another wolf emerged from the left. It cautiously moved forward after spotting Sam. Like the other, it, too, sniffed the air. With two wolves in her field of vision, Sam weighed her options. Which would be easier to shoot? One was too far to the side, the other lurked in the shadows. She waited. If she fired at one, the other would flee.

The dire wolves crept closer before other pack members appeared. They were aware of Sam, but focused on the dead wolf instead. Sam set down her rifle and picked up another. She had previously loaded it with a magazine to allow her to take multiple shots. After disengaging the safety, she selected her newest target, the wolf to her left.

The sound of gunfire startled the pack. The wolf spotted in her scope fell to the ground after being shot in the chest cavity; it was too easy. Sam pulled the rifle to switch positions, but the sight caught on the grating. This delay gave the wolves time to separate and disappear into the woods. Sam cursed and frantically looked for another target.

After the frenzy and their flight, something caught Sam's attention. The newest kill lay where it fell. The creature appeared smaller and weaker than the other wolves. She scanned back to the original kill. The pack had dragged its body to the trailhead before abandoning it. Sam did a double take. Why would one wolf sacrifice its life so the others could drag a carcass into the woods?

The first rays of sunlight poked through the trees from the east. Sam was confident the pack would not return. Instead, they would retreat deeper into the forest. They had already fed during daylight. However, the wolves had lost two additional pack members. Sam doubted they would risk further loss. It could prove disastrous for the pack and lead to their collapse. She hoped it was the beginning to their end.

Sam slid the earmuffs over her head until they fell to her shoulders. She pulled the plugs out of her ears, chucking them into her backpack. While waiting for her friends to arrive, Sam secured the weapons, rolled the sleeping bags, and packed up her items. After a moment of rest and listening to the hum of the generators, Sam picked up a walkie-talkie.

"Dale. You up?"

"I've been up since the first shot. Hard to sleep through the gunfire. Are you okay? I've been worried about you."

"I'm good. Shot another one, but the pack fled. My damn rifle got caught up in the grating."

"Do you want me to unlock the door now?"

"No. Wait for everyone to arrive. I don't want to take unnecessary risks. We'll chill during this beautiful sunrise and fantasize about a hot shower and clean sheets. Man, I can't wait to spread out and stretch. This metal barrel sucks. Smells, too."

"I hear you. Sleeping upright in your truck wasn't comfortable, either. Hey, I think your friends are turning off. I see their truck now. Hang tight for a little longer. I'm on my way. Over and out."

DAY FOURTEEN

"Let's hurry! I want this space cleared out and activity free. Move it, move it!"

There was a flurry of activity in the small area as everyone worked together to pack up the equipment. Sam's colleagues had hitched the culvert trap to a truck, but the generator and lighting were still in the field. Dale stood watch with his rifle loaded, ready to take down approaching wolves.

Tony arrived at the scene after receiving a message from Sam. Like her, he was ecstatic about the dead dire wolves. He watched Sam open a tarp and spread it across the grass. Tony stood on a corner to hold it in place while she dragged the small carcass into its center. He left Sam to finish her work and wandered to the wolf at the tree line.

"I wouldn't stand there," Dale said.

"Why? It's dead, right?" Tony asked. He looked at the carcass and nudged it with his shoe.

"If one of these things is in the bush, it'll grab you before I can shoot. You'll be on today's menu. Best to back up and widen the space between you and the forest."

Those words motivated Tony to move immediately. He stood behind Dale and watched the activity from afar. With help from her friends, Sam wrapped the remaining wolf carcass in a new tarp. After enclosing both wolves in the canvas, they slid the bodies into the back seat of her truck. Sam offered her appreciation before her colleagues left. Dale and Tony joined Sam next to the pickup for further instruction and additional information.

"Sam, where are you taking those?"

"Tony, I am taking these bad boys, or girls, to a secret place. You said, in so many words, you don't want to know anything about this operation. Right?" Sam said. She gave him a wink and slammed the rear door with her hip.

"What's your plan for today? Tonight?"

"I'm not sure yet. We'll stash these carcasses, shower, and rest. I'm hungry, dirty, and exhausted. Aaron's on his way back to the park. He texted that has good news. I assume it's confirmation these things are dire wolves. Before I do anything else, we need his advice to catch the rest of the pack."

"Wouldn't that be the most damn thing? Dire wolves in Yellowstone? Where do you think the others are hiding?"

"I'm hoping they stick around this area, at least tonight. I don't foresee the wolves leaving before then. They lost two pack members, possibly the alpha or beta. Hey, it looks like everyone is on their way out. Let's get going, too. I don't want to give the wolves a reason to flee."

"Sure thing. If you need me, you know how to reach me. I'll be back in my office keeping the masses of pains in the asses away. Everyone wants to know every detail of your hunt."

"Thanks, Tony. It's much appreciated."

Sam watched the other vehicles from her party head north. She pulled up to the pavement, but parked the pickup on the shoulder instead of heading south. With binoculars in hand, Sam jumped into the bed of her truck and scanned the forest for several minutes. She hoped the wolves would reappear to look for their missing pack mates. There was no movement, prompting her to return to the driver's seat.

"Nothing?" Dale asked. He was still gripping his rifle, wanting to take down a wolf or wolves. Although impressed with Sam's shooting skills, he desired his own kill. It didn't bode well for his masculinity. His friends would tease him and demand he surrender his man-card. He imagined the conversation and laughter playing out when he returned home. "Why don't we give the culvert trap one more try? I can stay inside tonight."

"I'm not sure they'll fall for it a second time. We'll concoct a new plan to catch the wolves off guard. Let's dump these guys off with the frozen she-wolf and head back to the cabin. I'm curious about Aaron's findings."

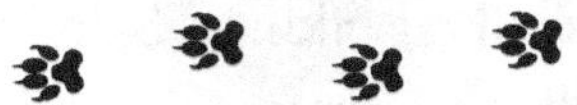

Sam stumbled out of the bedroom, more tired than when she laid down for a nap. It wasn't the sound of approaching tires on gravel that woke Sam, but another nightmare. She sat up, delirious and sweaty, before she realized she was in the safe confines of her bedroom. Sam glanced at her phone's clock and balked. It was much later than she had hoped. There was still much work to do before sunset, and she wanted to talk to Aaron before taking him to study the dead wolves.

Dale wasn't able to sleep during this time. Sam slept through the first few of her alarms before Dale crept into her room and turned it off. The annoying sound carried through the small cabin, preventing him from catching rest, too. To bide his time, Dale gorged on food while tinkering with Sam's laptop. He reviewed her research and tracked their tagged bears.

"Good afternoon, Sam."

Aaron sat on the couch and addressed Sam when she entered the living area. He had just arrived and wore dressy clothing. There was little doubt that he was a scientist or had just left a university's campus. Sam acknowledged him with a half-smile and a nod. She took a seat across from Dale at the kitchen table. He looked glum, as if something was eating at him. Sam was afraid to ask.

"What's up, Dale?"

"While you were sleeping, I was poking around your laptop. I don't know if I ran the one report incorrectly, but something's off with the mama bear in Hayden Valley. She hasn't moved in two days. Tag number 74..."

Before he finished speaking, Sam grabbed the laptop from Dale. She slid it across the table and swung the screen around to look at the data. The image of the bear's movement looped over and over. Dale was right. The GPS on her collar tracked the sow entering the forested area near the dire wolves. The grizzly's activity now remained dormant.

"We need to check on this bear. Something's not right. If the wolves killed the mama and her baby survived, I need to get her. We need to go now."

"Sam, maybe it's a faulty signal? We can't go into this area, not without reinforcements. That's where the wolves are. Let's think this through and not react based on emotion."

"Not wolves, dire wolves," Aaron said. "The DNA testing is incomplete, but I compared specific markers. The lab will email the reports when they're finished. They're also running additional tests, so I can be one hundred percent certain. Based on the information I looked at this week, I'd bet my career on it. These are dire wolves. Can you believe that? Dire wolves."

Sam thought about what Aaron had said, but her mind raced back to her grizzly bears. Until now, the bears had avoided the new predators. It couldn't be faulty equipment, and the mama bear didn't wiggle herself out of the collar. There was too much of a coincidence. The zig-zag pattern of her movement reflected an animal in distress. Something stalked her and her baby until she stopped or until something stopped her.

"I get that, but we need to go. I need to know what happened to my bear."

"Let's not rush and make a stupid move, Sam," Dale replied. "This may sound farfetched, but what if this is a trap? I've seen movies like this. The bad guys kill or maim someone to use as bait and lure their target out of hiding. What if the wolves are doing this to get to you?"

"That's preposterous! How would a wolf know I track grizzly bears? Why do they want me?"

"If you secured the collar, the device may smell like you. The dire wolves watched you last night. They know what you look like. They also know your scent. It's familiar to them. You've been to Hayden Valley, the river, the marina, the employee housing, the campground, the lake. You took two of theirs, and they want to take you. It's payback, Sam. We know nothing about these creatures. The dire wolves haven't perfectly aligned with the behavior displayed by gray wolves. Maybe they are up to something? It may be a trap, just like the movies. Please, Sam."

Sam and Dale turned to Aaron. They sounded like an old married couple, going back and forth. They needed input from a third party to solve their differences. Anything Aaron said would only fuel the conversation, possibly directing their anger towards him. He thought for a moment before finally speaking.

"During my entire career, educators have conditioned me to believe dire wolves are big, stupid predators. They have small brain cavities. Therefore, they aren't as intelligent as today's canines. We have recovered dire wolf remains by the thousands in the La Brea tar pits. They came to take advantage of an easy meal, those stranded in the sticky asphalt. We assumed they were more like scavengers, hence the large numbers recovered amongst the other mammal bones. Everything you've told me, everything I've heard, it makes no sense. My brain can't wrap itself around this discovery. It contradicts everything in the scientific community, everything I know and understand. Until several days ago, it was an extinct species. Our knowledge about dire wolves is based on bones and bone fragments. Now, I realize how little we know. Anything is possible at this point. We need to study their behavior, movement, social organization, their age, diet. I can go on forever."

"We don't have forever, and we will not study them. I'm going to kill them, Aaron. We have until tonight, which is a few hours from now. How do we entice the wolves to leave the safety of the forest? Better yet, I'm making an executive order. Let's search for my bear and its cub. I'm getting sidetracked by this dire wolf nonsense. If you like, we can drop you off at the restaurant. We stashed the two additional kills in the freezer. They're fresh, not frozen, so you shouldn't have difficulty handling them. Are you up for it?"

"Absolutely!"

"We'll drop you off and pick you up later. Make sure you stay locked inside the restaurant and don't speak to anyone," Sam said.

"I'd rather spend time with dead ones than face the living, especially on their turf. You have my word, Sam. I won't do anything to betray your trust. I want to be part of this discovery. It's a once-in-a-lifetime event."

"Good boy, Aaron. Let's ship out, guys. Dale, grab the guns and ammo. I'll grab a jacket and get my equipment. Let's track this mama bear and her baby."

They recognized nothing in the forest. The sun began its descent, and the wind meandered through the trees. Sam was unsure if she detected movement from the wolves as the thicket swayed and rustled under the darkness cast by tree branches. Her truck's headlights added to her distress by casting additional shadows within the depths.

"You're not going in there, are you? We can't see anything. What am I firing at? If I shoot blindly, I may hit you."

"Dale, the last transmission we received was located straight ahead. The bears should be there. If I walk a straight line, I'll find her. Or them. Them as in the bears, not the wolves," Sam said.

"Yeah. Do you realize the wolves will know you're here as soon as you step outside the truck? They're undoubtedly watching us right now. Isn't that what you said?"

"Have I said that? It sounds like you're trying to talk me out of this?"

"Let's not get started on your carbon footprint. You've driven a heavy vehicle off-road and plan to trudge through the flawless brush. How does that align with the values and responsibilities of someone working in the park?"

"Mr. Dale Wright, I'm wondering whose side you're on? Shouldn't you be preparing your rifle?"

"I'll tell you what. I'll go in with you. We're a team, right? Whatever happens to you might happen to me. Or just me. The blood on your hands should be easy to wipe off. When I'm gone, you can continue studying the grizzlies. After all, you'll possess the collar and its tracking information. Perhaps you can name a boar after me? Or number it twenty-two, like my age?"

"You're mad, Dale."

"I think you're stalling. You and I have every right to be scared shitless. There is something large, with massive sharp teeth, waiting to feast on our frail bodies. Let's call it a night. We can check in with Aaron and review the video footage. We'll see how many of these things have survived. How many are in that forest, waiting for you to step into their territory? I'm guessing there's at least one. One that can tear you apart before my finger can pull a trigger. Seriously, Sam. I won't think any less of you. The sow and her cub are dead. There's nothing more we can do for them. Let's take out these dire wolves first. Afterward, I can help you recover the grizzlies and the tracking collar."

"What if mama bear held off the wolves long enough for her baby to climb a tree? The cub might starve to death."

"The wolves already killed a human baby despite a fight and flight. They won't hesitate to take out a bear cub. Let's be smart about this. Yes, it's a probability that the cub survived. No, it's not worth risking our lives for a look. Who will protect the bears or educate the visitors if something happens to you? Nicole and the W.O.L.F. TEAM?"

"That was a low blow. You reek of desperation, Dale," Sam responded. She finally broke her gaze with the forest to look at Dale.

"You are an intelligent, strong, and beautiful woman. It would be a shame if the wildlife community lost someone like yourself."

"How do my looks affect my work? You are grasping at straws! I'll give you points for the intelligent part, though."

"Let's go with this scenario. The wolves tear up your face. You survive, and now you're left with atrocious scars and missing chunks of flesh. We are in the middle of nowhere, so you can't get the cosmetic surgery you require. Anyway, that leaves horny young men with no career aspirations. Yep, horny young men like me. We'll roam the earth, seeking some sort of direction in life. If only that beautiful wildlife biologist were to visit our classroom on career day to speak about her bears? But she no longer exists. Sounds pathetic, I know."

"That is the worst persuasive speech I've ever heard. I truly hope you're not that shallow of a person, Dale. Did I persuade you to become a wildlife biologist? Which elementary school did you attend?"

"I made that part up. We never met before, and no, I'm not that shallow. Beauty is only skin deep, blah, blah, blah.

The horny part was true. I had to insert some sort of fact you'll believe. As you said, I'm grasping at straws."

"Let's get out of here. I'm not sure which is worse, you or the wolves. Just this once, I'll give you a victory. I don't want to be locked in this truck with you any longer. The real Dale is finally emerging. Maybe we should arrange for a conjugal visit with your girlfriend to ease your self-diagnosed horniness?" Sam said. She winked at him before starting the truck and leaving Hayden Valley.

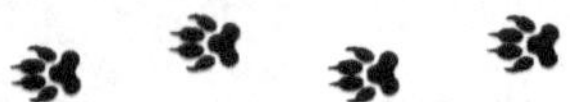

Aaron squatted outside the freezer, jotting notes on his notepad. When Sam and Dale entered the restaurant, he barely acknowledged them. The fluorescent lights buzzed and flickered, more so than during previous visits. Sam couldn't help but imagine it as a hallway of horrors, especially with three dire wolf carcasses stashed out of sight.

"So, what's the verdict? What can you tell me about the pack by looking at the remains? Did I bag the alpha or cripple the pack?"

"Mmm," Aaron responded. He finished scribbling and sketching before closing the cover. "Did you retrieve the collar and find your bears?"

"No. Dale convinced me to hold off. Did you even hear what I said a moment ago?"

"Sorry. I was in deep thought. What was that?"

"What can you tell us about the dead wolves?"

"Oh, boy! Did you collect some great samples, or what? Follow me into the freezer. They're still on display. Watch your step and be careful. It's a little tight."

Sam and Dale followed Aaron into the freezer. Despite coming from the same pack, they were different sizes yet still larger than a gray wolf. Each wolf's coat was a similar reddish color, but one was a tad lighter and one slightly darker. Aaron grinned from ear to ear, excited to explain his observations.

"Bear with me while I speak and save questions until I finish talking. I'm not trying to appear rude, but this discovery is astonishing, and my brain is all over the place! Let's get to it!" Aaron said. "Okay, we have three dire wolves from the same pack, correct?"

"Yes," Sam replied. She wasn't sure if it was a trick question. Aaron bobbed his head when she responded.

"Okay. I've arranged the wolves in size order. The first one is a small female wolf, a she-wolf. She was the specimen you collected last night. The middle is the original she-wolf that I used to collect tissue samples. The third is a male. I'll get to him last. Let's start with the similarities. All three are fairly young. Their teeth are free of disease except for the first she-wolf. Again, their coats are thick and healthy except for the first she-wolf. Each has a hearty muscle mass and strong bones, except for the first she-wolf."

"Why do you continue saying they're young and similar if they're not?" Sam asked.

"Quick question. Why did you kill the smallest one? Tell me how it played out last night."

"The male emerged from a game trail much earlier. I shot and killed him first. The female approached from the left a few hours later. She was alone in the field. The rest of the pack watched on the game trail within the forest boundaries. Because she was the easiest shot, I took her down."

"It makes sense now. One more piece of the puzzle. The smallest she-wolf is probably the omega. She is like the runt of a litter. An omega is normally the smallest female, male, or both a male and female in a pack. The omega may be an outsider or the youngest littermate. Because this pack just appeared in Yellowstone, I'll assume she is the alpha's offspring. We'll run DNA testing later to confirm this. Getting back to my observations, the pack keeps the omega around for several reasons. Sorry if this is too much information. Let me get to the point. She's small because she's on the bottom of the pecking order. She will eat last, after the others. If you look at her muzzle and around her face, she has many scars and injuries that have healed. The omega is like a punching bag. The other wolves in her pack will vent their aggressions on her. Enough to cause injury, but not kill her."

"So, why does she stay with the pack?" Dale responded.

"It's her family? For safety? If she left the pack, other wolves would kill her. She's not strong or healthy enough to survive on her own. Plus, she knows no other way. It's like humanity, children that grow up in abusive relationships are likely to continue them into adulthood. Okay, let's get back to this wolf. You stated she was alone. That's another trait of the omega. Although they are part of the pack, they are not part of the pack. The omega is like an outcast and will bring up the rear. That is why she approached from a different direction."

"Will a pack sacrifice the omega for the good of the pack?" Sam asked.

"I don't follow?"

"I shot the male between the culvert trap and the tree line. He lay dead until the omega showed up. While she distracted me, the others dragged the male's carcass to the forest edge. They only abandoned him when I turned my attention to the pack. Why would they do that?"

"They dragged him? Are you sure?"

"I'm most definitely sure. I thought maybe it was the alpha, and they wanted his body back. To mourn or something. I'm not up with wolf culture and practices."

"Wolves don't mourn in the same sense as we do. Possibly cannibalism? He's a healthy and large male. They have documented gray wolves eating their own, especially when food is scarce. Do you know when the pack last ate?"

"Yesterday, they ate some people. Sounds kind of odd saying, but yes, they took down cyclists that stopped for a bison stampede."

"I saw that on the news, but the details were sketchy. Anyway, wolves will eat people, but we're not their preferred food source. They need a higher fat content to stay healthy. Although they're eating us, we don't provide the nutrition they require to build muscle and grow healthy coats. Especially with winter approaching."

"So, what role does this male play in the pack? Is he the alpha?"

"I highly doubt it. It's possible, but not probable. You most likely eliminated the scout and beta."

"The other male I spotted was almost as large, if not larger. How are you sure?" Sam replied.

"The scout is often the beta, second in command after both alphas. He'll search for prey ahead of the pack. If something were to happen to the alpha male, the beta will probably replace him. The beta will breed with the alpha female and now identify as the new alpha male. Of course, everything I've told you is based upon our knowledge of gray wolves."

"Yeah. There's no telling what this pack is capable of. Let's wrap these carcasses up and lock the building. We need to review camera footage and get a headcount on this pack.

Once we know how many are remaining, I want to come up with a new plan. They've overstayed their welcome."

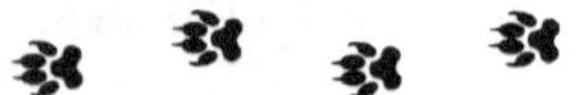

Grainy and printed images of the dire wolves lay sprawled across the kitchen table. Sam, Dale, and Aaron leaned over the printouts to identify the individual characteristics of each wolf. They referenced them against the clear photos on the laptop before marking the papers with highlighters and tagging them with neon flags.

"What do you think? Do we agree on the number of wolves in this pack?" Sam asked. She felt as if they had looked at each photo a million times. Sam was tired and couldn't handle another round of comparison and debate. She rubbed her eyes until someone spoke.

"Based on these images, yes," Aaron replied to Sam. "Unless other dire wolves remained off-camera and avoided the lens. For example, any pups that may have remained in a den. But I don't think that applies here, given our knowledge about the pack, their movement, and the season. It's too late in the summer. Anyway, look at the dire wolf on the outskirts, right there. It looks like the omega. She's smaller, and those lines on her muzzle resemble her facial scars. The one leading the pack looks like the beta. That daunting pair behind him is likely the alphas. Yes, it's safe to suggest we have identified and counted the entire pack. The strongest wolves to the weakest ones."

"Yeah, I agree with Aaron. I think we have eight more wolves to track down and hunt. There are eleven different wolves in these photos," Dale said.

"Agree! Next on the agenda. How do we track down and hunt the remaining members of this pack? I think they're intelligent and won't fall for the culvert trap trick again. Aside from me jogging around the open fields to attract their attention, what do you men suggest?"

It was getting late, and the three collapsed onto the chairs that surrounded the table. Sam glanced at the kitchen cabinets, contemplating whether a shot of vodka would stimulate her think-tank. She was sleep-deprived and running out of steam. Dale looked at her disapprovingly until Sam caught his gaze.

"Let's look at this another way," Aaron said. He interrupted their stare-off.

"Shoot away! All ideas are welcome."

"What have the dire wolves hunted since they've appeared in Yellowstone? What have they accomplished?"

"I hope this isn't a trick question, as my brain is shutting down. They've hunted deer, elk, moose, bison..."

"No. Well, yes. That's not the answer I'm looking for. You know this, Sam. What have they hunted?"

"Man? They've put quite a dent in the human population this summer."

"Let me try again with a new question. What is the opposite of the dire wolf's prey?"

"Ugh, Aaron! You're making me think way too much. I'll go with other predators. That's the opposite of prey. Is that the correct answer? Dale, help me out." Sam asked. Dale looked at her with sleepy eyes and shrugged his shoulders. When he yawned, Sam yawned as well.

"Exactly! According to what you've told me, the dire wolves have chased the other predators from the park. Most notably, the gray wolves. Plus, the dire wolf pack slaughtered those gray wolves that were left behind. Correct me if I'm wrong?"

"You're on to something. I think I follow. Keep going, Aaron."

"The dire wolves view other predators as a threat. What if we lure them to a location somewhere in the open, where we can eliminate them? We can use another predator to do that for us."

"How? It's difficult to capture wolves. And to use as bait? Don't even consider my grizzlies. I won't risk their lives or ours. Unless... unless we borrow some stuffed wolves or bears from the museums and visitor's centers?" Sam said.

"But the dire wolves like movement. Easier said than done, I guess? It sounds good in theory, but we need to make it work. How can we make stuffed animals work? Think, think, think." Aaron asked. He stood up and paced the cabin.

"Come on, Sam. You're a native. How did you discount wolf urine? That's easy to come by. Someone in the area should have a bottle or jug they'll donate? We can spray the hell out of the area to lure them into the open," Dale replied.

While Aaron grimaced at the mental image of a jug of wolf urine, Sam grinned. The potent liquid was used to scare and deter garden pests. Someone would have it, especially in Wyoming. Herds of deer could annihilate someone's vegetable garden in one visit. Sam knew plenty of people that would have the urine stored in their garages and workshops.

"That's a great idea, Dale! We can spray a trail leading to us."

"Where will we ambush them? How will we ambush them?" Aaron asked.

"They like the brush. We can lure the dire wolves from one forested area to another. I'm sure we can find the perfect location in Hayden Valley. There are lots of clusters of trees," Sam said.

"We can set up tree stands and shoot from those! With a clear shot from above, we'll take down the rest of the pack. We'll end their carnage within minutes."

Dale was excited about this plan. He had more experience stalking prey by foot, but once used a tree stand while hunting wild boar in Texas. The tree stands offered better vantage points and would keep him and Sam safe and away from danger. They could sit idle for hours, waiting and watching for the dire wolves.

"Yeah. Yeah. That will work, I think. I'll send out some texts tomorrow morning to round up supplies. I'm sure we can get everything set up before nightfall. Oh, and night-vision goggles. Just like the poachers used. I'll put out a request for those, too," Sam said. She scribbled notes and looked at Aaron. "Have you ever fired a weapon?"

"Do I look like I know how to shoot? I've never touched a gun in my life. I'm from the city, not the bush. My work tools are nothing more than a brush and dental pick. I'm handy with kitchen knives, though. I can slice a mean head of cabbage for kimchi."

"Are you serious? I need you to kill wolves, not feed them Korean delicacies. You are Korean, right? Regardless, I'll request a stand for you, too. If you can't shoot the dire wolves, you can help spot them. You'll be our extra set of eyes in the trees. And for the record, I met a spectacular young lady from Los Angeles this summer. She could probably shoot better than anyone in this cabin."

Sam stood and stretched before leaning over the table to stack the papers. Dale had since fallen asleep, his arms crossed, and his head dropped. Sam gently nudged his shoulder until he stirred and finally rose. He meandered down the hallway towards his bedroom while Aaron tucked a sheet around the couch cushions. Sam locked the door and started turning off the lights.

"Thank you for including me on this adventure, Sam. Everyone at the museum will be so envious when this is over. Notably, when I waltz through the door with a fresh carcass in hand. I feel like I'm living in a dream, on cloud nine, to be exact. Someone needs to pinch me."

Aaron adjusted his pillow, then plopped on the sofa, lifting his feet and covering his body with a blanket. He stared lovingly at Sam, failing to hide his admiration. She glanced at him, shooting him a smile as she tenderly blinked her eyelashes. Her eyes sparkled when she finally spoke.

"Not a dream, my dear Aaron. This here is a nightmare. Your cloud nine is a puff of steam emitted from our little slice of hell. A pinch won't be necessary," Sam said. She turned the remaining light off, pitching the cabin's interior into darkness. Aaron listened to her feet shuffle atop the wood flooring before her bedroom light switched on. Sam raised her voice. "If you're not careful, Aaron, something will bite you. Not just any bite, but a chomp and chew. Tread lightly on these lands and sweet dreams!"

DAY FIFTEEN

After breakfast, everyone piled into Sam's truck. They planned to scout locations for setting up the tree stands for this evening's hunt. There were multiple clusters of thickets in the meadows, perfect for setting up their trap. Sam wanted to select one with sweeping views and limited obstacles. However, it needed to be accessible to vehicles, especially her pickup. No one wanted to march through open fields with arms full of equipment. They would be easy targets with no protection.

Sam's truck traveled north towards Hayden Valley with Aaron in the back seat. Unlike his previous experience with Johnson, Dale refused to surrender his passenger seat to this newcomer. And like his experience with Johnson, he felt threatened by another man's presence. Specifically, around

Sam, his summer crush. Dale lifted her cell phone from the console and read the messages when it chimed.

"Looks like we have everything. Someone's dropping off tree stands at our cabin around eleven. The wolf urine is on the way. That guy said traffic in Jackson and into the park is bumper to bumper. His wife will meet us at the marina around noon."

Additional messages popped up from different people. Sam was thankful for clear cellular reception today, as they needed help from the community. She didn't want to waste time by leaving the park for in-person visits. Dale continued to skim through and read the messages that applied to their project. As the sun blazed through the trees, he shifted positions to avoid the glare on the phone screen.

"The guy sending the wolf pee added that he included some old jugs of buck urine. He said to use whatever we need, throw away the rest. His wife doesn't want it anymore and is thankful to have more space in their workshop," Dale said. He glanced at Sam when he thought of a use for the bonus material. "That could come in handy. We can trick the dire wolves into thinking our fake wolves are tracking some fake deer. Predators and prey, that's what they like to hunt."

"I wonder how many jugs of pee he was storing in his workshop. Are there any more important messages? Did anyone mention night vision goggles? Those are an important part of our plan."

"Yeah, Tony just sent a text. Not about the night vision goggles, though. Tony said to be careful because activists are rallying in the park today. They will interfere with our hunt until politicians pass legislation to protect the dire wolves. He's looking into it. In the meantime, he's sending help to clear them out and offer us protection. Godspeed!"

"Wow! A sad state of the times. Everyone's okay if the dire wolves kill people, I guess. I'm all for the conservation of animals, but these things don't belong here. It's no different from boa constrictors wiping out small reptilia and birds in the Everglades or lionfish decimating the fish population in our coral reefs. What a bunch of jackasses. I wonder what lies ahead?"

"Who knows? I highly doubt this is the last of the dire wolves, anyway. This pack could be one branch from a giant family tree. It wouldn't surprise me if the Canadian wilderness is full of them. Let the protestors save those to the north."

The three remained quiet as Sam proceeded down the road. She occasionally peered into the rearview mirror to watch Aaron's reaction to his surroundings. He stared out the side window, wide-eyed and oblivious to those in the front seat. Sam doubted he heard any of the conversations. She realized he had never traveled to Yellowstone National Park.

"First time here, Aaron?"

"Hmm. Sorry, yes. Yellowstone has always been on my bucket list. I've been so busy with work that I've only traveled as far as Yosemite. It's beautiful here. Maybe when this is over, you can give me the grand tour? I'd love to see more of the wildlife."

"I bet you would," Dale said. He mumbled under his breath. Sam heard his comment and shot him a disapproving glare.

"Dale and I would love to give you the grand tour. Aaron, you haven't seen half of it. We haven't even touched on the springs or geysers. Yellowstone is a remarkable and one-of-a-kind place. Did you know it's the first national park in the United States and possibly the world? Whoa, what do we have here?"

Sam slowed the truck and pulled off to the side of the road. Her passengers grabbed their seats during the bumpy exchange, until the pickup came to a stop. Sam reached for her binoculars without taking her eyes off the activity ahead. Just beyond the clearing, she spotted a line of vehicles parked on the shoulder, bumper to bumper. There was little doubt these were the activists Tony mentioned.

"I don't think Tony is aware of the number of protestors in the park. From what he texted, I assumed there would be a few activists. This is a highly organized rally. These people snake along the road as far as I can see."

"Let me have a look? Are you sure they're protestors? Maybe they came to look for dire wolves?" Dale replied. He grabbed the binoculars from Sam.

"Yeah. Those are protestors. Native Americans? I see a lot of colorful clothing, feathers, some headdresses. Some of their outfits are from Wyoming. I'm not sure about the others. We need to get closer for a better look."

"Native costumes? Can I see?" Aaron asked. He grew excited, wanting to look for himself.

"Not costumes, clothing. It's offensive to call tribal clothing a costume. Costumes are for Halloween. Wait, I think I see a W.O.L.F. SUV. They parked their vehicle between trucks, halfway down the line. There-"

Sam yanked the binoculars from Dale. She scanned the line more slowly until she spotted the vehicle. There was little doubt that W.O.L.F. had organized this event. Upon closer inspection, Sam noticed the protestors. They stood in the beds of their trucks, singing, yelling, and waving flags and banners at passing motorists. Traffic slowed as visitors crept along to take videos and photos.

"I think we need a change of plan. If I drive forward, the protestors may block us in. I wouldn't put it past

Nicole to lie about us and exaggerate the truth. She probably instructed them to stop a crazy redhead in a pickup truck."

"I agree, but not about the crazy redhead part. It could turn nasty quickly. If the protestors turn their aggression towards the truck, they could strand us until help arrives. Who knows how long that will take?" Dale said.

"No one's touching my truck. From the look of it, we won't penetrate this line. That means we can't select a location to set up our equipment. We only have so many hours of sunlight, and we need this time to prepare for tonight's hunt. Change of plans, boys. Let's return to the cabin. I'm going to wait for the supplies to arrive, and you two are going on a brief trip."

"I'm not doing this. It's stupid," Dale said. He pulled his ball cap over his eyes to hide his face.

"I think it'll work. No one will suspect a gay couple in a little red compact car of any wrongdoing. You should be able to slip by and get video footage without raising suspicion. Besides, look how cute you are!"

Sam stood facing Dale, repositioning his hat and running her hands over his shirt to remove wrinkles. While she did this, he glared at her with a scowl on his face. After his clothing check, Dale reluctantly took a seat next to Aaron in the car and lowered his window. Sam leaned into the vehicle, resting her chin on her folded arms. She failed to hide her amusement regarding their insecurities.

"This doesn't bode well for my manhood. If my girlfriend finds out, she may rethink our relationship."

"You have nothing to worry over. Aaron and I will never mention this again. Right, Aaron?"

"You got that right. Although, I have to agree with Dale. What if someone videotapes us? If it gets back to my coworkers, they may think the dire wolf tale is a cover-up for a lover's tryst with another man. I am single, you know? Also, should I be worried that Dale is wearing my shirt? You didn't give me a wardrobe check? You're toying with my manhood, Sam."

"How pathetic! You boys are something else. What century are we living in? If it bothers you that much, pretend you are brothers. I need you to do this for me. If I go, they'll know we're up to something."

Aaron and Dale looked at one another, exchanging chuckles. They would play along with Sam's plan, at least for now. When she backed away from the car, Aaron started the ignition.

"Make sure you scout out a place to set up and let me know if Tony had any success clearing these people out. I'll head to the marina shortly for a supply grab. That lady should be there soon. I'll meet you for lunch. My place, lover boys!"

"You owe me, Sam!" Dale responded. He shook his head before raising the window and putting on sunglasses to shield his eyes.

Sam winked as they reversed and drove away. She glanced at her phone for a time check and any new messages. There was much work that needed to be done before nightfall. A trip to the marina was in order, so she didn't keep the lady waiting. Sam jumped in her truck for the quick trip up the road.

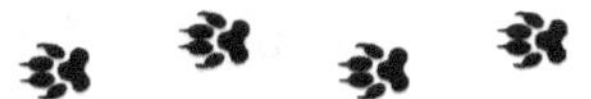

While Dale and Aaron were gone, Sam collected the jugs of urine and a few tree stands. She didn't expect them to be gone as long as they were. To pass time, she cleaned the rifles they would use to take down the rest of the dire wolf pack. Sam emptied cartridges and refilled them with the ammo after giving everything a quick inspection. There would be no room for error tonight. Everything had to be in perfect working order.

When Sam heard a car approaching on the gravel, she grabbed one rifle and headed to the front door. The boys had finally arrived. She stood on the stoop with the safety off as she swept the property for activity with her rifle's scope. Both Dale and Aaron looked alarmed when they walked toward her.

"What's with the rifle?" Aaron asked.

"I have a box of urine in the bed of my truck. Some bottles have leaked or spilled over. I'm not taking any chances with you two out here. The dire wolves could head to our cabin for all I know. Hurry inside."

After everyone was inside the cabin and the door secured, Dale headed to his bedroom to change. He returned to the living space, shirtless, with mussed-up hair. Aside from a slight farmer's tan, Sam found his upper body pleasing. He purposely and slowly flexed his muscles while unfolding his shirt. She had never seen him without clothing and enjoyed his little show.

This must be Dale's ruse to prove his masculinity. *After all that I put the poor boy through. Tsk, tsk,* Sam thought.

Aaron emerged from the bathroom in new clothing. He donned a camouflage Yellowstone t-shirt and khaki shorts.

Somehow, during their leave, they had found time to shop. When he spied Dale's messy hair, Aaron muddled his own. Sam rolled her eyes in response to their childish behavior.

"Have you two recovered from your assignment? The show you're putting on is pretty pathetic."

Sam collected her weapons and stored them before heading to the kitchen for food. She spread out bread, cold cuts, and condiments on the tabletop. During a second trip, she grabbed the plates and utensils. All the while, the room remained silent while the guys took a seat at the table. Dale tapped on his phone screen until he pulled up images he had taken during the ride.

"What took you so long, anyway?"

"Traffic. It's terrible. Protestors created a gridlock traveling in both directions. There is no way we'll access any areas in Hayden Valley to set up the tree stands. I'm not sure what you want to do?" Dale asked.

Dale slid the phone across the table towards Sam. She set her butter knife down and pushed the makings of her sandwich to the side. While she browsed the images and video, the guys helped themselves to the food on the table. Sam looked between them, waiting for someone to speak.

"Not good," Sam said.

"There's no way Tony will clear these people out before sunset. If we're going to act tonight, I'm not sure how we'll go about it. Did you get the supplies while you were here?"

"Most everything. I didn't get any night vision goggles. Our plan's a bust if we can't secure some."

"Can't we use artificial lighting?" Aaron asked.

"Been there, done that. It's good only if the wolves walk into the lighting. Most are smart enough to avoid it. Plus, there are too many shadows. If we're going to do this, we need to do it right. I think we only have one more opportunity. If we blow it, we're done. Tony's been quiet today. I think he's staying off the radar because the shit is about to hit the fan. Dale, who might have goggles? Ideas?"

Dale put a finger up and reached across the table for his phone. He did an internet search, clicking and tapping while Sam watched. She took it as a cue and used the break to eat and conduct a web search on her phone. Aaron remained quiet, unsure what they expected of him.

"Nothing," Dale said.

"Same here. There's a night vision rifle scope at a store in Idaho Falls. That might work. Wait, not available at this location. The closest one is in Casper. We can't get it before tonight. What do you guys suggest?"

"I can make a run for it. The probability of anything happening tonight is slim. Where's Casper from here?" Aaron replied.

"It's about a six-hour drive from here. Give or take, depending on traffic. From what you've said, maybe even seven hours of drive time?" Sam responded. "We don't have that kind of time."

The three sat silently, deep in thought. While brainstorming, they finished their lunch. Dale cleared the table while Aaron pulled up the night vision rifle scopes. He wanted to know more about them. Especially if they were to come up in conversation.

"Maybe we do?" Dale said. He sat across from Sam, watching her for a reaction.

"Maybe we do what?"

"Maybe we have that kind of time, Sam? If we rush today, we may make mistakes. Let's take Tony's advice. He said to go off-grid and disappear. Let's send Aaron to Casper to purchase the scopes. After lunch, we can pack everything we need for a few days. Food, clothing, supplies, weapons."

"And go where, Dale?"

"The last place someone would expect us to hide. All we've talked about recently is Hayden Valley. That's where officials will look and activists will continue to protest. This place may be an even better area to lure the dire wolves. They're familiar with this spot and associate it with food. We'll have total privacy to set up and eliminate the pack. No park officials, no W.O.L.F., no activists. We can take our time and do this right. The best part is Aaron can find us when he returns tomorrow. His little car can easily navigate the road."

Dale stared at Sam with a grin and a twinkle in his eye. It took her a moment to process his description of the location, but Sam caught on. She came back with an enormous smile of her own.

"The campground?"

"Yes, think about it. The campground has been closed and blocked off since Johnson and Gabby's death. It's a no-man's-land. We can easily hide the truck and no one can see anything from the main road. Since the deaths at the Piscary Bridge, you've only talked about taking down the pack in Hayden Valley. We've told everyone that the wolves are traveling north. That's where they expect to find you, us. No one will suspect a thing."

"How do we keep them focused on the valley? What if they catch on to our change of plan?"

"Easy. Let's order the scopes and send Aaron on his way. When he's gone, we pack up anything and everything we'll need for a couple of days. This evening, just before dark, we can head north. We'll make sure the protestors and W.O.L.F. see us on the loop. Perhaps they'll think they've scared us off? When we know we're not being followed, we exit the park. We can reenter at the south entrance after dark and duck into the campground. No one will know where we are. They'll think we're gone."

"How do we lure the wolves to the campground? I was planning to leave a trail of urine from their trailhead in the forest to our tree stands in Hayden Valley. What if they don't come back?"

"My turn to talk," Aaron said. "The La Brea tar pits currently occupy a small city block in Los Angeles. A half-mile by a quarter-mile? That doesn't sound very impressive, right? Despite its size, we have recovered millions of bones and thousands of dire wolves. Why? The La Brea tar pits are sticky asphalt. It's like a glue trap. The animals got stuck and died."

"How does this apply to the rocky ground and forests by the lake in Yellowstone?" Sam replied.

"I was getting to that. Despite the risk of death, predators came to feast on the trapped mammoths, camels, and ground sloths. Not just a few predators, thousands of them. Dire wolves, bears, saber-tooth cats, American lions, the list goes on. They came to this small parcel of land, and not by chance. They came because there was always prey, easy prey. If what we know is true, these dire wolves will return to feed again. They'll return to feed on this speck of land in this giant nature preserve. Just like their ancestors did at the tar pits."

"You have a point. What if these people scared them off today?"

"Possible."

"Possible, no. I doubt it's even probable," Dale said. "We know the dire wolves were in the area when we searched the cabins and employee housing. The noise scared them, and they remained frozen in place. How do we know? When everyone left that evening, the wolves moved on. That same night, they killed the men at the Piscary Bridge. Then the pack headed into the outer borders of Hayden Valley. If you ask me, they're still in that area. The wolves will lie low until the coast is clear. Remember, they have remained hidden from man since the ice age. It's their most effective defense and has contributed to their survival."

"True."

"If we can drop a urine trail at the beginning of Hayden Valley to the campground, they'll likely return. It's not a far stretch. They can easily travel that distance in a few hours, maybe less. Like Aaron said about the predators in the pits, they'll come back for an easy meal. They associate the campground with food. Food that doesn't fight back. I think we can do this. It's the best plan we have to work with."

"How do we mark the trail to lead them back to the lake? Who will do this without getting caught or drawing attention to us? We can't use my truck, or can we? Whom do we trust?"

"Let's not waste any more time. We need to get Aaron on his way and pack. Let's think about this while we work. Worst case, I'll leave a trail after dark tomorrow. We know they don't move until then, anyway."

"Wrong. The wolves attacked the cyclists during daylight," Sam said.

"Yeah, while pursuing a bison calf. Worst case, I'll bike to the clearing and spray the urine. Maybe the wolves will follow me back instead," Dale replied. He winked at Sam before rising to pack his gear.

Sam watched Dale leave the room with a blank expression on her face. Until now, she had led the charge to eliminate the dire wolves. Dale was maturing into a man this summer. He was correct about the location and luring the predators to the campground. When Aaron cleared his voice, she turned her attention to him and forced a smile.

"Sorry. Let me order these scopes, and you'll be on your way."

"Are you ready to do this?" Sam asked.

"Ready as I'll ever be," Dale responded.

The last few hours were excruciating and slow for Sam and Dale. After Aaron's departure, they packed gear and equipment for the next several days. The supplies were in a heap by the front door, out of sight from prying eyes. With all the activity in the park, they didn't know who was watching from where. They wanted no one catching on to their plans.

To prepare for their absence from the cabin, they locked windows, drew the curtains, and closed bedroom doors. They collected anything that acknowledged the dire wolves and stashed it in a backpack to take with them. Sam feared W.O.L.F., activists, or reporters would force entry into the cabin after they departed. They left no valuables and nothing to tie them to the recent activity in the park.

When their work was complete, they sat at the table and listened for activity outside the cluster of cabins. Neither spoke a word, afraid they'd miss something if distracted. During this time, Sam thought about the cardboard box with the animal urine in the back of her truck. She wished it was strong enough to attract the dire wolves to their neck of the woods. It would save her the hassle of tracking and killing the pack elsewhere. Sam would rather shoot them from the safety of her summer home. If only she were that lucky.

The sun had finally started its descent, prompting the pair to load the truck. There was a small window of time for the activists to witness their departure from Yellowstone. It was easier to lose them in the darkness if someone was following. No one knew the back roads and turnoffs better than Sam. The timing meant everything tonight.

"I watch, and you load," she said.

Sam grabbed her rifle and scanned the area surrounding the cabins. While she provided the two with protection, Dale loaded his arms and shoulders with the straps of bags and backpacks. Even if the dire wolves appeared, they couldn't reach him through the supplies that hugged his body. He quickly dumped them in the back seat before grabbing the remaining equipment. After Dale emptied the cabin, he locked the door. He left interior lights illuminated and a radio blaring to give the illusion that someone was inside. Both took a moment to relax when they took their seats in the truck.

"I expected the activists to stop us at our cabin. Nicole knows where we live. I wonder why she hasn't sent a group down here?" Sam said.

"The news crews were in Hayden Valley today. Nicole probably wanted to put herself and her minions in front of the cameras instead. If she split her group up, the numbers wouldn't look as impressive."

"I'm so thankful we don't have access to television. I can only imagine what Nicole's preaching to the world. Hopefully, the viewers see through her bullshit. Hey, I need to stop for gas. We won't get very far with what's left in the tank. All these quick trips back and forth have sucked me dry. Grab my credit card so we can get in and out. I don't want to stay any longer than we have to."

Sam navigated the familiar gravel lane, eventually turning onto the main road. Headlights traveled in both directions as tourists headed back to their accommodations. She was thankful that no one had taken an interest in their movement. So far, everything had gone as planned.

"It's a little too quiet in these parts."

"That's going to help with our hunt. All the action is in Hayden Valley. That's where they expect us to turn up. If we drive by and the activists see us, they'll think they won. I expect they'll stay even longer to keep you away. Nicole's not as smart as she appears. We got her, Sam."

"I hope you're right, Dale. What if they don't see us?"

"They will. Lower your window and flick those long red locks into the wind. No one will miss you. Especially the men," Dale responded. He watched her reaction from the corner of his eyes. Sam forced a grin, unlike herself and her bubbly personality. The stress of the previous days and the upcoming hunt was showing.

As they passed the campground, Dale turned in his seat to check the entrance. Although he couldn't see anything, the lane leading to the campsites was dark and free of activity. He noted the same for the employee housing turnoff and the marina. The park still blocked all three locations with barricades to restrict access, but no longer staffed them with security officers. Dale was relieved to know that they could slip inside, unnoticed.

The protestors came into view when Sam's truck emerged from the forested area. Their line of vehicles remained parked on the shoulder, still bumper to bumper. It appeared they planned to spend the night in their cars or camp in the bed of their trucks. Their energy had dwindled in the heat of the sun. No one appeared to notice Sam pass in the fading light. Or so she thought.

"What do you think about the group now compared to earlier today? Have you seen a W.O.L.F. vehicle yet? I hope Nicole's not abandoning these people to sleep in her air-conditioned camper tonight. It looks like she's leaving them to do the dirty work."

"Yeah. I don't see any signs of Nicole. We definitely would've seen one of their vehicles by now."

"I think you're right about everything. This line of cars wouldn't let us pass to access the meadows. There is no way we could get back to our previous location, even to spread some urine. We need to think about how we'll do that without them noticing. Man, I can't believe how long this line of cars is. I have to give them credit. They're a strong-willed group of people."

Before she could continue, a pickup abruptly left the line of vehicles and stopped in front of Sam. A man hopped out of the passenger's seat and approached her truck. He gripped something that reflected light from her headlights. Sam leaned out the window for a better look. She moved her hand to her waist until it touched the cold metal of her pistol that hung from her belt. Dale looked nervously out the windows to ensure no one was approaching from elsewhere.

"You can stop right there," Sam said.

The man stopped and lifted his hand that gripped the object. He clicked a button and started talking to someone. Relieved that it was a walkie-talkie, Sam shifted her hand away from the pistol. She listened to the stranger confirm it was Sam in the pickup, and he was talking to her now. After ending his brief conversation, he pulled a flashlight from his belt and shone the light into the truck's bed. He peered into the back seat before looking at Sam and Dale.

"Where are you going? It looks like you are skipping town," he said.

"Yes. This is not what I signed up for. I've been working in Yellowstone for years. My job is to protect the animals, not slaughter them. I want out before things end badly. I have a reputation to uphold," Sam replied. She was doing her best to lie and not arouse his suspicion.

"You already made them end badly for three of our wolves. How many more of our spirit animals will you murder? Do you understand the significance of these beautiful creatures? They symbolize loyalty and family, amongst other things. We will not allow you to take any more."

"I didn't understand their importance to your people until today. I was under the assumption that this was a new predator that was killing people, innocent people. Or so they led me to believe."

"Who told you?"

"Before I answer that, what have you learned about these wolves?"

Sam was trying her best to prevent their exchange from escalating. She grew annoyed with this man's referring to these monsters as wolves. Dale realized where the conversation was heading. He feared Sam might say something that would interfere with their plans. He put a hand on her leg and leaned over.

"I'm sorry to cut this conversation short. I need to get to Bozeman for a flight. Do you mind if we go on our way?"

"It's a little late for a flight tonight. Don't you think?"

"It is. My flight is at seven-thirty tomorrow morning."

"Where are you going?"

"Dallas."

The man peered through the window behind Sam again. He used his flashlight to inspect the bags and backpacks before tucking the light under his armpit. He pulled a cell phone out of his pocket to look up flights on the internet. While the man waited for the pages to load, he waved for traffic to pass. Those held up behind Sam's truck grew impatient.

"What flight number?"

"Here, here's my itinerary," Dale responded. He flashed his phone's screen at the man while he compared the information to his search. His lips twisted before he finally spoke.

"I'll let you pass. If you know what's best, you'll leave Yellowstone and not return. This is our land, and these are my animals. It is not your will to do as you like. We will not allow you to assume the role of God."

"Thank you," Sam said. "Can I get your name?"

"Who I am is not important. We are all the same people with the same beliefs. Go before I change my mind."

Sam put the truck into drive and swerved around the man when he stepped to the side. She nodded her head and offered a quick wave of thanks. Dale watched in the side mirror to make sure no one followed. Neither said a word until they were sure the only cars behind them held tourists.

"What the fuck was that?" Sam asked. "Bozeman? A flight? His land? I'm playing God? What dimension did I just enter?"

"That was the first time anyone scared me shitless. While we were waiting at the cabin today, I ran through every scenario in my head. Just to be safe, I made a screenshot of a flight itinerary. Lucky for us, he only glanced at the schedule. Holy crap!"

"I wish I knew who that was. He wasn't a local. I'm not sure where he came from. Where the hell did Nicole find these people?"

"I took a picture when the truck stopped. We have the plate number and a grainy image of the guy. I didn't take additional shots because I didn't want to get caught," Dale said. He expanded the picture with his fingers.

"Aren't you the sly guy? Great job, Dale."

They continued up the road, following the Yellowstone River as it snaked along Hayden Valley. A large herd of bison grazed in the northern meadows. Sam took that as a promising sign. The mammals appeared relaxed as they ate tender shoots of grasses or the calves nursed. Young bulls butted heads while some rolled in patches of dirt. Seeing their behavior was encouraging. That meant the dire wolves were not in this area.

After topping off the gas tank in the Canyon Village, Sam and Dale changed direction. Instead of driving for the nearest exit, Sam headed deeper into the park. The activists would expect her to follow this route to Bozeman if they were following. It validated the plans they shared with the strange man in Hayden Valley. Sam was even more thankful for the change of direction because it would save them time.

Without warning, Sam made an abrupt right. She drove onto a dirt road surrounded by trees before she reached the next intersection. With the headlights off, she made a U-turn to face traffic. To her relief, no one was on the road to witness her odd behavior. Sam and Dale waited patiently, watching the cars pass and looking for signs of anyone that might follow their trail.

It was now pitch black, and traffic had all but stopped. When they deemed their reentry safe, Sam turned on the headlights and hastily proceeded to the intersection where the road divided. No one approached from behind or in either direction. At that moment, Sam turned south on the Grand Loop Road. It was time to return to the campground and set up for the slaughter.

DAY SIXTEEN

fter turning south the previous night, it took Sam almost four hours to reach the campground. Dark skies and many animal crossings slowed their drive. Unlike the east side of Yellowstone, the rest of the park was still teeming with wildlife. It surprised Sam that the dire wolves had made such a devastating impact around the lake during such a short period. Not once did she slow for deer or moose by the lake.

Sam chose a spot in the back of the campground, nestled in the trees and away from prying eyes. Unless someone knew where to look, they would not find her. Although they had planned to stay close to the restrooms, Sam reconsidered. No one had removed the yellow crime scene tape from the door, and she imagined the sights and smells of the dried blood and missed brain matter. They would sleep in the truck and pee in the woods instead.

Before bedding down for the night, Sam touched base with Aaron. He had arrived in Casper earlier that day. Aside from the scopes, Aaron purchased three ghillie suits. He intended to provide everyone with additional camouflage during the takedown. Sam thought it unnecessary until Dale convinced her that the shaggy shades of green might confuse the dire wolves.

Several messages came through from Tony. Rather than read or acknowledge them, Sam deleted everything. They had come too far to abandon their plans and return to the cabin. She would not quit until the wolves lay dead around her feet. Sam couldn't wait to display their bodies for the world to see.

Dale slept through the slamming door, the bright sun, and the various bird calls. When the pickup bounced, he stirred. Dale pulled the sleeping bag away from his face and lifted his seat from its reclined position. Panic struck when he noticed Sam's blanket and pillow heaped in a pile on her seat.

"Sam!"

"Back here. It's time to get up. We have a slight problem," Sam said. He noticed her silhouette behind the rear window.

Dale rolled out of the truck and stretched his limbs. Despite the space in the cab, it wasn't ideal for a good night's rest. He longed for an oversized bed in a cool, darkened room with a woman by his side. When he noticed Sam's back turned to him, Dale walked behind some thick brush to empty his bladder.

"So, what's the problem?" Dale responded. He shook, tucked away his goods, and zipped his jeans. He approached Sam as he wiped his hands down the sides of his legs.

"I've checked these tree stands, but only one is whole and safe to use. They wore the teeth out on these cinch straps, and they won't grab the straps. See," Sam said. She locked the cinch and pulled the frayed straps through the metal piece. "Those climbing sticks are bent or rusted. I'd be afraid to put any weight on them."

"It looks like only one of us is going up the tree."

"I am."

"No. I won't let you. You'll be safer in the truck."

"Don't give me the macho man crap. Wyoming is the equality state, and I can do this just as well as you, if not better. Your ass is staying down here. Let's set this up and tweak our plans for tonight."

"You're right. Wyoming is the equality state. Do it yourself," Dale responded sarcastically. Sam punched his shoulder when she noticed his smile.

Over the next hour, they selected a mature lodgepole pine directly across from the restroom. Sam and Dale worked together to secure the ladder of aluminum sticks to the tree. When the pieces were in place, Sam shimmied up the trunk. She carried the stand fastened to her back. Sam tethered the equipment to the tree, tightening the cinches before lifting the platform upright. Sam further tightened the straps to remove the slack. When she pulled the stand downward, she shook it. The platform wouldn't budge.

Sam removed her lineman's rope and tethered herself to the safety rope. She sat on the tree stand, looking out towards the campground. From atop the tree, she had a clear shot of the rooftop. It was still stained with blood. Sam had an idea. She tethered herself to the lineman's rope once more, released the clip to the safety rope, and descended from her stand.

"I have an idea. From up there, I have a clear view of the area. What if we replicate Johnson's plan the night the dire wolves killed him?"

"What do you mean?"

"We pull my truck up against the building, giving them easy access to the rooftop. The dire wolves traversed that route before and may associate it with an easy meal. Once they're up there, you pull away. The wolves will be stuck with nowhere to go. During this time, I can pick them off. It'll be like shooting fish in a barrel."

"What if they jump down and get away?"

"That's a pretty steep drop. The wolves will probably injure themselves."

"We can't chance it. What if we lay something down around the building to ensure the wolves injure themselves?"

"Like what? Nails and boards?" Sam asked.

"Can we text Aaron and have him stop at a home supply store for some bird spikes? The kind the park uses to prevent birds from landing on trusses in some of the buildings. We can lay them out in various places around the restroom. If a wolf lands on a strip, it'll prevent them from going anywhere. The spikes are pretty long and can inflict serious damage."

"Great idea! I'll text him now," Sam said. She pulled her phone out and sent a message instructing him to purchase every bird spike between Casper and Yellowstone.

"How will we lure them to the rooftop?"

"We have a bed full of metal bars from the tree stands, sleeping bags, a couple of pillows, and a roll of duct tape. Do you think we can create a fake person? How creative are you? It'll be too alluring for the dire wolves to pass up."

"It sounds like a plan. You'll need to help me as I'm not creative or artsy. My creation might scare these damn creatures away."

"I'll help you. One last thing. How will we spread the urine to lead the wolves here?"

"We know they prefer to hunt in the dead of night. There have been no attacks lately, which means they're probably hungry."

"How do we know they didn't eat any protestors last night?"

"Give me a sec," Dale responded. He grabbed Sam's phone and pulled up the internet. After waiting for the area news to load, he searched for updates. "Nothing. No news is good news. Just a bunch of hype and speculation about the new creatures hunting in Yellowstone. Apparently, it's a slow news day."

"So, what's your idea?"

"I'll have Aaron drive me from the outskirts of Hayden Valley to the campground. I'll dribble the crap along the road until we run out. It'll be nice and stinky. Let's rig something up to make it easier. I don't want any of that stuff on me."

Sam thought about the details and the impending work required to make tonight's hunt a success. She glanced at her phone's clock, relieved it was still early morning. They had one opportunity to make their plan work and ensure things moved smoothly. Sam tucked her phone into her pocket again. She looked at the tree stand and the restroom building. There was no more perfect place for her to exact her revenge on the creatures that took the lives of Johnson and Gabby.

"Maybe I'm stepping out of line, but you didn't seem very upset over Johnson's death," Dale said. Sam's lack of emotion had weighed on him since the dire wolves killed her friend. Only once did she show a hint of grief.

There was an awful silence that made Dale regret saying those words. Sam responded with a long-drawn sigh as she dropped her head. When her hands went limp in her lap, the sandwich she held fell apart. Salami and bits of mozzarella spilled from the bread to the ground. A chipmunk watching from nearby scampered to claim the morsels as his own.

"My father raised me himself after my mother died. Without my mom, I fast became a tomboy. My dad was part of the forestry service and always worked in the field. He took me with him and homeschooled me between cutting trees and prescribed burns," Sam responded. "I think he was afraid of losing me, too. He was overprotective, as were the rest of the men on his crew. Not only did I have my dad, but I had many dads. They treated me like one of the guys. Not in a bad way, but if I got hurt, they'd tell me to shake it off. Don't cry, toughen up, that sort of thing. It hurt losing Johnson, but I hide it. Killing these dire wolves will help me cope with his loss."

"So, how close were you to Johnson?"

"We were more like drinking buddies. When we weren't working, we hung out in the cabins. He was a good guy with faults. Johnson came from a wealthy family in Calgary that expected him to be exactly like them. He was disinterested in the city life and growing up in their shadow. Instead, he fell in love with wolves during a camping trip and took a particular path in life, his path. But that's a different story."

"For another time?"

"Yes, for another time. At least Johnson died doing what he wanted to do. If a bear takes me, I will die a smiling woman. The dire wolves — anyway, isn't there something better we can talk about?"

"Yes. That damn dummy we created looks pathetic. Are you sure the dire wolves will fall for it? Should we douse it in buck urine to make it more appealing?"

"Nah. That might confuse the wolves. I have a better idea."

Sam jumped from the truck's bed and rummaged through a bag in the back seat. After he listened to her zip the bag shut, he recognized the clattering sound of ice cubes as she pulled something from the cooler. Sam returned with deodorant and pepperoni.

"That's an odd combination," Dale said. He furrowed his eyebrows, then raised them when he understood her intent. "You're going to make it smell more human?"

"Exactly. That's what the wolves will expect."

"Isn't it too early? What if the smell attracts them now?"

"I don't think it's strong enough. I'll slather up the dummy with human scents if you check my phone for an update from Aaron? He should be here soon. Afterward, we'll clean up and rest. There's not much else that we can do until dark."

Sam set her phone's alarm for the late afternoon. After their work was complete, knowing they had a late night ahead of them, Sam and Dale returned to the truck for a bit of shuteye. Before the alarm went off, a message chimed from Aaron. Sam grabbed the phone from the console and read the text.

"Time to wake up, Dale. Aaron's back. We need to help him around the barrier and finish setting up."

Dale groaned and grunted as Sam responded to Aaron's message. She yawned as water pooled in the corners of her bloodshot eyes. The two had fallen fast asleep in the cool shade of the trees while listening to the lapping waves of the lake. She stretched her arms and back before starting the truck and emerging from their hiding place.

Aaron waited until Dale dragged the barricade far enough for him to pass. Sam watched from her seat with a loaded rifle raised towards the sky. She was ready to defend Dale if the dire wolves emerged from the thicket. Aaron followed Sam into the campground after Dale returned to her truck. He backed his car into a spot across from the restrooms and beside the tree stand. If something were to go wrong, Sam would be close to shelter.

Over the next hour, the three laid and secured the bird spikes around the building. They staggered them where they expected the wolves to land if they jumped from the building. Sam and Dale next attached the scopes to the rifles. They finished by storing weapons and additional ammunition in the tree stand. Sam had enough firepower to eliminate every animal around the lake. She left nothing to chance.

When the work was complete, Sam called for a review of everyone's roles and responsibilities. Before settling in the cab of her truck, they made sandwiches and grabbed snacks to fill their growling bellies. After taking their seats, Dale and Aaron listened to the master plan.

"When we finish this exchange, you two will spread the urine from the start of Hayden Valley until you reach this site. Use the stuff sparingly so we don't run out. It won't take much, anyway. Aaron, when you return, back up and park in the exact spot your car is in now. If someone follows you, go to our cabin, lose them, and double back. Try not to waste time. Aaron, you will wait in your car with the doors unlocked. Leave the windows cracked open and the radio off so you can listen. Stay still and quiet. Don't move, don't use lights, not a sound. That goes for you too, Dale."

Sam stopped to catch her breath. Dale and Aaron didn't dare interrupt her instruction since she was serious, intense, and spoke with authority.

"Dale, you're going to wait in the pickup next to the restrooms with your windows cracked. You will not move until you see me flicker my flashlight. I'll be in the tree stand, watching it unfold and conducting a headcount. Don't make any assumptions about the number of wolves. I don't want to rush this step and miss one. Once you see my signal, gun it. Turn the truck so you're away from the building and in position to shoot."

"Where am I shooting?"

"I'm getting to that. As soon as Dale moves the truck, I want both of you to turn on your lights and high beams. Aaron, you will sit in the car and not make a move. Dale, you will shoot any wolves that land on the ground. Use the handguns if they're too close. I have an excellent position in the tree stand and can take down the wolves on the rooftop. When we're confident that the wolves are dead, you will provide me with cover when I come down from the tree stand."

"What else do you want me to do? I feel you two are doing all the work," Aaron said.

"Nothing. I've already said it twice, nothing. Don't leave the car under any circumstances. I don't want anyone shot or injured during the shootout. The only thing I expect you to do is to turn your headlights on when Dale moves the truck. Don't forget, leave your doors unlocked, so I have a safe space. Aaron, your work will begin when the wolves are dead. At that point, they're all yours to do with as you please."

"What will you do during this time?" Dale responded.

"Before you leave, I'll get settled in the tree stand. I'm going to watch the area intently for movement. With some luck, the dire wolves will have already started this way. After their arrival and with the aid of the night vision scope, I'll count out the eight dire wolves. When I'm confident about their numbers and our timing, I'll signal for you to move. It shouldn't take long to execute the entire pack. When we finish shooting, I'll signal again with my flashlight. I'll come down, and we'll go from wolf to wolf to ensure they're all dead. I'll text Tony to let him know our work is complete. At that point, I expect some backlash from the park, but we'll cross that bridge later."

Sam dug through the console and pulled keys from a hiding spot. She handed them to Aaron.

"What are these?" Aaron asked.

"Those are to the restaurant and freezer. If the park gives us any hardship, I want you to duck out of the chaos and steal back the frozen dire wolf carcasses. Those are yours. Take them and run."

"Won't I get in trouble?"

"I'll assume any responsibility. Tonight might be my last time working in the park, anyway. They may as well tack on additional violations."

"What if the dire wolves don't come?" Dale asked.

"They'll come. We'll be sure of that."

Sam glanced at the clock on her cell phone screen. The sun had started its descent, and they needed to get the ball rolling. For a moment, she questioned their plans and preparations. *What if Dale is right? What if they don't come?* Sam didn't have time to second guess any part of the arrangement. They had to make this work tonight.

"Let's finish eating, boys. It's time to suit up in these fine ghillie suits Aaron purchased and move into place. When you're finished with your dinner, chuck the leftovers on the rooftop. We'll provide the dire wolves with their last supper. That's the only mercy I'll show these monsters."

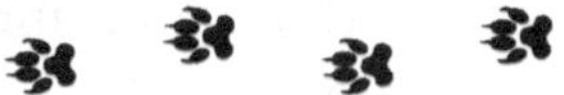

Sam watched the rental car move away from the campground from the tree stand. After dinner, things didn't play out as expected. Sam's ghillie suit impeded her movement up the tree. Bits of dangling string and fabric caught on the sticks of the ladder and bark of the trunk. When she returned to solid ground to remove the camouflaged clothing, she reeked of tree sap.

Instead, she retrieved a heavy coat from the truck for warmth and protection. The brown shade of her jacket blended well with the trunk of the old lodgepole pine, and the fabric slid across the rough bark. Sam took her seat above the men and checked that the safety lines were secure. She gave them a thumb's up to proceed with their part of the plan.

Dale stashed the box containing the urine in the backseat and behind Aaron. As the smell wafted through the interior of his car, Aaron opened the door and threw up his dinner.

After emptying his stomach, he dry-heaved instead. Dale laughed throughout the incident while Sam yelled from the treetops. She wanted them to bury the vomit before leaving the campground. When he heard the anger and concern in her voice, Dale did as Sam instructed. He used his boot to swipe loose dirt and rock to cover the waste.

After composing himself, Aaron lowered the windows for fresh air. Dale took the backseat opposite him and prepared the bottles for scattering. As they pulled away, Sam listened to Aaron yacking and Dale laughing. She hoped they wouldn't attract attention from protestors during their assignment. Sam cursed them in silence.

Sam sat back against the trunk and lay a rifle in her lap when all was quiet again. Her back and bottom already ached from the hard chair she settled in. It would be a long night, especially if the wolves made them wait for hours. Instead of wallowing in self-pity, Sam sat forward and scanned the tree lines while replaying the steps she'd take to kill the dire wolves.

It was dark when the men finally returned. Sam listened to their movement and watched the vehicles move into position. Aaron called up to Sam, asking if she needed anything. Sam lectured him about the unnecessary noise and yelled at him to return to his car. Again, she reminded him to leave the doors unlocked. Aaron hung his head and did as Sam instructed.

For the next five hours, they sat and watched. They listened to the critters scatter amongst the brush, the birds calling out to one another, and the waves slosh against the shoreline behind them. The men fought with fatigue and drowsiness in the warmth of their cars under the sliver of moonlight. Sam toyed with her night vision scope, scanning the campground for movement.

By three in the morning, Sam panicked. There were no signs of the dire wolves, not even a scout probing the area. Sam replayed every preparation, scenario, and review of errors in her planning. Most everything done tonight was her idea, and she would take the blame for any failure. Sam didn't want to let either man or herself down.

Another hour passed, and Sam struggled to stay awake. She hoped the men were alert, as she had no way of communicating with them. Sam longed for a walkie-talkie for human interaction and conversation. Maybe she missed something? Sam stretched and exercised with the rifle balanced on her lap. She carefully rotated her neck and any joints free of ropes and harnesses.

As blood and oxygen coursed through her body, Sam noticed a change in her surroundings. It wasn't the noise that caught her attention, but the silence. Something was nearing her location and startling the little creatures of the night. She quickly raised the scope to her eye and swept the campground. In the distance, she recognized the familiar outline of a dire wolf. It emerged from the trees, followed by others.

One, two, three, five, seven. Where is eight? There you are. Let's stay together, nice and tight.

As Sam finished her headcount, the wolves split when they approached the restroom building. They combed the area for other predators or prey before stopping to regroup. Sam continued to watch their interaction as they communicated through expression and body language.

You know you want it. Go check out my pathetic excuse for a man. He's waiting on the rooftop for your arrival, Sam mouthed with her lips. She was careful not to allow any sound to escape from her throat for fear of startling the pack.

Once again, the dire wolves split up and retreated away from the building. Sam panicked as they put more distance between themselves and the tree stand. If she took a shot, she could hit some. The other wolves would undoubtedly run or scatter, and she would miss this opportunity. Sam wouldn't take that chance. It had to be all or none. Instead, Sam continued watching their movement while her adrenaline surged and collapsed.

Much to her relief, the dire wolves only took cover in the brush. They faced the building and spotted the familiar form hunched on the rooftop. She watched them intently, urging them to move from their hiding spots and onto the building. Something didn't sit well with the pack. The wolves continued to observe the familiar figure propped on the building, but they wouldn't move.

Sam gently swept a free hand over the pockets of her jacket. Her fingertips explored every opening to search for an object to throw. If she created noise on the rooftop, it might pique their interest. Her search only led to more disappointment. Sam needed everything in the tree stand to take down the wolves. There was nothing she could sacrifice or spare.

Dale had seen the pack when a silhouette first appeared in his side mirror. Unsure if it was his imagination, he carefully turned in his seat and raised his scope. Dale's heart raced when he focused on one creature. The dire wolves had finally arrived. Like Sam, his heart dropped when they fell back from his sight. He watched as the wolves settled at the edge of the brush, their eyes directed at the figure sitting atop the building.

"No, no, no!" Dale whispered. *I know you want the pepperoni on that rooftop. We placed it there, especially for you. Don't go wasting my food.*

Aaron almost nodded off again. Instead, he stretched his facial muscles and smacked his cheeks to wake up. He looked into the darkness, but saw nothing. While the ghillie suit provided some warmth in the cool early morning air, it itched something fierce. He scratched and rubbed his body, bringing temporary relief to his dry and irritated skin. Before settling down again, Aaron debated checking the time. His fingers found the power button on his phone, but stopped short of pushing it. If Sam caught him lighting up the interior of his vehicle, she would go ballistic. He sighed and laid back in his seat, waiting for a cue to act.

Humph! Aaron let out a slight grunt. He was ready to call it quits and return to the cabin.

The pack rose in unison, glancing at each other before turning to the alpha male. Something excited them, sending them into a frenzy. Sam listened to the muffled sound of an old twangy country song. She glanced toward the truck when a flash of light caught her attention. Dale had thrown his phone from the window onto the rooftop. He somehow flipped it through the window opening and into the narrow space between her truck and the fascia. The phone landed upright, still blaring music and casting an ominous glow.

The dire wolves split and circled the building, watching the rooftop as they moved. Sam watched their progress through her scope. Dale quietly propped the rifle on the seat next to him and turned forward. His hand trembled and hovered over the key in the ignition, waiting for Sam to signal. When he felt the truck bounce repeatedly, his adrenaline surged. The wolves were finally making a move and using the pickup bed to propel themselves upward.

One, two, three. Sam counted. *Four, five, six. C'mon! Hurry, seven and eight. Fuck it! We're pushing forward without you.*

Sam balanced the rifle against her shoulder and into an eye socket with her finger next to the trigger. She grabbed the flashlight with her free hand and rapidly flickered the beam towards Dale. All but two of the wolves were on the rooftop. Sam couldn't risk losing this opportunity while waiting for the strays to join the rest of the pack. The engine turned over instantly, and Dale shot forward, leaving the wolves nowhere to go.

Sam aimed her muzzle towards the dire wolves on the ground. Two shots rang out in succession, causing both to fall. She turned the rifle towards the rooftop while Dale turned the truck, activated the headlights, and flicked on his brights. Although Sam used a night vision scope, additional light aided her effort.

Aaron struggled to find the headlight switch in his rental car. He panicked and leaned on the horn, causing it to beep without interruption. The earsplitting noise further confused the dire wolves that looked for an escape. They darted back and forth on the rooftop, searching for the truck.

When both vehicle lights illuminated the building, Sam positioned her rifle towards the most threatening wolf in the pack, the alpha male. A grin crossed her face as she slipped her finger over the trigger. Six wolves remained, and Sam was ready to finish them. But first, she would take out their leader.

Before Sam could eliminate the alpha male, a dire wolf

moved in front of him. Sam adjusted her shot for the new target and aimed at its chest. She pulled the trigger when certain she wouldn't miss, and the creature fell.

The sound from the rifle reverberated within the campground, bouncing off the trees. The resounding noise panicked the remaining dire wolves, and they darted back and forth on the rooftop. They looked for a way down, recognizing someone had cut off their escape.

"Five!"

Five dire wolves remained on the rooftop. Sam couldn't hide her enthusiasm as adrenaline coursed through her body. She would yell each time she took a shot, hoping Dale could hear her voice over the commotion. There was no longer a need to stay hidden or quiet.

One wolf misjudged the distance from the rooftop to the ground and jumped. He landed on the bird spikes, impaling his torso when his paws and legs gave out. Sam adjusted her rifle, but a shot rang out from below. Dale finished the distressed creature as it floundered, knocking additional spikes away from their places. Sam was delighted to have him take part in the slaughter. Dale took pleasure in yelling a number at their countdown.

"Four!"

Sam aimed her rifle at another dire wolf that teetered on the roof's edge. She didn't have a clear shot because the wolf was facing her as it prepared to jump. Before it vaulted from its crouched position, Sam aimed between its eyes and pulled the trigger. The wolf collapsed, its upper body hanging over the side. Half of the wolf's skull was missing, and its blood pooled on the ground below.

"Three!"

Sam selected a new target, passing on the alpha male.

An enormous wolf looked in Sam's direction, the alpha female. The surviving dire wolves had finally recognized Sam's position in the tree, given away by her muzzle flash. Sam studied the alpha's gaze, knowing they held the same hatred for one another.

Sam lifted the scope to her eye and aimed the crosshairs at the wolf's chest. The predator started pacing, making it difficult for her to make the shot. Sam predicted the wolf's next move and pulled the trigger, missing and hitting the roof instead. Sam aimed the rifle and shot again. This time, the wolf fell before taking another step.

"Two!"

Two wolves remained amongst a pile of blood and furry carcasses, the alpha and its offspring. Sam weighed her next move and selected her next victim. Because the alpha male was the leader, she would kill him last. Sam wanted the predator to witness the demise of his pack. He would never select another mate, procreate, or kill again.

One blast, one hit, and one wolf remaining. Both Sam and Dale yelled with euphoric voices.

"One!"

Sam could hardly contain her excitement about eliminating the last pack member. She lined up the alpha male in her crosshairs and cursed the foul beast under her breath. A shaky finger grasped the trigger and pulled. There was a click and silence. Sam's eyes widened when she realized she was out of ammunition. She popped out the magazine and pulled a loaded cartridge from her pocket. She locked it into place and raised the scope to her eye.

The alpha male recognized the impending danger and leapt from the building. The wolf disappeared to the opposite side of the building and out of Sam's sight. Dale turned the truck around to track the missing predator with the truck's headlights. She watched the pickup stop after maneuvering around trees and bushes.

Sam engaged the safety on her weapon, swung the rifle strap around her shoulder, and stood on the platform. She swapped out her safety harness line for the lineman's rope. Without hesitation, Sam descended the ladder and stopped short of the ground. Although she was eager to chase after the last dire wolf, she knew it was dangerous.

"He's over here," Dale said. He yelled over the truck's engine and turned it off when he noticed Sam straining to listen. "The wolf injured itself during the jump. He's not going anywhere."

"Spot me, Dale," Sam responded. She carefully navigated the last steps of the stick ladder until her feet hit solid ground. Sam swung the rifle around her torso, off her shoulder, and disengaged the safety.

"What do you want me to do?" Aaron asked.

"Pull your car around the other side of the truck and keep your headlights directed towards the wolf. Stay inside until we tell you otherwise."

Sam cautiously walked around the building, avoiding the bird spikes. She listened for movement, but only heard the panting and labored breathing of the distressed creature. When she rounded the corner, the alpha male came into view.

Rather than ending the alpha's suffering, Sam squatted on one knee to observe the beast from a safe distance. She wanted the wolf to see her face before she snuffed its life. Sam raised the rifle's muzzle and aimed it at his chest as it wallowed and whimpered. Although she could have used her handgun, Sam wanted to ensure the dire wolf's heart would never beat again. She pulled the trigger of her high-powered rifle, and the wolf's movement stopped.

A tear rolled down Sam's cheek as she dropped the rifle to her side, and it hit the dirt. She wanted to sob tears of joy, but she couldn't move. Fearful she'd topple over, she put a hand on the ground to provide stability as she wiped away tears with her free hand. The nightmare was finally over.

The men watched Sam from their vehicles, unsure if they should comfort her or allow her time to process the events. Both stayed in place, waiting for her directive. While Dale waited, he pulled his rifle through the window and secured the safety before placing it on the seat next to him. He would give Sam a few more minutes.

When Sam heard a rustling and the sound of something running towards her, she looked up. The alpha male still lay dead. It wasn't him making the noise. There was no time to react as something pushed Sam to the ground. Her face hit the hard gravel, narrowly missing a set of bird spikes.

A dire wolf's teeth sank into Sam's back as it pushed her body into the earth. Sam emitted a bloodcurdling scream and pulled herself into the fetal position despite the weight bearing down on her. She locked her fingers together and around her neck for protection. The creature's hot breath, which reeked of rotting meat, nauseated her senses. The wolf continued to explore her flesh with its teeth, biting and nipping. It searched for a way to stop the flow of oxygen into her lungs and end her life.

Dale and Aaron had noticed the creature emerge from the darkness and run at Sam. An unarmed Aaron lay on his horn while Dale grabbed the rifle strap and jumped from the truck. He couldn't risk shooting Sam from a distance during the struggle. Dale jerked back towards the pickup and stumbled when the rifle's strap hooked on the gearshift and stopped him cold. He panicked, causing a delay in his reaction time.

Frustrated with its lengthy assault on Sam, the dire wolf latched onto her leg. Its teeth sunk into her calf until blood seeped from the wound. Stimulated by the taste and warmth of her body, it readjusted its bite for a firmer grip. The wolf shook Sam violently as it attempted to free the flesh from her body. It would eat her alive as it pulled her towards the forest.

Sam released her hands from her neck and dug her fingers into the ground to stop the movement. The violent attack continued, and she failed to stop the wolf from tossing her back and forth like a ragdoll. Sam's hand reached for the pistol on her belt, but the wolf noticed her movement. It latched onto her arm as Sam flipped her body and used her free fingers to dig into the predator's eye socket.

The wolf yelped and released her arm. Sam flipped over to assume the fetal position again, but the wolf latched onto her leg one more time. Seconds felt like hours during the assault. Sam was weak from shock and blood loss. She summoned all her energy for one last fight when the world suddenly went still after a loud bang. The wolf's weight came down upon her.

Dale had abandoned his rifle and ran for Sam's instead. It lay only a few feet away from her, but she was helpless to do anything. He scooped up the weapon, pushing the bolt forward and pulling it back to load a bullet into the chamber. The predator never noticed him as Dale crouched to the ground and aimed the muzzle at his chest. Dale whistled for the wolf's attention and took the shot when it released Sam. The last surviving dire wolf fell dead.

Together, Dale and Aaron pulled the wolf's body off Sam. Dale returned to the truck for a cell phone and a first aid kit that Sam kept stashed in the backseat. He moved as quickly as his feet allowed while Aaron flipped Sam over and assessed her wounds. Dale returned to the bloody scene, texting for help with the supplies tucked under his arm.

Sam stared at the sky while the men tended to her broken body. She noticed the vivid colors of the sunrise reflecting off the clouds. Sam was unsure if she was still living or transitioning to the next world. She heard the soothing and familiar voices of her mother and father. They greeted her and offered the warmth of their embrace. Before Sam surrendered herself to the darkness, her parents pushed her away. Sam's nose and lungs burned from the overpowering scent of ammonia. A sudden rush of oxygen surged through her head and body, causing Sam to jerk upright.

"Whoa, whoa, whoa," Dale said. He tossed the smelling salts to the side and eased Sam back onto the ground. "Stay with me. There'll be no sleeping on my watch. Let's focus on the positive, Sam. I think you took out the entire pack. All but one, no, two. You need to credit me with two kills when the media comes knocking at your door. You did it! Can you believe it's finally over?"

While Dale cradled Sam against his body, Aaron put pressure on her leg injury. The bleeding wouldn't stop as he wrapped it tightly with gauze. The sterile white bandages turned bright red before Aaron finished securing it in place with a roller bandage. Panicked, he sent Dale to the truck for blankets and rope. Aaron shifted all of his weight against Sam's leg until Dale returned.

"Cover her with blankets. Hurry! Okay, now help me make a tourniquet with the rope."

"She might lose her leg if we use a tourniquet," Dale responded. He understood it was necessary when Aaron loosened his grip on her leg and more blood seeped out.

"She'll lose her life if we don't stop the bleeding. I think the wolf tore an artery. The blood keeps pumping out. Sam, how are you holding up?"

Sam mumbled a response. She was still conscious, but shook uncontrollably. Dale and Aaron rubbed her body to create warmth after the tourniquet was in place to slow the bleeding. They engaged Sam in conversation, although she could not communicate with words. Sam only responded with grunts and groans. Dale would smack her cheeks and threaten her with additional smelling salts if she closed her eyes.

"Should we get her in the truck and meet the medical responders?" Aaron asked.

"No. Wait here. I told Tony to send a life flight. They can land in the campground. There's plenty of open space. We need to keep her awake and warm."

While Sam fought against sleep, she focused on Dale. She watched the concern in his expression and admired the reassuring smiles he flashed when they made eye contact. Sam felt pity for the young man as he fought alongside her and offered protection. Dale never released his grip and rubbed her shoulders when he felt her quiver. When he finally moved aside, Sam knew help had arrived.

Dale held a firm grip on her hand as they loaded her onto the stretcher. Sam continued to focus on his boyish charm as they placed an oxygen mask over her face and administered pain killers. Dale walked beside her and still gripped her hand when the crew moved her towards the chopper.

When they slid Sam into the helicopter, Dale squeezed her hand tightly once last time before releasing his grip. There was nothing more he could do when they closed the door and signaled for him to move away from the rotors.

Although he had never cried publicly, Dale couldn't stop the flow of tears that streamed down his face. An arm patted Dale on the back and draped around his shoulder. He glanced to his side. Aaron stood next to him with swollen and bloodshot eyes. He, too, failed to hide his emotions. The crying men chuckled at one another, their faces dirty and stained with Sam's blood. After the helicopter lifted and veered southwest, Dale and Aaron watched it until it disappeared behind the trees. They prayed it was not the last time they would see their beloved Sam.

Seven Months Later

"May I have this dance?" Dale asked. He extended his hand towards the stunning woman that sat alone, watching the evening's festivities from across the room.

"Why, most certainly. I thought you would never ask," the woman responded.

There was a ceremony in a small church on the opposite side of this small mountain town. Afterward, attendees moved on to the property of a prominent ranching family for the celebration. They had transformed the barn into a large wedding venue to host family and friends.

String lights zigzagged across the ceiling, casting a yellowish glow on the guests below. A live band played country tunes, the beer flowed, smoked meats and hearty sides filled trays and dishes, and the guests laughed while throwing horseshoes and playing cornhole. Everyone enjoyed this moment, ignoring the blizzard outside that battered against the weathered wooden doors.

"Leave the cane. You can lean on me for support. Besides, didn't the therapist tell you to stop using it?"

Sam grimaced at Dale's suggestion and propped her cane against the wall. She stood and adjusted her dress, something she was unaccustomed to and felt uncomfortable wearing.

Dale took her hand and led Sam onto the dance floor, careful to keep her pace. He wrapped one arm around Sam's waist and gripped her other hand before they swayed to the music.

"I recognize that grip. I remember very little from that night except you holding my hand. If it weren't for you, I would not be here. Honestly, Dale. I'm not sure how I can repay you?"

"No need to think about that. You would've done the same for me. Anyway, how's the leg holding up?"

"What leg? Do you mean my stump?" Sam asked.

"Sorry, let me rephrase my question. How is the prosthetic leg working for you? Can it keep up with my Sam?"

"I'm taking it one day at a time, Dale. At some point, I'll get the hang of it. Besides, I'm already experiencing some benefits of having only one leg."

"Such as?"

"Such as half-priced pedicures. I have one less leg to shave, so I'm saving on water. A six-pack of socks means twelve days between loads of laundry, my least favorite chore. When I return to the field, I don't have to worry about a predator gnawing on my leg. They'll get a mouth full of plastic and titanium. Ah, I can be a sexy pirate girl for Halloween," Sam said, followed by her signature laughter. Her nose crimped, and her eyes sparkled in the cute way Dale found attractive.

"When will you return to Yellowstone? Did Tony sort everything out? I know he was busy getting W.O.L.F. banned from the park, but I've heard nothing else. Boy, did Nicole piss off the wrong people."

"There's been a change of plans. My choice, Dale."

"What do you mean?"

"I've accepted an opportunity I couldn't pass up," Sam said. Dale squinted his eyes and turned his head slightly, as it was unexpected news. "I'm teaching at a college in Anchorage this fall. Next summer, they'll grant me a fellowship to research brown bear populations on Admiralty Island. The students and I will determine if the overfishing of natural salmon populations will contribute to a decline in bear numbers in the forthcoming years. That's the principal source of their diet on the island. The best part of this trip—"

"Is this my cue to ask what the best part of the research trip is?" Dale responded.

"Why, yes, Dale. Thank you for asking. The best part of Admiralty Island is the absence of wolves. It's one of three known islands in Alaska devoid of those detestable and disgusting creatures."

"You don't want to help Aaron track and tag the dire wolf packs in Canada this summer? If he's wearing fishing gear and his greatest weapon is a car horn, he probably needs your help."

"Are you kidding? I never want to see a wolf again, especially a dire wolf. He can keep and study them to his heart's content."

"So how will the great state of Wyoming survive without the great grizzly expert and aficionado?"

"Wyoming doesn't need me, and the bears have been here long before us. You'll do well, Dale. I'm sure you'll make me proud when you don that red and khaki game and fish uniform. Besides, I think it's a wise move to study antelope.

Especially with a little one on the way," Sam responded. She winked at Dale. "I'll tell you what. You wasted no time getting married and planting your seed."

"Yeah. The experience in Yellowstone got me thinking about my life's purpose. When I returned home, I realized my girlfriend was the greatest thing going for me. She's beautiful, honest, faithful, and smart. I didn't want to lose her."

"I thought I was the greatest thing going for you?"

"You're like a Sasquatch, the Loch Ness monster, and the Mothman combined. Everyone glimpses you, but no one can catch you, Sam."

"Are you calling me a monster, Mr. Wright?"

"You know what I mean. Come on. One more dance before the missus gets jealous," Dale responded. His eyes looked glassy, and he forced a smile.

"Don't pout. The dire wolf may have taken my leg, but it didn't take my spirit. I'm the same old Sam," she responded. Sam wrapped her arms around Dale's neck and kissed his cheek. "You know I'll always be here for you."

Dale pulled her tighter and led Sam into a slow dance. He realized it might be the last time he spent with her, as their lives were moving in different directions. Dale would always maintain his boyish crush on Sam. She was the one that shaped him from a young college graduate to a full-grown man in one brief summer season.

The events in Yellowstone instilled fear and respect in Dale towards nature and wildlife. Rather than pursue a career researching predators, he accepted a job in Pine Creek to track the annual pronghorn migration. Dale thought it safer, especially with a new wife and a baby on the way. Unbeknownst to him, Dale was about to face something even more horrifying in the coming years. A new predator would stalk the residents of his small Wyoming mountain town.

ACKNOWLEDGEMENTS

There are countless people to thank during the creation of my first novel, especially my family. My husband and children listened to my endless enthusiasm over Dirus. I'm sure I bored them to tears on over one occasion with my constant drivel.

My mom hates horror, but she was the first person to read and unlock each episode as I published it on Kindle Vella. My siblings, extended family, and friends gave me valuable input and creative advice. I am honored to be surrounded by an incredible group. There is no way to express how much this support has meant to me.

When I started publishing on Kindle Vella, I reached out to other writers for help and advice. Their response was astonishing. This talented group never hesitated to support me and my endeavors. If you haven't already done so, check out the thousands of stories on this platform.

I would never have published Dirus without employing a professional editor. Thank you, Vicki Greer, for taking on this task. You have such a brilliant eye and vastly improved my work. You are also an excellent fact checker, saving me from embarrassing mistakes.

Once teacher inspired me to write. It took a few decades to reach my goals, but her words and encouragement stuck with me throughout life. Ms. M, I still imagine your enthusiasm when I turned in my stories. Instead of unicorns and rainbows, we shared a love of monstrous creatures.

Finally, this book and these words would mean nothing without readers. Thank you for supporting a writer like me!

ARCTODUS

A Novel

PROLOGUE

A thick blanket of snow no longer concealed the tunnel's entrance. Although the sun had yet to reach the north face of the mountain peak, its heat penetrated the last discards of winter and melted the once-frozen land that now glistened a blinding white. The sky was void of clouds and wind but glowed a still and bright cornflower blue. It was silent except for the clumps of snow and ice that thumped as they fell from the branches of the trees and hit the exposed rocks and ice-packed surfaces. Another sound echoed from beneath the earth. A deep, snore-like rumble reverberated through the tunnel as it traveled through the exposed entrance. The seconds shortened, and the noise became more frequent as its body recognized the change of seasons.

A fallen lodgepole pine with its twisted and rotted root system, still clutching masses of dirt and rocks, marked the den's opening. Inside, the narrow tunnel walls were damp with condensation and matted with dense hairs. Melted snow seeped through the structure and dripped from the roof, pooling onto the floor. A constant deluge of water created a stream that flowed towards the entrance, navigating small branches, rocks, and clusters of smashed and rotted pinecones. Heavy breathing continued, deafening from inside the passageway that sloped upwards into a darkened abyss.

The hole widened and blackened as it opened into a large chamber. Any hints of daylight evaded the expansive sleeping quarters. A thick bed of dry fir boughs and duff lined the floor, collected before winter for added warmth and comfort. Unfazed by the outside world, the creature remained curled up with its face tucked into its body. Its breathing continued to increase, and body temperature and heart rate rose. It licked and suckled on the pads of its softened paws to shed them of old and callused cells. Instinct drove him to toughen the bottom of his footpads for the spring hunt when he'd have to maneuver over beds of rock and dry grass in search of prey. The bear stirred more frequently as the temperatures continued to rise. A bird vocalized outside the den, the sound echoing inside the chamber. Spring had arrived, and it was time to awaken from a deep slumber.

Although he should have emerged in mid-March, it was now close to May. He appeared at the entrance, covered in snow that had brushed against his fur as he dragged himself from the den. As he enjoyed the fresh air, he relieved himself of a plug; feces, hair, and dead cells. This plug prevented him from defecating during his slumber. The bear stood on all fours and stretched before collapsing onto the ground. Still groggy, he napped yet again. His enormous body was leaner now, as any fat added during the previous seasons had nourished him throughout the long winter. His muscle mass and bone structure were unaffected by the extensive period of inactivity. Nature perfected his body to prevent it from breaking down during this extended rest period, recycling the waste products to create protein and increase his lean body mass. He kept his strength during winter for protection and for hunting in the spring. He was a formidable predator that only functioned to eat, sleep, and mate.

Over the next several weeks, he remained listless as his body metabolized. He would sleep often and showed no interest in food. The warming sun changed the landscape as more birds returned to the area, and chipmunks and pikas emerged from their winter dens. He noticed the transformation, but preferred to slumber. Whenever a spike of energy hit, he would rub against the rough bark of the trees to scrape away his thickened and light-colored winter coat. He would no longer need the added hair as the sun and heat intensified. The ground and skies were a flurry of activity as the bear's den collapsed from the weight of the saturated earth. He would now have to find another fallen tree and soft dirt to build a new burrow for the coming winter. First, he would need to feast and gorge. With his body fattened up, he would spend almost a week digging and tunneling before collecting a ton of bedding for his next long slumber. But his thoughts weren't on the work ahead. He continued to rest and watch and wait.

Soon, his bodily functions would return to normal. He became more active, exploring the surrounding area. He would sniff the air, searching for signs of a rotting carcass, victims of starvation, and brutal winter conditions. However, the winds carried no such scents. Hunger set in. Unlike previous years, his natural prey hadn't returned yet. The colder weather and snow cover prevented their reappearance. In spring, the elk would return from their winter-feeding grounds in the valleys to the secluded forests in the higher elevation. Here, they would feed on the lush spring vegetation in the fields, and the cows would give birth to increase the numbers in their herd. A newborn elk would provide the bear with nourishment and energy for hunting the larger prey. He preferred the thick muscle of an adult elk, deer, or moose.

The lack of food and driving hunger pangs forced the bear to leave the area he had occupied during his lifetime. He would travel to lower altitudes and expand his range in search of his first meal. The bear would face a race that drove his ancestors into hiding, a race that almost wiped out their existence. He was familiar with their scent and the sounds they made in passing. He would cower in the shadows of the trees and remain hidden amongst the boulders. From these spots, he watched the strange forms walk in lines along rough pathways that weaved throughout his terrain. Until now, he had avoided them with an unknown fear. Now, extreme hunger diminished this fear and emboldened his spirit. Men weren't to fear. Men were food.

ABOUT THE AUTHOR

L.J. has traveled throughout the world and has lived in multiple states, settling in her favorite location. She lives in the foothills of a small Wyoming mountain town that inspires and drives her love of writing creature horror stories.

When not writing, reading or watching horror movies, L.J. enjoys wildlife photography and exploring the isolated trails with her family.

www.ingramcontent.com/pod-product-compliance
Lightning Source LLC
Chambersburg PA
CBHW021227310726
48971CB00006B/1714